# BLACKBEARD'S LOST TREASURE

A LUCAS CAINE
ADVENTURE

## CALEB WYGAL

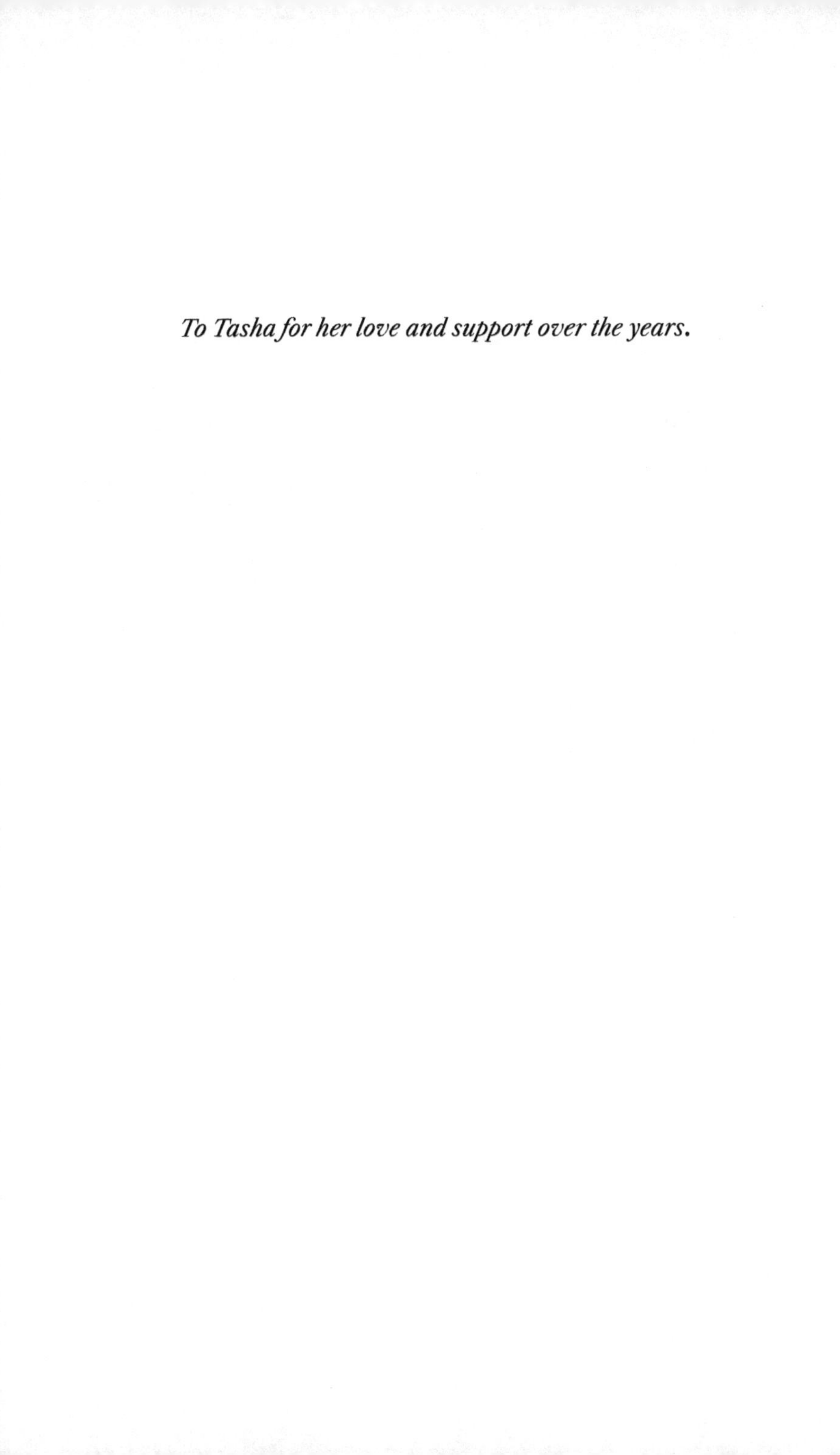

*To Tasha for her love and support over the years.*

But dead men tell no tales, they say! Except old tales that burn away The stifling tapestries of the day: Old tales of life, of love and hate, Of time and space, and will, and fate.

Haniel Long, 1888

# PROLOGUE

F EB. 13, 1717, 11:22 a.m.

Captain Ignacio Azarola hoped he had minutes to live. He feared the future that awaited him back in Spain if he somehow survived.

A week earlier, Azarola departed Havana harbor aboard a galleon named the *Nuestra Senora de Atocha* loaded with one of the last large shipments of silver and gold that would ever be found from the wreckage of the eleven ships of the Spanish Treasure Fleet, which sunk a year and a half earlier. Salvagers planned more dives, although as soaked chests, crates, and boxes of treasure were brought to the surface and tabulated, the accountants discerned there couldn't be much remaining.

The day was cool and blustery, creating choppy swells in the shallow Atlantic. Thick clouds lay overhead, casting a dull pall over the cold late-winter waters.

With plumes of dark gray smoke spilling out of several holes in the hull made from cannon strikes, the *Atocha* struggled to stay afloat. The lanteen-rigged bonaventure mizzen at the front of the ship disappeared in a well-aimed volley of cannon fire. The decks and remaining mizzenmasts slanted to port.

A terrible storm the previous day caused the *Atocha* and her protecting ship, the *San Jeronimo* to separate and lose sight of each other. The onslaught of waves had propelled them apart. Endless torrents of sideways rain limited visibility to a few feet. When the storm subsided, the two ships floated miles away from one another. The winds pushed the *Atocha* towards the Georgia shore and the *Jeronimo* further out to sea.

This had made Azarola uneasy. Before leaving Cuba, his crew removed most of their cannons because of the enormous weight in the holds. The ship, pregnant with tons of gold, silver, and jewels, had already sat low in the water before the first salvo of cannon fire struck. Then, when the ship stumbled closer to shore, it foundered on a sandbar. They were stuck.

As the *Atocha's* crew tried to collect their bearings in the shallow water after the storm subsided, a smaller sloop bearing a British flag had approached. It came from behind a small island. Although tensions between Spain and England were better now with the treaty, Azerola was still wary. He hoped they were just locals coming out to see if the newcomer needed help.

The ship came across their bow and heaved to their windward side about three hundred yards away, which Azerola thought odd. He thought they would have done the opposite to make it easier to catch the wind and get underway once they were finished helping the *Atocha*.

*Although it may be the Brits being Brits*, he thought. *Always making things difficult.*

Something tugged at the back of Azerola's mind, keeping him alert. Many bays, inlets, islands, and shoals lined this length of the Atlantic coast, making it a popular hiding place for bandits. What made him suspicious was that he discerned he was still half a day's sail away from reaching British controlled waters. They were just north of the Spanish stronghold of Savannah, headed towards the safer waters of Virginia.

He ordered his men to arm themselves and be at the ready. He closed his left eye and brought a spyglass up to his right. He saw three smiling men on the top deck of the approaching ship with more joining them from below decks. They appeared ready to help Azerola.

He took the spyglass down, set it aside, and let out a relieved breath. Help was about to arrive.

Or so he thought.

As the sloop came to a relative halt, a crew member pulled down the British flag and raised the most terrorizing flag he had ever seen in his many years at sea. When a ship raised a pirate flag, it was meant to intimidate other ships. Imagery such as skulls, skeletons, and hourglasses on the flags often told of the death and torture about to come to their prey, although many pirates lacked imagination and used a traditional Skull and Crossbones flag.

What this flag depicted chilled Azerola to the core. On it, a skeleton had a raised goblet in his right hand and a spear piercing a bleeding heart in the other. The goblet was raised in a toast to the Devil. The spear and blood-dripping heart were self-explanatory.

The men alongside Azerola on the top deck gasped in fear. The deck of the other ship was now filled with about seventy or so angry, filthy, shouting, pirates launching fusillades of threats and curses at the Spanish sailors.

The sloop drew closer.

Azerola recognized an attack was imminent. If the pirates came close enough to come aboard, it would be all over.

He commanded his men to prepare for battle. "Arm yourselves! We fight for the crown!"

After another moment of his men staring slack-jawed at the marauding vessel, they jumped into action. He saw several modifications on the sloop across the water. Fourteen cannons lined the starboard side facing them. Azerola knew that was about double the amount a sloop normally carried. He thought the added weight of the cannons might slow the pirates down, although with his ship floundering, the speed of the two vessels mattered little. They were close enough together for the ordinance men who fired the cannons to be able to aim with precision. If the pirates wanted to pierce the foredeck, they would be able to with ease. If they wanted to bring down the *Atocha's* masts, it wouldn't be a problem.

The sloop drew closer.

The muscles in Azerola's neck and shoulders tensed. He saw his men casting nervous glances at the approaching vessel.

He raised his spyglass to his eye again to get a better view of what he faced. The pirates were filthy and wore ragged clothes. He saw many of them were missing teeth and had visible scars. Some had raised cutlasses in one hand, and—Azerola did a double take—in a few instances, which was their only hand. He counted three who had one arm. Their other arm was no doubt lost in a vile manner. Others wore prerequisite eye patches for a pirate. He saw at least two who had a pointy hook for a hand.

The sloop drew ever closer.

The pirates on the sloop looked like they had seen their share of battles and endured many fights before now as they drew alongside Azerola and his ship. He risked a glance out over the ocean to see if he could spot his protecting ship. Their return would be the only hope he and his men would get through this unscathed. To his disappointment, all he saw besides the swells in the ocean and the dark clouds above were a trio of seagulls in flight.

There would be no help coming.

The sloop was twenty feet off to starboard. He could almost smell them.

Without warning, five of the sloop's cannons fired. With pinpoint accuracy, the pirate ship crippled the *Atocha*. Although no one died in the volley, three sailors caught some splinters, drawing blood.

He was about to order his men to counterattack when he saw the pirates stop their clamoring and become still. Tendrils of gray fumes wafted from the recently fired cannons. The men on the sloop stepped aside and gave a wide berth for someone to step through.

Azerola's men had been ready to respond but stopped to watch what was happening on the other ship. Black smoke poured from the hull of the *Atocha* where three cannonballs had penetrated. Azerola hoped the dark plumes would be a signal to the *Jeronimo*, although any help at this point might be too late.

All was quiet except the sounds of the waves splashing against the wooden sides of the ships and a squawking seagull who dared to venture close. As it sailed over the sloop, it became quiet before flying away.

Even the seagull recognized this was not a place for an innocent bystander to be at this moment.

Then Azerola saw why the pirates parted. A frightening man who stood a head taller than the rest of his crew appeared and stepped forward with a confident bearing. Azerola heard his men gasp. One young crewmember to his left began sobbing. A few cowards covered their eyes.

To all outward appearances, the figure on the other ship resembled a demon. A long, black heavy coat hung from his broad shoulders. A cutlass swung from his right hip and a leather holster containing three flintlock pistols hung from his right shoulder and disappeared around his left hip.

What captured everyone's attention, and put the men at unease, was the figure's head. A black tricorne hat was perched atop his head. Two lit hemp fuses stuck out from either side of the hat, causing a dark cloud to cover most of his face.

His most notable feature, however, was his long, black beard that spread out over most of his face and fell below his chest.

He was a giant among the men, and his countenance put everyone—on both ships—at unease.

In all Azerola's travels across the oceans and around the world, he had never seen something that frightened him more. He realized his death was close at hand. He was outgunned, his ship was dead in the water, and had no foreseeable help coming.

The demon stepped to the sloop's edge and stared across the water at the Spanish ship. He viewed every Spanish sailor who dared to look at him right in the eye. Finally, his gaze settled on Azerola who stood in the center of the Spanish sailors across the short distance.

Azerola gulped. When the pirate saw this, he knew he had won.

Azerola spoke little English. While he didn't understand many of the words and insults hurled at him and his men, he surmised the intent: Give us what you have in your stores or die.

He knew that wasn't an option. If he relinquished the treasure down below, he faced either being executed or spending the remainder of his life in a Spanish prison . . . if he made it back to Spain alive. Losing such a treasure was an unforgivable offense.

The pirate captain shouted something to Azerola. His lieutenant stepped to his side and translated, "He calls you a bastard with a whore as a mother."

Azerola winced. The pirate continued his verbal assault.

"He says," the lieutenant hesitated before continuing with his translation, "he says for us to lay down our weapons and let them come aboard or they will cut off our hands and feet, gouge out our eyes, burn off our testicles and then kill us by chopping off our heads and throwing the bodies overboard for the sharks to feast upon."

Azerola resisted the urge to release his bladder. He glanced about and saw two of his crew who could speak English was unable to do the same. He felt cold perspiration form on the back of his neck.

He had two choices: to ignore the demand and attack the pirates, dooming himself and all of his crew to a gory death, or give in and let the pirates come aboard and rob them of the treasure below decks. That would spare his crew, although either way, Azerola knew he was a dead man.

***

In the end, Azerola did what he had to do. He acquiesced to the pirate's demands. He might be a dead man walking, but there was no reason to sacrifice his men to these butchers.

The pirates slung grappling hooks across the narrow gap and pulled the two vessels together. Azerola instructed his crew to step aside and allow the pirates to have complete access to the *Atocha*. The first wave of pirates crossed with evil grins directed at the Spaniards and disappeared into the holds below.

When pirates captured a ship, they hoped to find goods such as sugar, tobacco, indigo, rum, or spices. To find actual silver and gold was a rarity. Azerola almost wished he could have been below when the pirates saw what lay in the *Atocha's* holds.

Standing on the other side of deck wall, the demon captain with the black beard remained in place—as much for intimidation of the Spanish as to direct his own crew. The dark cloud surrounding the man had disappeared. The hemp fuses sticking out of his hat had burned out.

While the dark cloud had scared the Spanish men witless, it was replaced by a set of piercing blue eyes that delved deep into the soul of anyone who made eye contact.

After a few minutes, one of the first pirates to go across to the *Atocha* reappeared and rushed up to the pirate demon. He spoke quietly to the bearded man. Azerola comprehended what the conversation was about: treasure, real bonafide treasure.

The conversation ceased and the bearded pirate considered the situation for a few heartbeats before giving instructions to his man. After the man scurried back below the *Atocha*, the bearded pirate locked eyes with Azerola.

"My second in command, Mr. Hands," the pirate said in perfect Spanish, "tells me you have great quantities of silver and gold on board."

Azerola gulped again and nodded.

The bearded man fixed the Spaniard with a threatening glare, took an aggressive step onto the *Atocha*, and stood inches from Azarola. He smelled a mixture of sweat, rum, and ganja coming from the pirate.

The man was *stoned*, Azerola thought, and now he knew about the treasure below.

The stakes just got much higher.

The pirate unsheathed his cutlass and held it to Azerola's throat. "You must be one of King Phillip's salvage ships."

Azerola tried to say something, but the words caught in his throat.

"Speak you filthy swine!" the pirate shouted. The action caused the blade to graze the skin on Azerola's Adam's apple. A trickle of blood fell onto the blade, rolled down and off the steel and splashed on the deck.

"Yes, yes," Azerola stammered. "It was brought up from the wreckage of the treasure fleet. Please, please take all you want."

To Azerola's relief, the pirate lowered the sword and stepped back a pace. He felt cold sweat ooze down his back and into his breeches. His men stared on at the confrontation in silence. Their fates would be decided in the next few moments.

The pirate pursed his lips and considered, holding eye contact with Azerola. "Where is your protective vessel? I know Governor Corioles wouldn't allow a ship carrying so much treasure to sail these waters alone. Where is it?"

"I do not know," Azerola said quickly. "The storm yesterday separated us. We have not seen them since last afternoon."

"Yes, a nasty swell that was," the pirate agreed and contemplated.

Then, a dark-skinned deckhand appeared at the edge of the sloop and gestured out at the ocean. "Captain Teach! Captain Teach! A Spanish galleon! A Spanish galleon!"

The bearded man, who Azerola presumed was Captain Teach, turned, and saw where the young pirate pointed. On the horizon, behind the pirate sloop, the *Jeronimo* appeared.

Azerola heaved a huge sigh of relief. Help had arrived, although he realized he wasn't safe . . . yet.

Teach made a quick decision. He recognized that with the arrival of the larger Spanish warship he was now the one at a disadvantage as far as position and firepower. He didn't have enough bodies to take control of the *Atocha's* guns and the ones on his sloop. He did have speed on his side and time. He figured the warship was still a good twenty minutes away from being within firing range.

He shouted to a group of ten pirates waiting to board the galleon. "Quick! Go below and take whatever you can in one trip. Be fast. Tell Mr. Hands and the others already below to get back here!"

"Aye, captain!" the man said, and led his crew across to the galleon and into the storage area below.

Teach turned and gave Azerola a contemptuous glare. "You got lucky," he said, and then turned and shouted to the rest of the cowering mariners in Spanish, "I am currently taking on recruits. If you wish your lives to be spared, you can join me. I will give ten pieces of eight to any who abandons this garbage," he said gesturing at Azerola. "Head below, grab the first chest containing treasure you find and hurry back aboard my ship."

Most of the sailors held firm, loyal to their flag. A handful of men, however, took a step forward.

Azerola thought about his life back in Spain. He had no wife or kids, a small home and little family remaining. If the pirate let him live, he could spare himself a life of the unknown upon return home. He didn't know what pirate life was like, but it had to be better than death.

"You have five minutes to get aboard my ship," the fearsome pirate captain shouted, setting the men off in a rush to the doorway leading below.

To Azerola, Teach said, "What about you, captain? You're a dead man if you stay either way."

Azerola discerned that to be true. He had seconds to make a life-altering decision.

***

Much later, as Azerola drifted off to sleep in a cramped bunk on the *Jeronimo*, on their way back to Spain, did he realize that neither Teach nor the pirates had harmed any of his Spanish crew. The only harm caused to his crew after the canon blasts subsided was the red scar on his own throat.

**7:02 p.m.**

Gentle waves lapped against a seagull's webbed feet as he stood on the shore. He was hungry, occasionally poking his beak into the sand trying to procure a small morsel.

Small waves came from three rivers coalescing together just a few hundred yards from where freshwater met saltwater and the open Atlantic Ocean, forming a shallow basin. Offshore, pelicans sat on the surf without a care in the world. Dolphins frolicked along the shore.

Across the basin, the glowing orange ball of the sun passed behind a narrow band of clouds on its way to rest for the night, filling the skies with brilliant hues of red, orange, and yellow. The rainbow of colors reflected off the calm, wide swath of water. A sliver of a moon already appeared in sky twenty degrees out over the ocean. The way the land curved here created a perfect vista during the evenings.

Life was easy for this little seagull. Quiet. He spent his days around this small island, soaring through the salty breeze, floating in the surf and hunting for food with his friends.

This day was different. Pirates landed for the first, although not the last time in the area, and were hard at work.

A small tribe of Indians had inhabited the island by themselves for hundreds of years before Europeans arrived in the early 1600's. The Indians traded land to the white men for cloth and other trinkets.

The first Europeans recently settled on the opposite end of the island along a riverbank after receiving a large land grant from one of the Lord's Proprietors. He was the first foreigner to call this island home.

The pirates on the opposite shore did not know about the new settler . . . at this time.

The Spanish Navy was searching for this band of pirates. However, the pirates and their cunning new captain were a step ahead of the Spaniards. The pirates recognized they were outmanned and out-gunned. The rest of their pirate fleet were busy antagonizing shipping lanes farther to the south.

With their faster sloop, the pirates raced north into a region of the Carolinas they thought was unsettled. As the crewmen buried the treasure on the shore of this island, the captain noted the location on a scrap of fibrous paper.

As a child, Edward Teach attended well-regarded schools in Bristol, England. Not only was he literate—a rarity in those days among pirate crews—he was well read. The pirate wanted to unload the treasure in the event the Spanish army based in Savannah caught and boarded them. If he had no treasure aboard, they would have nothing for which to hold him. Before today, the young captain had yet to assail any

Spaniards. What he did to the English or French was of little concern to Spain.

When Teach finished with a hastily scrawled map of the area so he would know where to return, he folded it, and tucked it into his frock coat near his breast.

Back across the sound, the seagull watched as the strange men dug a hole in a sand dune near a large tree. A shadow fell across the bird as it felt a heavy hoof land in the sand near him. Startled, the seagull flew away in search of food in a safer place.

Atop the horse, a man observed the pirates and their activity across the sound. He was alone and knew it would be dangerous to stay on the beach within the eyesight of the pirates. Before he trotted away, he spotted a black flag fluttering off the back of the pirate's ship. The flag depicted a white skeleton spearing a heart with his left hand and holding up a wineglass in the other, as if it were toasting the devil.

The man had not seen this terror-inspiring image before, but it would not be the last time he laid eyes upon it.

The ship had a single word painted near its stern: *Revenge.*

***

**April 17, 1982**

Travis Cole did not believe in God.

The gun pressed to the back of his head caused that belief to waver.

His parents were professors who worked in the geology department at the University of North Carolina at Chapel Hill. Staunchly atheist, the couple had never seen evidence of a god in their studies and imbued Travis with that belief as a child. It was sometimes tough for Travis as he grew up near Raleigh, North Carolina on the fringes of the Bible Belt. When other classmates celebrated holidays such as

Easter and Christmas, he abstained. They thought he was weird and oftentimes shunned their brainy peer. When pressed as to why he did not get presents for Christmas, Travis was often met with glassy-eyed stares when he explained to them that he didn't believe the person described as the son of God in the Bible could make that claim because there was no God.

Now, Cole hoped he was wrong. He was raised to believe that once a person died, that was it. There was no ascension to heaven. No meeting at the pearly gates with an angel who judged if he was good or bad. Cole knew one of two things would happen upon his death: cremation or burial. He was twenty-four years old and the thought of leaving a will with instructions of what to do with his body in the event of his death had never occurred to him.

What started as a side project in his spare time had spiraled out of control and led to this. He'd stood firm and now it was going to cost him his life. He made a promise he couldn't keep.

Now, he was on his knees. He felt the cold steel of a strange pistol pressed against the back of his head. Sweat poured down his forehead and dripped onto a puddle around his knees. His jeans were soaked with urine and blood.

He couldn't help it. The fear was overwhelming. He didn't want to die. He was too young to die.

But it was going to happen.

The man pressing the gun to his head had killed before. Several times, in fact. Although Cole did not know this. Cole had asked for the man's help in gaining access to the ruins of what was believed to be the last known home of Blackbeard the pirate.

***

**One Day Earlier . . .**

As Cole tramped through the underbrush, he looked up to see a snake coiled around a branch in a tree ahead of him. He thought the snake was looking at him and hesitated for a moment. This was the third snake he had encountered since leaving his car at a guardrail blocking the end of an unnamed road and disappearing into the forest.

His friend warned him of snakes lurking in the marshland. Mosquitoes too. He hoped a liberal spraying of bug repellent would keep that pest away. To this point, he didn't think he'd been bitten. He might not have learned that until he went back to his motel room and stripped off his already wet clothes. He imagined this decrepit piece of land must have been much more alluring—and habitable—three hundred years ago when it was last tenanted.

He thought his surroundings resembled more of a jungle than an area near the shoreline of the Pamlico Sound. A thick canopy of longleaf pines and oak trees shrouded the otherwise sunny sky above. When he stepped out of his car and grabbed his gear from the trunk, he figured he couldn't have asked for a more pleasant day to go exploring. Once he stepped into the tree line, it felt like the humidity tripled. His long-sleeved cotton shirt clung to his body, soaked in sweat.

Cole followed in his parent's footsteps and wanted to be a geologist while dabbling in paleontology. After graduating from college, Cole went to work for the North Carolina Museum of Natural Science in Raleigh. He was a low-level research assistant collaborating with the Director of Collections for Geology and Paleontology. It was the first step on what Cole hoped would be a long and winding career.

In the year he worked for the museum, he had been on multiple historical digs around the state. The subjects ranged from the geology of the Appalachian Mountains on the western side of North Carolina to suspected Native American sites in the central Piedmont region to a dig of a giant sloth from the Ice Age. He hoped to take his experience on a long weekend off and immerse himself in a subject that interested him.

Like many raised near the Outer Banks, Cole grew up with an interest in pirates. Blackbeard in particular. Cole's parents urged him to read and learn as much about that chapter of history as he could as a child. They took him to Bath and Beaufort when they held pirate festivals as a child.

Treasure hunters had combed the region over the centuries looking for evidence of Blackbeard's treasure. Cole had no new information when setting out on this side project.

While the student interns from North Carolina State at the museum were on Spring Break, his bosses gave Cole the week off. He took this time to go to the Outer Banks and see what he could find.

The Plum Point section just outside tiny Bath, North Carolina is the site where the ruins of Blackbeard's home once rested. This slice of land was a snake and mosquito infested marshland. Over the centuries, people came and fought their way through there, although no one had done any serious digging since people from East Carolina University came in the 1970's.

Cole and the man who granted him access to this zone had shared a history class at North Carolina State University a few years before. The man was interesting in many ways. He was the star of many school plays, his father was a famous local entrepreneur, and he had no visible hair—no hair on top of his head, no eyebrows, no facial hair, and no hair on his arms or legs. None. While his classmates made fun of him, Cole took the time to get to know him. When Cole asked him why he didn't have any hair, he said he suffered from a rare case of alopecia but was hopeful that over time and with treatments, he'd regrow his mane.

They shared an interest in pirates, and Cole came to find out the source of the young man's interest was that his family owned the land the dreaded pirate Blackbeard once inhabited. The man said he hadn't gone to Plum Point often and agreed to grant Cole access to the site on one condition: if he found something, the man wanted to see it.

Now Cole understood why the man—or for that matter, hardly anyone—came out this way. The area wasn't the most hospitable place to trek along the Carolina coast.

He pushed his way between a thick row of bushes and came to the edge of a thick, green stream. He consulted his map, and hoped the murky water before him was the appropriately titled Teaches Gut. He looked along the bank of the stream for a good spot to cross. He was going to have to get wet to cross over. If he didn't have a twenty-pound backpack strapped to his back, he could have jumped across without any problem. He didn't want to throw the pack across because there were sensitive and expensive tools in it. That and he didn't see anywhere to be able to get a couple steps of steam going before leaping.

He shook his head, swatted aside an insect hovering near his right ear, and picked a spot to cross a few steps upstream. He had on a pair of waterproof Merrill hiking shoes and water-resistant pants, so he was prepared to get wet. He waded in and sunk into water up to his waist. The stream was deeper than it appeared from the bank. The water was cool, not cold; he felt a soft current against his right side, although it wasn't going to be enough to stifle his crossing.

After slipping on a rock halfway across—and getting wetter in the process—he climbed up on the bank and took a sip from a water bottle. He gathered his bearings and consulted a map of the area. He just needed to endure about three hundred more yards of dense undergrowth off to his general left to arrive at his destination. He hoped.

The foliage on this side was thinner than what he had pushed through so far. He figured it was because he was nearing the ruins of Blackbeard's home and three hundred years ago, he had his men clear the land around it.

Cole stopped for a moment when he heard a plane flying by over-head. With the sparser trees now, he was able to see the blue sky and the white contrails from the plane zoom by. He was getting close. He could feel it.

He crunched over more undergrowth. It became more grassy than brushy the closer he got to his target. A snake slithered across his path, causing Cole to jump back and shout. The long black snake paid him no attention and soon disappeared into the bushes. Cole let out a breath.

*I hope that's the last one*, he thought to himself of the snake but figured that it wasn't likely. He hated snakes—and the umpteenth mosquito he just swatted off the side of his neck. He took a moment to reapply bug spray before continuing.

A few minutes later, he stepped into a clearing overlooking the Pamlico Sound. He soon saw why Blackbeard chose this site to build his home. The section was elevated, offering views of the water all around. You could see every ship—whether enemy or friendly—coming into and leaving Bath from this vantage point. There was no shore. No sandy beach. A rocky wall fortified Plum Point, causing would-be intruders to think twice before trying to invade. Cole imagined a dock protruding from the edge of the land that allowed Blackbeard to come and go as he pleased, conducting any type of business he pleased. Then-governor Charles Eden's home was also nearby.

It took Cole a good hour to find his way here, amid a thick forest and over two creeks. As isolated as Plum Point was from civilization, he imagined it was even more remote three hundred years ago before the encroachment of homes along the water's edge on both sides of Plum Point. Perfect for someone who values privacy.

Sea grass covered every part of the land here except where a few trees and shrubs dotted the clearing. A space filled with oddly shaped humps of grass and about a hundred feet in diameter was near the back of the clearing, farthest away from the water. Cole trudged off in that direction, hoping these clumps hid the ruins of Blackbeard's home.

He reached into his backpack and withdrew a compact pickaxe with a telescoping handle. He would use this to clear away any brush and chip at any rocks or wood necessary. If this were a museum-sanctioned project, he would have to mark off the areas he wanted to excavate and take numerous notes, explaining step-by-step every action taken. He came out here of his own volition and had limited time to explore. He would do this his way.

Besides, he thought, he wanted to get away from the mosquitoes and snakes and get back to his air-conditioned, pest-free motel room as soon as possible. He would have to repeat the same daunting trek through the forest to get back to his car.

He made his way to the region where he assumed Blackbeard's home once stood. He turned and gazed down the bluff at the water and thought the eyewitness accounts of Blackbeard were probably true—that he was an intelligent man. Cole could see across the water for miles and spied several ships crossing the choppy waters. The welcoming smell of salt water permeated the air. Coupled with the thick and forbidding forest he had just traversed; this was a place few invaders would attempt to conquer. Not now nor three hundred years ago.

He approached the nearest clump of grass and looked down at its length. It was about two feet tall in a few spots and extended about thirty feet from end to end. Cole stood in the middle and prodded at the bulge with the pickaxe. About twelve inches into the thick, dry grass, the metal of the edge of the axe clattered against something hard.

"Hmm," Cole grunted, and attempted to clear away the grass. While the top layer of grass was faded and dry, the inner couple of inches were wet and brown and in the lengthy process of decomposing. He pulled back what he could, revealing gray, rotted wood.

*This must have been a wall to the house,* he thought.

He stepped over the wall and into the interior of the lumpy section. Any furniture or additional trappings of life from the early eighteenth century disappeared from this site long before the walls crumbled and rotted away. He did not know what he was hoping to find, he just hoped to find *something*. The thrill of discovery sent his pulse racing.

He poked, prodded, and kicked at different spots where he figured the perimeter of the house used to be. He located a chipped, clay plate and several rusty, bent metallic eating utensils. Nothing he could say definitively belonged to Blackbeard or to his sixteen-year-old bride. He placed his findings into a large Ziploc freezer bag and wrote the day's date and location on it using a black magic marker. He placed the packet in his backpack. The odor from the marker gave him a bit of a buzz.

After an hour of combing through the clumps, he stepped over one of the deteriorated outer walls. He walked around the perimeter of the ruins searching for artifacts. A few billowy trees separated by about ten feet lay between the eastern wall and the edge of the bluff. Cole pictured Blackbeard disembarking from his vessel at the imagined dock and walking in between those trees, returning home to his bride. He had read where the pirate often brought friends with him on those return trips, so they could all have their way with his teenage wife.

Times were different back then, Cole thought, shaking his head. What we consider savage, they are oftentimes thought of as commonplace.

Near the rear of the area, at a point farthest away from the water, he saw another clump about twenty feet from the nearest wall. Grass climbed over something in a four-foot-by-four-foot section. It was a few inches high in most spots. The humps around the edge were slightly higher. Cole wondered if this used to be an outhouse, or a storage shed. He jabbed the edge with his foot and hit something solid. He took the pickaxe and ripped away a part of the covering grass to reveal the same decayed wood used on the house.

He stuck the head of the pickaxe into the middle of the small space and pushed. He wanted to step into the area, although if this was an outhouse at one time, he didn't want to fall into the waste pit. He wasn't afraid of getting trapped, he was afraid of the possible snakes and, well, he didn't want to get into where Blackbeard may have taken his bowel movements—even if the feces and urine would have been long gone. It just seemed gross to him.

He had nothing to fear. The pickaxe hit a solid bottom two inches below the surface. He bent over and used the pointed end of the pickaxe to scrape away the grass covering the area's interior. A few black insects scurried away while Cole worked. Thankfully, he saw no snakes. He hadn't had to swat at any mosquitoes in the past ten minutes either, or he hoped it would stay that way.

After he finished clearing the leaves of grass, he stepped back to see what was now exposed. The wood on one side was higher than the other and he saw an opening towards the center of the elevated area. Not a shed, this was the outhouse, Cole thought. He placed a foot inside the space and tested it before stepping in. The first foot held firm. Satisfied, he stepped into the lower section. He bent over to look down inside the hole. It was dark, so he pulled a heavy-duty metal flashlight from his pack and ignited the beam. He aimed the light down the hole, and sure enough, saw a snake moving around the wet bottom about three feet down.

He didn't want to find any artifacts down there.

He straightened and let his eyes cast about at the open clearing. He had wanted to do this for a while. Come out to Plum Point and see if he could find anything belonging to Blackbeard. It disappointed him that he had only found kitchenware so far.

*At least it's something*, he thought. How many people made it out here over the past three hundred years and missed seeing the eating utensils and single, chipped plate?

He took pride in that, at least. It might earn him respect among his peers back at the museum.

Feeling a little frustrated, Cole slammed the pickaxe against the old floor of the outhouse. What should have been a solid *smack* was instead a hollow *thump*. Surprised, Cole repeated the action. Same result.

What was this?

He bent over and rapped against the soft wood with his knuckles. He figured that three hundred years ago when they built the house, they would have leveled off this area before the builders laid wood directly over the dirt. They would have dug a pit on the opposite side for the refuse. This part of the floor should have been solid.

He located a seam in the wooden planks and inserted the edge of the pickaxe in the dark groove. The board gave way with a rusty creak. Cole moved it aside. He flashed the beam of the light into the opening.

Thankfully, he didn't see any snakes. He did see a wooden box. His heart leaped into his chest.

He looked around, almost feeling like a thief pilfering something valuable while watching for the police. He reached in and pulled out the box.

It was wood. Cedar. Remarkably, it was dry. The closely placed planks of wood covered the floor. Cole thought it would have been difficult for moisture to make it through, even over the centuries.

Amazing. Who would think of hiding something valuable in the floor of an outhouse?

A smart, cunning pirate named Blackbeard was the answer.

Cole's chest hurt and he had to force himself to breathe. No matter what was in the box, this was the most exciting thing that had ever happened to him. He couldn't imagine finding anything else for the rest of his life that rivaled what was in his hands.

He took a deep breath and opened the lid of the box.

Jackpot.

***

Cole chose not to meet the man's condition of telling him what he found, although it was after the fact. That was what got him in his current situation.

He could still get out of this and grant the man his wish. However, he wouldn't do so in the interests of archaeology. He had made a significant, history-changing discovery. The problem was that he had yet to tell anyone at the office about it. He hoped someone would find the box he placed in the archives earlier.

After dealing with this man, Cole saw that he couldn't let him know what he had discovered. It may never have fallen into the right hands if he did.

Cole did not know it would come to this, and in the back of his mind, he held out hope that there was more to life than the physical form he was about to leave. His too short life flashed before his eyes.

"Cole," his friend said softly, "you knew the rules."

"I'm sorry," Cole pleaded and squeezed his eyes together, waiting for the man to pull the trigger.

The man did. Travis Cole's life ended.

# CHAPTER ONE

**Present Day**

*It must have been a mistake*, Darwin Trickett thought. *How did no one not see this before now?*

Trickett was a graduate assistant at North Carolina State University, working in the archives at the North Carolina Museum of History in Raleigh. His job was, for the most part, boring, although it would make a good entry on his resume down the line.

He was a massive human. Standing at six feet, eight inches tall and weighing close to three-hundred and fifty pounds, he had to squeeze himself between the already generous amounts of spacc in between shelving units in this dank, dark, musty storage room underneath the old part of the museum. At twenty-three years of age, he already had a rapidly receding hairline. The rest of his scalp consisted of dense, puffy, black curls. He wore a pair of black horn-rimmed glasses. He was so farsighted that the lenses magnified his eyes.

His appearance often frightened small children.

Those who took the time to get to know Darwin—who were rare—knew him to be a gentle, caring person who would do almost anything for his friends.

The museum opened a new research wing during the late winter of 2012, and now they were looking for low-paid, recent college graduates to sift through the archives in the old wing to clear out space. Boxes and crates filled the numerous storage areas, filled with artifacts and documents from various types of archaeological expeditions. Most of the contents of the storerooms came from projects and digs located in the Carolinas. There was a room for prehistory, ancient history, and recent history. In the grand scope of time, the museum curators defined "Recent History" as any time since Christopher Columbus landed in the New World.

Trickett sat on the floor in one corner of the Recent History section, digging in a cardboard box of unfiled papers and artifacts from what must have been a small project. A strong, musty odor emanated from the box. A common smell to Darwin. Lying atop a wooden plate, a manila envelope and other assorted kitchen tools was a scrawled note in a large Ziploc bag.

It read:

**Plum Point Artifacts**
**Travis Cole**
**Bath, North Carolina**
**April 16, 1982**

That was it. No notation of who worked on the project besides Cole or any indication of why the box's contents were important. He had been through dozens of crates and boxes, and all had standard documentation: Name of Project, Project Leader, Place, Date, Findings, and Assistants. Trickett couldn't place the name Plum Point, although he thought Bath was somewhere near the Outer Banks. It sounded familiar.

With no context to go upon, the various artifacts were meaningless. He pushed the contents around, hoping something would jump out at him. The interior consisted of different artifacts that came from everyday life such as plates, cutlery, a wooden box, and cups. Just like most of the other boxes he had sorted through thus far. He grabbed a manila envelope tucked along the edge of the box in hopes of finding some shred of information that would help him decide if he should keep the box or throw it away.

At the moment, he leaned towards the latter.

The packet was a standard manila envelope. It was thick, but not heavy. He released the metal clasp and lifted the flap. The musty smell returned, however unlike the odor in the rest of the box, it reminded Trickett more of an old library than anything else.

Inside was a leather-bound journal—the source of the smell—and another handwritten note. Again, the note did little to help Trickett. It read:

*From the Teach ruins.*
*This is presumed to be the diary of Mary Ormond.*

Trickett set the note aside. He wasn't familiar with the names, although he had a sense he'd seen or heard it somewhere before. He'd have to go back and check later and made a note to do so.

There wasn't an identifying name written inside the first few pages. The cover of the journal was black and unadorned. The pages were yellowed with age and frayed at the edges. Dates preceded many of the entries with the first one beginning in 1717. Whatever this was, it was almost 300 years old. Nowhere near being the oldest of the artifacts in this basement (there was most of an acrocanthosaurus claw in another room that was over 130 million years old); although that didn't mean he could take this any less seriously. Trickett thought the thin book was in amazing condition, considering its age.

He leafed through a few of the entries near the back of the journal, and was surprised at the intimacy portrayed. The entries depicted a woman much in love with a man and worried about him while he was away. In an entry near the end of the journal, she awoke to a surprise on her pillow: a gold necklace with a large ruby.

Some of the lettering was faded, although Trickett could still make out what was written. Of the few entries he read, this Mary Ormond did not mention the name of her lover. He figured that from the period and the coastal location where Cole came across this journal and from what he had read that the bearded man was the captain of a ship of some sort.

He thought the journal seemed interesting enough, at least, to catalogue. This might be the only thing he'd save from the carton. Trickett was getting ready to close the journal and set it aside when he fumbled it in his hands, causing a folded piece of yellowed parchment to come loose from somewhere in the recesses of the book and flutter to the floor.

He stared at the parchment in surprise. He wondered what was special enough about it that made Ormond tuck it away in her personal diary.

He picked it up between his chubby fingers, and unfolded the frail paper slowly. There was something sacrosanct about it causing Trickett to treat it with even more care than the journal. The parchment had a silken quality. This was expensive paper for the period in which it was made. The left edge of the paper seemed as though it came from a notebook of some sort. Like someone ripped it out in a hurry.

Darwin didn't know it at the time, but the words and lines on that piece of parchment would change his and other's lives as well as rewrite the history books.

# CHAPTER TWO

Lucas Caine was at his absolute limit. He had enjoyed moderate success during his first years of post-college life. Now in his early thirties, Caine had once been near the top of a successful chain of restaurants and now owned a growing bookstore. The restaurant chain, Mahoney's, was now under the ownership of a dining conglomerate, and his bookstore was on autopilot. He had hired a savvy library science graduate from University of North Carolina at Charlotte to take care of the day-to-day tasks while he went in search of a property for a second location for his business. In an age where brick-and-mortar bookstores went out of business on a daily basis, Lucas established a business model combining current technologies and old-fashioned book selling that consumers liked. With the original store doing so well in its Concord, North Carolina location, he decided it was time to branch out.

While his professional life was great, his personal life is what brought him to this low. Almost a year ago, he found out that his wife of five years, Kristen, had been cheating on him with their family doctor. He never suspected it.

Lucas noticed that she seemed to be going to the doctor quite often. When he asked her the reason, if everything was okay, she said she had things she needed taken care of and not to worry.

Then Lucas figured out their "code."

He noticed Kristen had begun frequenting a sub shop near their doctor's practice. He knew this because she would do a "Check-In" on Facebook when she went. When Lucas and Kristen went places, she didn't check-in anywhere. What made Lucas suspicious was when Kristen would check-in somewhere when Lucas wasn't with her and then a few minutes later their doctor would leave a comment on her check-ins with an emoticon. :)

This happened most often while Lucas was working at the bookstore. When he asked her about it, she said without hesitation that she had been cheating on him with the doctor and had spoken to an attorney about getting a divorce.

The news stunned Lucas. He didn't know what to say, how to react, or what to do. When he and Kristen were together, everything seemed normal, as it always had since they met. Perhaps that was the problem. After a few years of marriage, Kristen got bored with their day-to-day lives.

She wanted something new. Something to do. Lucas's business and the sizable severance package he received when he left Mahoney's made it so Kristen didn't have to work. At first, she continued to work at Not Just Franks in downtown Concord across from the courthouse. As time went by, she worked less and less until one day, she just quit.

Lucas was fine with that. In fact, he had suggested several times that she didn't need to work if she didn't want it. That maybe if she stayed at home, they could start a family. He didn't know if the affair came because of her aversion to having a child and she wanted to find a way out of the marriage. Communication between the two of them over family matters broke down, and Lucas had a hard time understanding her position on not wanting to start a family. She was three years younger than he was, still in her late twenties. He wondered if she still thought she was too young to have a child. Their friends of the same relative age had children. Maybe she didn't have the same goal and didn't know how to express it. When they talked about having children before they wed, she never once expressed any reservations.

She told Lucas she still loved him. However, the deplorable act she committed by sleeping with another man—a married man at that—made Lucas nauseous in the pit of his stomach. He still loved her on some level, but it was too much to bear.

A sense of self-loathing came over Lucas after that. For weeks, he couldn't look at his face in a mirror. He had done nothing wrong that he discerned. If he had, he may never know. That's the question that kept him up at all hours of the night: *what did I do?*

He doted on Kristen, bought her presents, took her out on dates and on spontaneous romantic getaways. Despite his busy schedule, he helped her cook, clean and keep the house tidy. He tried to make her life as easy as possible. As soon as she quit her job and the real prospect of having a baby struck her, she couldn't handle it or tell Lucas whether she had any misgivings.

It drove Lucas to the verge of madness. He didn't know what to do. If he went to a psychiatrist, he feared they would put him on medication. He wanted to figure it out and come up with a solution that caused him to come out better for it in the end. For now, he spent many nights with a half-finished bottle of Kentucky's finest.

Under North Carolina law, a couple has to wait one year before filing for divorce after separation. The state hoped couples would reconcile during that period. In this instance, there was little hope of the two of them getting back together. That waiting period was almost over for Lucas and Kristen.

Lucas's parents were saddened when they heard the news of their separation and rushed down from his home state of West Virginia to give him comfort and support. They stayed a week while he met with a divorce attorney and Kristen moved all of her things away from their house in downtown Concord.

Lucas's dad had appointments he had to keep the following week at a VA hospital in central West Virginia. They left town, leaving Lucas alone for the first time at home.

This day had been an overcast, cloudy day in early October. The leaves on the trees were beginning to change. The air was getting noticeably cooler. A few weeks ago, temperatures were in the low nineties. This morning, Lucas wore a light jacket during his morning jog.

As the seasons transitioned, so did Lucas's life.

He sat in a leather recliner in his dimly lit home office. The only light in the room originated from a single bulb under the cover of an antique wooden lampstand. Golden liquid sloshed around the small tumbler in his hand. An instrumental jazz station on Pandora played over the speakers on his surround-sound system. Around the house, several pieces of furniture departed with Kristen. A side-table here, a bookshelf there. From where he sat, he knew more of her things were gone in other parts of the house. Her pink razor, her body wash, her clothes. The picture of her and her departed aunt that once sat on the mantle now left a thin line clear of dust.

Her possessions were missing, as was her physical presence. In the past, even if she wasn't in the same room with Lucas, he could sense where she was in the house. It was small, just the right size for a childless couple. If she were in the bathroom tidying up, Lucas could tell from his chair. If she was in the kitchen baking, the smells drifted in from the kitchen, around the two-sided fireplace and into the den connected with his office.

He missed her, although deep down, he realized that she was never coming back. He hadn't yet figured out how he was going to move on.

Compounding that, he returned home the previous day from his grandfather Leland's funeral. He died from Alzheimer's disease, a malady that ran in the family. The slow degradation of his grandfather's mind devastated Lucas and everyone else in the family.

Leland had a strong influence on Lucas's life. He died a year after his wife, May, died of natural causes. Really, Lucas thought, he had died before she was gone. His mind started slipping long before her death.

His grandparents' three children got together when they realized their parents couldn't live on their own anymore. It took several months of argument and convincing before they agreed to be admitted to a nursing home. May's health was deteriorating and needed constant medical attention, and Leland couldn't remember where he was many mornings when he awoke.

Lucas visited the two of them shortly after they settled into their new room at the nursing home. His grandfather was an avid coin collector. Anytime Lucas came across a coin he thought was rare, he'd save it to give to his grandpa. Leland had a large safe deposit box at the bank containing rare coins valued at over thirty-thousand dollars. When the United States Mint released the state quarters, Leland had bought a display featuring each state's design. He gave it to Lucas upon his visit.

"Lucas," he had said, "I want to give you this. Don't tell your aunts I did so."

He handed Lucas a box containing the display. It was made of three folding, high-grade cardboard panels painted blue. There were slots for the fifty states. All of the quarters were there, except one: South Carolina.

"I came up one quarter short of completing the entire set," his grandfather had said. "I know that you of all my grandchildren will appreciate this the most. I wanted to give you this in hopes that you'll finish the project for me."

Lucas assured him that he would and accepted the gift. The display now sat on a bookshelf above Lucas's head in his office. The South Carolina quarter slot remained empty. Lucas had yet to complete his grandfather's mission.

His grandmother was under the impression that if her health improved, she would get to go home. She promised Lucas that she would make him his favorite meal upon her release: chicken and dumplings.

She never made it home.

Lucas remembered back to the last time he had seen his grandfather alive. Lucas had gone to visit him several months after his grandmother's death in the nursing home. The rest of his family had warned Lucas that Leland was not the same. When Lucas got to his grandfather's room at the nursing home, they hugged, and Leland invited Lucas into his room. They sat down and Lucas tried to have a conversation with Leland. It started out well, and his grandfather was his normal gregarious self. Although he joked about the weather and the food in the cafeteria, Lucas could tell something was off.

After a few minutes, Lucas realized as he stared into his grandfather's eyes, that the man he'd known his entire life, who had taught him how to play baseball, who had taken him to Washington D.C. as a teenager to watch his first NBA basketball game, who had spent countless hours walking in the forest outside his grandparent's home, teaching Lucas valuable lessons on life and how to be a man, that from the blank look in his eyes, this man no longer knew who Lucas was.

That was one of the most difficult moments of Lucas's life.

As he sat in his office, lost in thought, his phone buzzed on the wooden side table to his right. Lately, he hadn't taken many phone calls. His phone rang so often, he had turned the ringer off and set it to vibrate. He just didn't feel like talking to people. He glanced at the name showing on the screen and went "hmm" aloud.

He hadn't heard from this guy in a long time. He hit the "Accept" button and said, "Hello, this is Lucas."

The voice on the other end hesitated, breathing heavily into the mouthpiece for a moment before responding, "Hey Lucas. This is Darwin. How are you doing?"

"Well, not so great, Darwin, but it's good to hear from you. How's school?" Lucas hoped catching up with his old friend would get his mind off his current situation.

"I graduated back in the spring."

"Congrats, Darwin! I'm proud of you," Lucas said, allowing something positive to penetrate.

He'd known Darwin Trickett since he was a 16-year-old busboy at one of the Mahoney's restaurants in Concord. Trickett won a scholarship available to employees in a contest from Trent Mahoney, the now deceased owner of a restaurant chain. Lucas was the member of the home office who presented the award to Trickett, which he used to go to North Carolina State University in Raleigh.

Although he was more than a decade older than Trickett, he learned they shared many of the same interests in history and archeology. While Lucas graduated from the Business & Economics School at West Virginia University, Darwin went to college to pursue a career in archeology.

In some ways, Lucas was jealous of Darwin and wished he'd thought about that before choosing a major.

"What are you doing now?" Lucas asked.

"I took a job as an archivist at the North Carolina Museum of Natural History here in Raleigh."

"That's cool. What do you do?"

Trickett took a moment to consider how to describe his job. "Basically, what I'm doing now is parsing through the old storage rooms, trying to decide what to keep and what to throw away."

"That's interesting."

"Not for the most part," Trickett said bluntly. "You know the scene at the end of the first Indiana Jones movie where they have the Ark of the Covenant in a crate at a CIA warehouse?"

"Yeah."

"Well, what I'm going through is in a place such as that, although on a much smaller scale. You wouldn't believe how many artifacts are here that no one has investigated for decades. Nothing is logged into computer inventory database, which is what some other members of this project are doing in a different part of the museum. I can imagine how much funding went into the financing of these digs or projects that just sits here now."

"Who knows? It sounds crazy."

"Yeah, so I came across something that might interest you."

Lucas imagined plenty of things buried away in a museum that would interest him. "What is that?"

"The diary of Mary Ormond."

The name brought Lucas up short. He had to think about it for a second. It sounded familiar. He had to put what Darwin said into context. He was in a museum basement looking through old projects, so Mary Ormond couldn't be anyone in recent years. Darwin knows Lucas's interest in the historic and the ancient. Lucas remembered that the museum Darwin was working in had a focus on the Carolinas.

Carolina history. Carolina history. Ormond. Then Lucas thought *pirates* and it clicked.

"Do you mean Blackbeard's wife?"

"That's the one," Darwin chuckled. "It took me longer to figure it out than you, though. When Governor Charles Eden married the two, she became Mary Teach. She was, like, sixteen-years-old at the time."

"Dang." Lucas went through a period in his twenties where he studied a lot of pirate history. Not for any reason in particular. It was a subject he had found interesting since he was a child, and he saw a book in a small coastal bookstore while traveling in South Carolina that gave an overall history of pirates. Later, he had gone to the local library and picked up books focusing on Captain Kidd and Blackbeard.

Despite being the most notorious pirate in history, not much is known about Blackbeard's personal life. Most believe his given name was Edward Teach and hailed from Bristol, England. His transgressions were well documented, sometimes embellished, although not too far from what was probably the truth. Finding something from the point-of-view of one of his wives was unheard of.

"Where did you come across it?"

"It was just in a box, sitting in a manila envelope. There were other artifacts in there—bowls, spoons, etc.—but it was just unceremoniously dumped in this box."

Lucas shook his head. "I believe that would be an important find."

"Yeah, me too," Darwin said.

"Who was behind the project?"

"Some guy named Travis Cole," Darwin answered.

"Does he still work there?"

"Not that I can tell. I've never met him if he does. I studied the staff registry to see if he was one of those professors with tenure that comes and goes as they please, but he's not listed."

"Okay. Could you read any of it?"

"Yeah, it's in good condition. The lettering is faded on some pages and the paper is yellowed, maybe a little mold on the leather cover. Still a great find. I have no idea what it was in when they uncovered it. It must be nearly three hundred years old."

Lucas let out a long, low whistle. "What did it say? What did she write?"

"What little bit I've read is mainly about her waiting for Blackbeard to come back from his voyages."

"This would have had to have been after he resumed pirating?"

"Allegedly."

Blackbeard spent part of the last year of his life living around the Outer Banks of North Carolina in Bath. In 1717, he received an Act of Grace, which was, in effect, a pardon for his pirating actions from the Governor of North Carolina at the time, Charles Eden. The colony of North Carolina's seat at the time was based in Bath Town where the

Pamlico River joined the sea. This was where Darwin said the journal of Mary Ormond was discovered. In June of 1718, Blackbeard set up residence along the shore of the town, near Eden's home. Before that, some believed that Blackbeard lived on a farm outside Bath. Many believe that Eden granted Blackbeard the Act of Grace in return for a part of the pirate's booty. Land records show that Eden sold his home in April of 1718 when rumors surfaced of his arrangement with the infamous pirate, before Blackbeard moved into the area. They never located the tunnel.

"Lucas, the diary wasn't the biggest find in the box," Darwin said matter-of-factly.

Lucas had a difficult time imagining what would be bigger than the diary of Blackbeard's wife, Mary Ormond. "What is it?"

On the other end of the line, Lucas heard Darwin make a sound resembling a maniacal laugh.

"A treasure map," he said.

Lucas's jaw dropped.

# CHAPTER THREE

"A treasure map?" Lucas repeated as a question.

"That's right," Trickett confirmed. "The problem is that it's just a sketch of an area."

The revelation sent Lucas's mind spinning. For centuries, legends existed of the "Lost Treasure" of Blackbeard. Treasure hunters from all over the globe had come and gone from the Outer Banks of North Carolina where they hoped Blackbeard hid his treasure. Salvors have tried to uncover his treasure from the minute notorious pirate had his head lopped off on a November day in 1718 near Ocracoke Island.

The night before Blackbeard died in battle, someone asked him if Mrs. Teach, Mary Ormond in this instance, had knowledge of where he had buried his money. He replied that nobody but himself and the devil knew where it was. No cache of gold or money has been found to date.

In 1996, the wreckage believed to be Blackbeard's flagship, *Queen Anne's Revenge*, was discovered outside of Beaufort Inlet near Moorhead City. Divers recovered cannons, cannonballs, pewter platters, pottery fragments, anchors, and other artifacts from the wreckage. However, no one recovered any large chests of gold, silver, and jewels.

"What is it a map of?" Lucas asked.

"I have no idea."

"Tell me more about the map," Lucas said. "What does it look like? Did he write anything on it?"

Darwin explained that the sketch depicted what appeared to be an island shaped like a human kidney on the left side of the map. The island had a river with numerous tributaries that resembled veins. The artist divided the map into three sections. The island on the left sat farther in than where the mainland ended. The right side was the continent. The shore of the landmass began to curve inland near the right of the island.

There was no indication of where true north was. Darwin said Blackbeard had drawn a picture of either the sun or moon cut in half by a line in the upper-left-hand corner of the map. He couldn't figure out if depicted a sunrise, moonrise, sunset or moon set. If they figured that out, they might know where the true north was in relation to the map.

"So, did he really draw an X? Does X mark the spot?"

Darwin laughed. "Actually, he did. There's an X and a big tree on the rounded part of the bottom-right of the island. He made a note on the back. It's in different, more masculine handwriting than Mary Ormond's in the journal. The notation reads, "treasurre buried 23 paces in by the large oak under a falling sun near the cove where the dolphinss gather.""

"Any idea where that is?"

"I have no idea," Darwin said. "It's vague, and he may not have known the name of where he was when he buried it."

"So, it could be almost anywhere then?"

"Pretty much."

Lucas seemed to remember that Blackbeard's travels took him from South America to the Caribbean and as far north as Delaware Bay. A very large expanse to try to pin down from a few crudely drawn lines on a 300-year-old parchment.

"How did that happen? How did the people who discovered the journal not see it?"

"Well, the map was tucked into the journal fairly well and it's thin. I mean, I almost dropped the journal and jerked to catch the map when the paper fell out. It could be they never realized it was there. I haven't had the chance to ask anyone here about it yet."

"Why not?"

"There's no one here to tell," Darwin said. Being late on a Sunday night, Lucas could understand the staff wanting to spend time elsewhere. Darwin continued, "I found it a little bit ago. I'm taking a break, and I knew it had been a while since I spoke to you. I figured you'd be interested in this. I wanted to tell *someone.*"

"Thanks Darwin. Makes me feel special that you thought of me," Lucas laughed.

"You're partly responsible for getting me into college, and I wouldn't be here if it weren't for the Mahoney's. The company as it was doesn't exist anymore, and Quinn is dead. You're my one last connection."

Lucas fell silent for a moment. The mention of Quinn Mahoney brought back sad memories. The Mahoney's hired Lucas right after graduating from college. He threw his belongings in the back of his car and drove down to Concord where he went to work as an assistant for Mr. Mahoney's son, Trent.

A year into his employment, Lucas arrived at the office building in Concord to find Trent shot dead in the parking lot outside the front entrance. A high-security perimeter surrounded the building requiring anyone arriving at the gate to enter an access code to get in. Lucas was the last person to leave the evening before and the gate logs showed no one getting in between the time Lucas left and arrived the next morning.

With all signs of the murder pointing at Lucas, he took it upon himself to clear his name. In less than a day, Lucas broke up a mugging, met Kristen, was threatened at gunpoint, and discovered the person responsible. Quinn Mahoney died of a heart attack a few months later. The family sold the corporation shortly thereafter. By that time, Lucas was in the planning stages of his bookstore.

"It was a sad mess of things that happened with them," Lucas said.

"That it was," Darwin agreed. "How is the bookstore doing?"

Lucas caught Darwin up with his growing business, ending with, "Right now, I'm just taking some time off. I have someone taking care of the one store and waiting to hear back on a property for another."

"That's great!"

"Thanks," Lucas said with little conviction in his voice.

Darwin picked up on that, and asked, "What's the matter? Thought you'd be happier about it than that."

He didn't want to talk about it, but informed Darwin of his impending divorce from Kristen, leaving out the scandalous details.

"Man, that's tough," Darwin said. "I'm sorry to hear that."

"Thanks," Lucas said in the same dry tone as before.

"Look," Darwin said, "part of the reason I called was to see if you wanted to go on an adventure? I go on vacation starting on Monday, tomorrow, and don't have any plans. It's difficult for a guy such as me to make travel plans when all I own is a moped."

Darwin didn't drive a car from what Lucas remembered. Darwin never had the money for a car. Picturing Darwin cruising along the side of the interstates on his moped made Lucas smile, although he thought that might be illegal. "What sort of adventure?"

"How about a treasure hunt?"

"You're not serious."

"I am," Darwin stated. "Look, no one knows about this journal or map from Blackbeard yet. I've already snapped a picture of the document with my phone. When I go to the museum director and tell him about the map, it'll take weeks before they even consider following up on this. And when they do, they'll send a team that I guarantee doesn't include me to investigate. I've seen how they work.

This bureaucracy can be glacially slow. There's nothing in my contract with the museum that says I can't use anything I've learned from this job outside these walls. I might not be able to take the actual artifacts. With this, I don't need them."

"I don't know," Lucas said doubtfully.

"Look," Darwin said, getting excited, "this is an opportunity to find treasure that's been missing for centuries. People have been looking for his treasure since before Blackbeard's headless body stopped twitching. Haven't you ever wanted to be a part of something like that? I called you because I remembered this stuff interested you and that you might be able to help me out."

Lucas hesitated, "Well . . . the map is vague."

"So? It's a start. C'mon man, after what it sounds like you're going through, you know you need to get away. We could be onto something *big*."

Lucas let out a breath and thought about it. He didn't have much on his plate during the coming week except for trying to forget about Kristen. He'd barely been out of the house since she left, only to go on business or get food and to his grandfather's funeral. He was falling into a deep depression. Perhaps a short vacation would be good for him.

Besides, he didn't feel anything would come of Darwin's findings. Many people had tried and failed to uncover Blackbeard's treasure. What if Darwin had stumbled onto an incredible find? What if before someone at the museum got around to following up on Blackbeard's map, he and Darwin located it?

He'd kick himself for the rest of his life if that happened. The next question Lucas asked himself was: *why not?*

"Ok, let's do it."

# CHAPTER FOUR

Lucas spent the next day, Monday, arranging his affairs for the upcoming week. Darwin said he would be off for one week, so that is how long Lucas planned on being away. Through Sunday.

He communicated with his assistant, Margaret, about what to do. It was almost an unnecessary task. She could run things and anticipate his needs without him. He wasn't concerned.

He packed a suitcase, clothes, and duffel bag with toiletries and then booked a couple rooms in a motel in a small town named Chocowinity. It was the closest hotel he could find to the town. It was about twenty minutes from their destination of Bath, where Travis Cole found the journal.

Lucas threw his things in the back of his late model four-door Jeep. It was of the soft-top variety, and the interior noise could get loud when driving on the interstates and highways. The trade-off was when the weather was pleasant outside, he could unsnap the vinyl cover and stow it away, allowing the Jeep to become an open-air vehicle. Lucas loved to cruise around town, in the mountains, and at the beach like that. He didn't miss the compact, sporty car he traded in for the Jeep at all.

His first stop after leaving Concord was to pick Darwin up in Raleigh, just off the North Carolina State campus. He got on I-85 and drove east through Concord and past Salisbury. Once he got by that area, the traffic eased off and he was able to put the Jeep on cruise control. It gave him time to think as he hurdled towards Greensboro and the Triad region of central North Carolina.

In between arranging his affairs and packing, Lucas had time to refresh himself on the infamous Blackbeard and research Bath or "Bath Town" as the settlers called it during the 1700's.

At that time, Bath Town was the capital of North Carolina. It is located on the shore of the mainland. From there, it was about a two-hour ferry ride out to Ocracoke Island—the place where Blackbeard ultimately died.

Charles Eden was the second governor of North Carolina, and he resided on the outskirts of Bath Town. He was known for his campaigns to end pirating in the area. Blackbeard and another well-known pirate, Stede Bonnet surrendered to Eden. In return, they received a King's Pardon, exonerating them of their seafaring crimes. Both eventually returned to their old nefarious ways.

Perhaps what Eden is remembered for, however, was the implication of being in collusion with Blackbeard. On Bath Creek, Eden's estate was near Blackbeard's home. Rumor had it that a sixty-foot-long tunnel led to Eden's home from the creek. Although no one ever proved it, many of the colonists believed Blackbeard would bring his ship up the creek to the tunnel entrance and pass plunder through there to Eden's basement. The locals thought this happened twice.

In return, Blackbeard received the pardon and a nice estate of his own nearby. When the pirate returned to his old ways, Eden turned a blind eye on his neighbor. Many believed this was another sign of them working together.

Perhaps the biggest clue was that discovered on Blackbeard's person following his death. They found a handwritten letter from Eden's treasurer, Tobias Knight, addressed to Blackbeard, requesting the pirate's presence as soon as possible. Lucas saw a copy of the letter while doing research online on an old website.

Knight's estate in Bath Town rested between Eden and Blackbeard's residences. Knight was later put on trial for being an accessory to piratical acts associated with Blackbeard and his crew and was acquitted.

Bath is North Carolina's oldest town. It is just over one square mile in size and holds a population of fewer than three hundred. From above, it looks like a pointed piece of land, jutting out into the Pamlico Sound, similar to shark's tooth. Bath is a rarity among towns on the Atlantic seaboard in that it remained almost unchanged as the townsfolk kept the blight of commercialism away. Many antebellum homes and buildings still stand, and he read that Bath makes for a relaxing tourist destination during the summer months.

This was where their expedition would begin. Many treasure hunters have ventured to Bath with hopes of finding Blackbeard's treasure. They dug holes and poked around, although they always came up empty. Darwin and Lucas hoped Blackbeard's map would point them to the X.

Lucas and Darwin decided to start from the last place Blackbeard lived, and if the treasure wasn't there, they would try to trace it all of the way back to Blackbeard's known beginning as a pirate using the newly uncovered map as the first clue. They hoped the journal would help to unlock clues as to the treasure's location along the way. The journey would last at least until Darwin had to be back to work at the museum the following Monday.

They wanted to try to speak with the natives of Bath to get their thoughts. As Lucas studied the legend of Blackbeard, he noted some disambiguation in what was known of the legendary pirate's life. Most people believed his given name was Edward Teach and he hailed from Bristol, England. However, some in eastern North Carolina thought the man who would become Blackbeard grew up around Bath Town, and his father was named Edward Beard. Beard owned 375 acres on the west side of Bath Creek.

Five months before his death, Blackbeard sailed up the Pamlico Sound to Bath Town where he met with Tobias Knight to discuss a pardon. Upon arriving at Knight's doorstep, the treasurer was believed to have said to the pirate, "Well, well, young Edward. I was not sure I would ever see you in Bath Town again. I know your families will be most glad to see you, too."

Blackbeard had not been in those waters since spending several years in the Caribbean and South America. If the quote were true, then that would indicate that he could have grown up in the Outer Banks. Nothing exists to prove this, nor has anything been found to disprove it.

If Blackbeard grew up in the Carolinas, then he likely knew every nook and cranny along their coasts. He may not have needed to use place names on his map if that were so. If he recalled exactly where to go to retrace his steps, the crude drawing Darwin discovered would be all the experienced sea captain needed to find his way back to treasure.

Now past Greensboro in his drive to Raleigh, Lucas thought for the first time since he left Concord about Kristen. He cruised along on a relatively straight stretch of the highway, lined on both sides by rows of tall, verdant loblolly pines with a few interspersed billboards. He kept the radio off. The only noise in the cabin of the Jeep came from the tires rolling across pavement and the throaty growl of large trucks.

After a few months of Kristen being gone, and waking up by himself, Lucas began to understand what life would be like without her. As a teenager, college student, and now an adult, Lucas was never the type to have dozens of friends to call upon. While some people had their groups or cliques of friends, he was always content to have one or two close friends. Most of the time, he'd had a girlfriend of varying degrees of closeness. Of course, the closest of any of these was his now soon-to-be ex-wife.

The difficult thing to get used to was waking up to an empty bed. Kristen was warm natured and kept the thermostat in the house set to about sixty-three degrees year-round. It seemed as though there was always a chill to the house, and on nights where the temperature dropped outside, no amount of comforters and blankets could keep Lucas warm.

When that happened, all he had to do was roll over and put his arm around her. Without fail, she felt like a furnace. She'd had tests to see if there was a reason she couldn't keep her body temperature regulated without result. No matter, Lucas enjoyed her warmth on those mornings. It comforted him to know she was there.

After they married and moved in together, every morning when she woke up and looked at him for the first time, she would get a twinkle in her eyes and a smile on her face as though she were seeing a close friend for the first time in years. Looking back on it, Lucas realized that it didn't take long for her smile to fade.

The smell of her perfume from the pillows and sheets faded over time, as did the memory of her living in their house. Lucas thought several times about selling or moving into one of the other bedrooms of the house.

In Concord, he had limited friends to whom he could talk to about his separation. His closest friends weren't the sort Lucas could seek out for comfort. One, Greg Hanover, was a detective for the Concord Police Department. He spent most of his days investigating crimes and murders among the dregs of humanity. The other, Carter Washington, was a retired Navy Seal. Injuries forced him to retire after tearing the ACL in both knees during separate training exercises. He was still in great shape, and seemed as though he could kill anything that moved with his bare hands. He had little empathy for anything or anyone, although he was as loyal of a person as Lucas had ever met.

They were great guys to drink beers with and watch a game, but not so great when it came to delving into each other's personal feelings and affairs. He could always talk to his parents, although it felt awkward when he wanted to discuss the more intimate details.

So, he did the difficult thing and kept it all to himself. He'd never felt more alone in his life. He hoped this trip to the Outer Banks would help keep his thoughts off the domestic difficulties back home.

He didn't know it at the time, but by the end of the week, Kristen and his failed marriage would be the farthest thing from his mind.

# CHAPTER FIVE

Lucas picked Darwin up at his home on the south side of Raleigh. He emerged from his apartment carrying a duffel bag, a portfolio, and a lumpy pillow. He threw everything in the back seat and climbed in Lucas's Jeep. Darwin's bulk caused the Jeep to tilt to the passenger's side.

The GPS showed they had about a two-hour drive from Darwin's apartment to Chocowinity. They used part of the time to catch up with each other. Darwin told Lucas of his experience of going to North Carolina State. Lucas told the younger Darwin about his bookstore and life after leaving Mahoney's.

They turned off the interstate near Greenville and drove past East Carolina University before joining state road 33. The two-lane road wound its way across farmland and cotton plantations. Fluffy, white cotton balls perched on small bushes in enormous fields were all they saw for an hour. Lucas wondered if he had any clothes made from the cotton in those fields. After seeing how much cotton grew in this part of the state, he thought there was a good chance of that.

Eventually, the conversation drifted to the reason for their trip: Blackbeard's lost treasure.

"Did you get a chance to look at any more of the journal?" Lucas asked.

Darwin shook his head. "Yeah, but there wasn't much of use for what we're doing. The entries began in 1717. She didn't meet Blackbeard until the next summer. She wrote a little bit about him, although the journal was mostly about her helping her dad on his farm. Even while she and Blackbeard were married, he spent a good part of his time either in town or out at Ocracoke."

"But he had a bunch of wives, right? I remember reading that somewhere."

"I spent all day yesterday researching his life here in North Carolina. In the two years he spent as a pirate, he had something like fourteen wives. He'd go to a port, meet a girl, and marry her on the spot. Sometimes he'd have his ship's mate do the ceremony."

"Were they legal?"

"Looks like just his marriage to Ormond. I imagine he married a girl just so he could get her in bed then leave her at port. He didn't care. With Ormond, Governor Charles Eden performed the ceremony, so there was some legality there, at least. She was the only wife written about after he took the King's Pardon, and he allegedly ended his pirating days."

"She didn't write anything about the treasure?"

He shook his head. "Not that I read. She mentioned him surprising her with a necklace before he left for the last time. Didn't say anything about it coming from a cache somewhere. He may have given her the map and told her to hold on to it for him but not explain what it was for."

"Didn't he say the night before he was killed that "nobody but myself and the Devil" knew where the treasure was?"

"And the longest liver should take all," Darwin finished the famous phrase and then chuckled. "Don't you believe his wife could have been the Devil?"

Kristen's face flashed across Lucas's mind. "I see what you mean."

Darwin explained that he couldn't bring the journal or the map. He was able take a couple clear pictures of the map using his phone and printed them off from home. They were in his leather portfolio with a few additional notes. He had to leave the journal behind at the museum.

"What did the people at the museum say when you told them about the map and journal? Did you find the guy responsible for the dig?"

A funny look crossed Darwin's face. "Well, nothing really. Most of the artifacts I set aside for a closer examination go and sit in a storage closet in the new wing of the museum. I felt the journal and map were important enough to escalate the process and took it to show the museum director."

"What happened?"

"He wasn't there. I told his assistant I needed to show him something important, and she explained he had to step away for a few days to take care of his sick mother. She told me to place what I had back in storage, and she'd tell him when about it when he got back."

"No one knows what you found?"

"Not really. I told the assistant what it was, and she thought it was interesting, although there's nothing for her to do about it until he gets back."

"That's good. It means we'll have a head start."

"Probably more than that," Darwin said. "It'll take them weeks to figure out what to do next."

"What about the guy who retrieved the artifacts?"

"Travis Cole. Couldn't find him. Like I said, I hadn't heard of him in the time I've worked there and couldn't find him on the staff directory."

Lucas stroked his chin in thought. "We could just Google him when we get time."

"Good idea," Darwin said and shifted gears. "I examined past digs out there at Plum Point."

"Find anything?"

"Not much. There were some in the 70's. All they found were pottery shards and a couple forks."

"So, what? Did this Cole guy go back after figuring something new out?"

Darwin shrugged. "Dunno." He went silent for a moment. "So, what are we going to do about it? The map, that is?"

Lucas didn't have a great answer handy. This trip was almost more about having a reason to get away from Concord for a while than it was about a wild goose chase to find a 300- year-old treasure. He still had not seen the map.

"I want to go out and talk to the locals in Bath and, if we can, make our way out to Plum Point where the journal was recovered to poke around. Then, if we can't find anything there, head out to Ocracoke."

"What do you think of trying to find local nautical charts to try to find a match for Blackbeard's map?"

"Absolutely," Lucas said. "Anything we can think of. I'm no expert when it comes to this. You tell me what we need to do. You're the archaeology graduate. Here's your chance to lead your first expedition."

Darwin smiled at that. "Sounds good. I spent so much time over the last forty-eight hours contemplating the map and Blackbeard that I failed to come up with a plan."

Lucas glanced at the GPS. "We should be in Chocowinity in about twenty minutes and then checked into our motel soon after. Why don't you start writing down what we should do once we're there?"

"No problem," Darwin said. He reached into the seat behind him and grabbed his portfolio. Then he had to maneuver himself in the confines of his seat to pull a Tweety Bird pen from his pocket.

He scribbled notes the rest of the way to the motel as the sun went down.

# CHAPTER SIX

A S THEY NEARED THEIR destination, the sun disappeared behind a thick blanket of clouds. There were few lights lit in the town, making it very dark. Chocowinity wasn't much of a town, Lucas thought. Rather small.

Rain fell on the Jeep's windshield in tiny drops. More of a heavy mist, making the driving conditions more difficult. Over the past week, remnants of a tropical storm stalled out over eastern North Carolina dumping large amounts of rain. As they got close to Chocowinity, the GPS alerted them to turn onto Route 17B.

They had a slight problem, however. After going about a mile on 17B, there was a temporary barrier from the Department of Highways blocking the road with a yellow and orange sign indicating a closed road ahead. Lucas turned around in the parking lot of a closed laundromat before detouring around to Walhurst Ave. That road bent back on itself, connecting Route 33 to 17B forming what resembled a giant square if seen from above.

The town looked a little worse for wear than its neighbors. Most of the boxy buildings were made of white painted cinderblock. Small businesses occupied the buildings that weren't abandoned. There was one stoplight in the town. There were few vehicles on the road. What vehicles they saw were typically beat up work trucks.

They made a left at the light. Then, tucked behind a closed restaurant was the brightly lit Baymont Inn. They pulled into the porte cochere, exited the Jeep, and went into the lobby.

A well-groomed young man greeted them at the desk. Lucas surveyed the room and was satisfied by what he saw. The building looked nice in stark contrast to the rest of the town. It felt out of place.

The desk attendant explained the recent rains had washed out part of Route 17A, and that was the reason for the detour. Lucas and Darwin checked into separate rooms and agreed to meet in the lobby as soon as they had their gear stowed.

Twenty minutes later, Lucas returned to the lobby with an Android Tablet tucked under his arm. The desk clerk had put on a fresh pot of coffee, for which Lucas was grateful. He saw a logo for S&D Coffee on the side of the coffee pot and knew he would be drinking a good cup of coffee as opposed to the swill many hotels offered.

S&D Coffee's corporate center was in Concord near Lucas's house and was a rapidly growing company due in part to them producing coffee blends for McDonald's and Dunkin Donuts. Lucas loved driving past the plant as they roasted the beans. It made the entire town smell of fresh coffee. If the wind shifted in the right direction, he could smell the roasting coffee beans from his house.

Darwin already had a paper cup of steaming coffee sitting before him along with his portfolio and a notepad. Lucas poured himself a cup and settled in across from his large friend.

Lucas studied Darwin as he concentrated on studying his notes. It had been over two years since Lucas saw him last. When Darwin left Concord, he was clean-shaven, and Lucas questioned his ability to grow facial hair at that point. Nevertheless, he must have developed that in his latter stages of puberty. He now sported a thick, long beard. He appeared wiser and more mature. Lucas didn't know if college life had been good for Darwin, although he seemed prepared to face the world.

He remembered Darwin as a quiet kid doing his first job as a busboy for Mahoney's. He came from a single-parent home. His dad had disappeared before Darwin reached Kindergarten. His parents had vicious fights before their split where a young, impressionable Darwin had a front-row seat. His mom taught him how to dial 911 when he was three should the arguments turn violent.

Young Darwin ended up calling the number three times before his dad left.

The circumstances of his early years left Darwin shy and reserved. He elected to hang out in the background during class, at lunch and at recesses. That became more difficult as he got older. When he was in fourth grade, he wore size thirteen shoes and was taller than all of the teachers in school.

In middle school, football coaches talked him into joining the team. He was larger than any other kid on the squad, but Darwin realized he had no interest in sports, particularly ones involving contact. When the coaches wanted him to get fired up and knock other players on their ass, he remained passive. The years of seeing his dad strike his mom made him abhor violence. He just wanted to keep to himself and read books.

He was a special person, and Lucas knew he had to treat him differently. Darwin finally looked up. Lucas asked, "So, what do you think?"

"The archaeological method isn't going to work here," Darwin said, tapping the table with a finger the size of a sausage. "We have no credentials."

Lucas could tell Darwin had given this a lot of thought during their car ride. "So, what? Give up and go home?"

"No, no. Not at all," Darwin said, shaking his head. "We just might have to go about things differently."

"How so?"

Darwin regarded the ceiling and collected his thoughts. "The archaeological method is a set of practices on how to identify and excavate a potential site. I went to the Badlands in Montana the summer before last to work on a stegosaur dig. It is a time-consuming process. Here we have two major problems: one is time; the other is that we don't have a site nailed down."

Darwin pulled out two copies of Blackbeard's map and handed one to Lucas.

"My thought is," Darwin continued while Lucas studied the map, "is to go into Bath and try to talk with the locals, as you said. Maybe see if they have a marina where we could show this to some of the people who trawl these waters. See if they know of a place such as this."

"Sounds good to me," Lucas said. At first glance, there was something oddly familiar about the area depicted on the map, but he couldn't put a finger on it. It might be one of a thousand places. He couldn't tell what the scale was. Every inch may well depict several miles or several yards. He assumed that if this map depicted somewhere along the Atlantic seaboard, then true north would be on the right side of the page. He smiled, "Sounds fun"

"Then, if that fails, we hop on a ferry and ride out to Ocracoke Island. That's where he spent a lot of time during 1718 and had a weeklong party with other well-known pirates. That's also where he was killed by Robert Maynard and his men."

Lucas took a sip of coffee and sloshed it around in his mouth before swallowing. *Not bad*, he thought. He could tell it was a cheaper blend S&D made. Still not bad.

The year of 1718 was the height of the Golden Age of Pirates, and Blackbeard was the most notorious of all. Darwin explained that Blackbeard, or Teach as the locals called him, spent six months in Bath Town after receiving his pardon and before his death. During that time, he married Mary Ormond, built a house, and possibly resumed pirating.

By that summer, piracy reached its peak around the world. The waters of the Atlantic and Caribbean were filled with the blood of innocent sailors, while the holds of many pirate ships were filled with grains, spices, rum, wine, slaves and other valuable trade commodities.

Teach and his crew returned to Bath one day in September with salvage, not plunder, from what they claimed was an abandoned French ship they discovered at sea. If they had boarded the ship and seized the cargo from the unwilling French crew, that would have violated the pardon. If so, Teach and his crew could hang for the offense.

Tobias Knight, the Collector of Customs, presided over a Vice Admiralty Court to investigate the matter. The court found the ship to be a derelict lost at sea. Twenty hogsheads—or large wooden barrels—of sugar were granted to Knight, sixty were given to Eden and the remainder was left to Teach and his men.

Teach and his crew liked to linger around nearby Ocracoke to watch the ships coming and going from northeast Carolina. While there, he met another well-known pirate, Charles Vane.

Vane had rejected the King's pardon several months earlier and was on the run from pirate hunters commissioned by Woodes Rogers, who was the Governor of the Bahamas. One pirate hunter was Benjamin Hornigold. Hornigold was Teach's pirate mentor who accepted the King's Pardon after Teach struck out on his own.

Vane arrived with other notorious pirates such as "Calico" Jack Rackham, Robert Deal, and Blackbeard's old first mate, Israel Hinds. Vane's reason for the trip to North Carolina from the Caribbean was to convince Blackbeard to sail south with him. Teach politely refused the invitation but hosted the visiting pirates on Ocracoke to a weeklong, rum-soaked party.

One man who wanted to see an end of the plague of piracy upon the settlers and explorers of the New World was Virginia Governor, Alexander Spotswood. He and the other Colonial Governors saw pirating grow to the point that its effect may well stifle the growth of the colonies. With the pirate-hunting actions set in motion by Rogers to the south, and the pledge to fight piracy along the American coast, the death of Blackbeard would send a message to pirates everywhere that they were of a dying breed.

Teach's meeting with Charles Vane on Ocracoke scared Spotswood. If the most feared pirate in the world and Vane merged forces, they would have a fleet large enough to lay siege to that part of the world. Although he was out of his jurisdiction, Spotswood commissioned two British war sloops to seek out and to, figuratively, cut off the head of the face of pirating, which they did, literally, when Blackbeard was beheaded in the battle that followed.

"Then the search for his treasure began," Darwin finished.

Lucas picked up his copy of the map and studied it. "And the search continues with us."

"Yes, and we're armed with something no one else has: Blackbeard's actual treasure map."

Lucas set the map aside and worked on connecting his tablet to the Wi-Fi in the lobby. Once accomplished, he started the Maps program and searched for "Bath, NC."

The application pulled up a wide view with Bath centered. Lucas zoomed in until the small town filled most of the screen. Lucas compared the image with the treasure map.

"There is a resemblance," Lucas said after a minute.

"How so?" Darwin asked with a measure of excitement in his voice. Were they on to something already? He hoped it would be that easy.

"The shape of the bottom of the island Blackbeard sketched out is similar to the layout of Bath. Bath is obviously not an island like what was drawn, and the mainland is at a different angle as well."

"What about the half-moon or sun drawn on the left side of the island? What do you think of that?"

Lucas scratched his head. "*If* what is drawn is one of those, and we can only assume that, then it can't be a sunrise. If you are out in Bath

Creek on the eastern part of town looking back to the west, then it looks as though the sun would set over the town. It doesn't look like, however, that there's a big area in which to do that."

"Okay, so it may not be a map of Bath," Darwin said.

"Looks that way. If Blackbeard was familiar with that locale when he drew the map, then I imagine he would have drawn it more like this," Lucas said pointing down at the tablet, "with place names, landmarks, and references."

"And we also have no way of knowing when this map was made."

"Yeah, it might have been at any point during his time as a pirate."

"He was a pirate captain, for what? Two years?"

"I believe so," Lucas said. "Something like that."

To consider that Blackbeard's rise to infamy took fewer than twenty-four months was staggering considering the time in which he lived. Today, with the rise of social media, news and rumors can be reported in the amount of time it takes to compose a 140-character Tweet. It doesn't matter if the news is about war breaking out in the Middle East or someone's aunt getting a new cat. News is instant and can spread across the globe in a matter of seconds.

In the early 18th century, the speed at which news traveled was only as fast as the fastest runner, horse, or ship. An Indian attack in the north would take weeks for word to travel to the southern colonies. For pirates, their reputation took months to spread. And spread across the world it did. Sailors, merchantmen, and ship captains quickly learned of the scourge that was Blackbeard. He and his fleet had the ability to shut down entire ports and the shipment of goods. Vital goods to the growth of the New World.

He wasn't alone. Other well-known pirates such as "Calico" Jack Rackham, Anne Bonny, and Charles Vane did their part to hamper the growth of North and South America. They would float along well-traveled shipping lanes of the Caribbean and Atlantic and attack any ship they thought might have plunder.

During the Golden Age of Pirating from 1715-1722, pirates made the transportation of anything a dangerous venture. This didn't just take place in the Americas. Other, more successful, pirates plied the waters of the Indian and Pacific Oceans. They did their part to place a dent in the spice and fabric trade.

There was something about Blackbeard, however, that captured people's attention. Something sinister. Something intriguing. For word of him to reach around the world as fast as it did, that told Lucas he must have been talked about by every sailor, captain, passenger and officer who sailed the high seas at that time.

"Yeah, two years sounds about right," Lucas said.

"I wish I had more time to research him further before we came out here."

Lucas shook his head. "It's okay. At least you conveniently had this week off anyway." He stopped and then asked, "What were you going to do on your vacation?"

Darwin gave him a blank look. "I didn't have anything planned. Not much I can do with just a moped and no money."

"What about your family? Think about going home to see them?"

"I haven't spoken to mom since my sophomore year."

"Why's that?"

He hesitated before answering. "She called to tell me she was moving."

# CHAPTER SEVEN

D ARWIN REVEALED THE NEWS without a trace of emotion.

"Oh, where to?" Lucas asked.

"Wyoming."

"Wyoming? Why there?"

Darwin scratched his chin and resumed his observation of the ceiling. "She said she'd met a cowboy ranch hand on a dating website for farmers and was going to go live with him."

Lucas gave Darwin an incredulous look. "A dating website for *farmers*? When was your mom ever on a farm?"

"Never that I know of. The closest she came to a farm was the produce section at the grocery store," Darwin said. "Just one day, she called, said she was leaving. Good luck."

"Wow. Just like that?"

"Just like that," he said. "That was the last I heard from her. She didn't say where she was going, leave a telephone number, or anything."

"Man, I'm sorry to hear that, Darwin," Lucas said.

He knew Darwin's father left him and his mom when he was a small child. Now, he's had both of his parents desert him. Lucas still had both of his parents. He couldn't imagine having neither of them, nor to have them leave in the manner in which Darwin's parents left. Poor guy.

Lucas took another sip of coffee and then asked, "What about your friends? Anyone there you could visit?"

Another sad shake of the head. "Don't have many of those either," Darwin admitted. "I kept to myself in school mostly. I suppose my size kept classmates from wanting to talk to me."

Lucas studied Darwin from across the table. He dwarfed the chair and table in which they sat. Lucas was well above average height himself, about six-foot, three inches. Darwin made Lucas feel small. Darwin's dark skin was almost the same color as his long, bushy beard, and his hair was unkempt. His t-shirt had holes around the collar and sleeves. He wore a pair of horn-rimmed glasses with thick lenses that he'd had since middle school.

When Darwin walked across campus, Lucas was sure his friend stood out like a sore thumb. With already low self-esteem, Lucas imagined Darwin spent at least the last four years of his life depressed. That is, if he wasn't depressed before college. Lucas saw how that would lead Darwin to withdraw from his peers and keep to himself.

At times throughout Lucas's life, he found himself staying distant from people, even his friends. He didn't know why, it's just the way he was. He would come out of his shell when he needed to, though. He empathized with Darwin to a degree.

"Well, buddy," Lucas said, "let's have fun this week."

As big and as rough around the edges as Darwin appeared, his smile lit up the room. If he smiled more, he'd look much more approachable, Lucas thought.

"Sounds great. I could use that."

"Good," Lucas said. "I could use a diversion myself."

"Why is that?"

Reluctantly, Lucas filled him in on the details about Kristen.

When Lucas finished, Darwin said, "Man, you're right. You could use a diversion. Dang, I'm sorry to hear that."

"Thanks."

"If that was what was in her heart, she didn't deserve you," Darwin said.

Lucas smiled at the sentiment. "Thanks, Darwin. Look at you wax philosophical on me."

He laughed. "Took a few courses in Philosophy at State. Can't much help it."

"That's good. Take any psychology?"

"Yeah, a little."

"Well, maybe I'll come lie on your couch later and we'll have a session I'll spill my soul to you about my marriage."

Another laugh. "I don't know about that. I'm not sure I'm the shrink you need."

No words passed between them for several minutes while they assessed the personal news about each other they just learned. The last sip of coffee Lucas took from his paper cup was cold. He set it aside and folded his hands before him. "Back to the matter at hand."

Darwin perked up, remembering why they were sitting in a small hotel near the North Carolina coast and more than glad to change the subject. "Yes, to that."

Lucas yawned and looked at the clock on the wall behind Darwin. "Okay, how about this? It's getting late. Why don't we hit the sack and reconvene here around eight a.m.?"

Darwin nodded. "Then head to Bath?"

"Yes, we'll go out, get the lay of the land, see who we can talk to, and try figure out if the treasure is there."

"And what if it's not?"

Lucas shrugged. "Then we'll try somewhere else. We have an opportunity to uncover history here, and I would love for us to be the ones to solve the mystery of Blackbeard's missing treasure."

"Amen," Darwin said. He stood up, collecting his folder and map, jarring the table in the process. "Sorry."

Lucas had a hand on his tablet and notebook to keep them from falling. "No problem, big fella. I'll see you tomorrow."

# CHAPTER EIGHT

D ARWIN ENTERED HIS ROOM and threw his duffel bag and backpack on the queen-sized bed filling most of the room. He stood in a standard-looking motel room by any standards. Neutral colors throughout, a TV on its way to being out of date. Mass-produced curtains tried to cover the windows. *It's better than what I have at home*, Darwin thought.

He walked to the back of the room and ducked into the bathroom. He relieved himself and then washed his hands at the sink where he stared at his unruly mop of hair on the top of his head in the mirror.

He hoped this trip was the start of a new phase in his life. He spent most of his childhood and time in college alone. Most of his classmates shunned him during his academic life. To them, he seemed too big, too weird. He didn't do himself any favors by not being the most outgoing person. He sometimes came off bristly, as in "look, don't touch." He didn't mean to be that way. His father's abandonment of he and his mom caused Darwin to be untrusting of most people. He didn't know why his dad left. He remembered them being close during his earliest memories of his life.

Then, things began to change. He remembered being afraid while his mother and father got into frequent arguments. The subjects of the spats were lost on three-year-old Darwin. He remembered they were loud and sometimes came to blows. He wasn't taught that hitting other humans was wrong—and his parents had no interest in teaching him that—he figured it out for himself.

After his dad left—a fuzzy moment in his memory—Darwin barely spoke. His mother became concerned, although she didn't have enough money to afford child counseling for her young child. Eventually, she came across a public program that offered free counselling for Darwin. However, because of the office's workload his sessions with a therapist were hurried. He was too young to understand what was happening and therapy did little good.

While his mom tried to hold a job and move on with their lives, Darwin was often under the care of his two aunts. He had no uncles. Like his father, they too were long gone. He spent the most formative years of his life without a strong male presence. He had no one to teach him the responsibilities of being a man, being a father, being a good contributor to society. The limited number of adults in his life taught him values, but his mother wasn't a pillar of the community. Darwin figured out during his teenage years that when she locked herself in her room, she was oftentimes doing various drugs.

She, like him, often sought to escape reality via numerous means. Darwin never once resorted to that type of escape, although he could have. His mom kept no locks on her door or nightstand. He could have sampled anything she did. In school, sometimes kids offered him pot—when someone would speak to him—although he never once tried it.

As he grew older, he became more aware of the environment and life surrounding him. When he turned thirteen, he realized he was aware of so much more than he did when he was ten. He first became aware of his personal space. That bubble around him and others. Similar revelations occurred when he reached sixteen and then eighteen. He reached the same revelation more and more as he progressed through school. This was because he learned cause and effect. How his, or someone's actions, affected others. Most of the other kids in his age group did not display a similar conscientiousness of the world around them.

Darwin never found school challenging and seldom studied for tests. He took little interest in most classes. That didn't stop him from earning high grades throughout middle and high school. He graduated near the top of his class with ease. He did best, of course, in the classes he enjoyed. He loaded up on science and advanced math classes when he could.

He read voraciously, mostly adventure fiction. Michael Crichton's *Jurassic Park* and its sequel, *The Lost World*, inspired Darwin to take an interest in archaeology. The treasure hunting of Dirk Pitt in Clive Cussler's novels kept Darwin up late at night, adventuring to exotic locales looking for lost artifacts or treasure. This was one way he escaped the home situation he lived in. He branched out later and learned about noted archaeologists Robert Bakker, Howard Carter, Hiram Bingham, and Robert Ballard. The stegosaur dig Darwin went on in Montana during the summer before his senior year of college was a dream come true. Now, he was on his own expedition. He wasn't digging for bones. He was digging for a long, lost treasure.

He learned to think for himself. He had to. His family wasn't going to help him to figure life out. From an early age, he had to take care of himself. He had to get himself up for school, pack his own lunches, including walking down to the grocery store to do the shopping for him and his mom.

He was smarter than almost all the other kids he knew. His teachers gave him an IQ test in elementary school where he tested out at near genius. He saw the decisions his family members made and recognized that they weren't the correct ones. He knew that much by the time he was in third grade. That led to him questioning what adults taught him at school, at church, everywhere. When he needed help with a particular problem, he often sought the guidance of his teachers. They were the most responsible and intelligent adults he knew.

In school, when teachers separated students into groups for projects, he would be the one who most often did all the work. It's not that his classmates didn't want to help. It was more that he didn't like the way others would want to accomplish their assigned task. He saw solutions while his peers still tried to identify the problems. Although he never intentionally used his size to intimidate them, they mostly acquiesced to his ways.

No one wanted to poke the bear with a stick.

Somehow, amid all the troubles he had at home, child services never stepped in. He and his mom never had much money. Government programs such as food stamps helped put food on the table.

When Darwin turned sixteen, he went to his guidance counselor and asked for help in finding a job. That led to him getting a job as a busboy at a Mahoney's location in Concord. He earned minimum wage, and after a month on the job, had more money than he had ever had in his life. He had no car, so he rode the city bus to and from work every day to save money.

He applied for and won a scholarship award during his junior year of high school from Mahoney's. All he had to do was write a paper on what going to college would mean for him. In it, he wrote about his childhood and familial situation. He knew that no one in his family ever went to college, much less graduated. He wanted to break the mold and show people that someone with his background could succeed.

During the process of entering and winning the contest, he became friends with Lucas. Although not old enough to be his dad, Lucas helped to guide Darwin through the murky waters of entering adulthood. Lucas provided the first strong male presence in Darwin's life. That is one reason Lucas was the only person Darwin called when he discovered the treasure map.

He scraped for everything he had, although it was little. He had already accomplished more than any family member he knew and recognized that he could do more. He just had to find an avenue in which to go.

He didn't know what would become of this trip, although Darwin hoped it would be what he needed to give him a boost as he entered the work force now that he had graduated.

# CHAPTER NINE

WHEN LUCAS ENTERED THE motel lobby the next morning, Darwin was already there. Had been for a while. Several empty plates and two Styrofoam cups sat on the table. He had a third in his hand when Lucas walked up.

"Did you leave me anything?" Lucas asked, gesturing at the counter where the motel had a continental breakfast set up. There was a microwave, toaster, three coffee urns, cereal and juice dispensers, mini-fridge, trays with various baked goods and fruits and a waffle maker.

Lucas smelled the aromas of the coffees and syrup for the waffles. His stomach growled.

"Not quite," Darwin laughed.

"How long have you been here?"

"Since about five. Couldn't sleep. That was when they started serving breakfast."

"Oh, okay. Well, let me grab something to eat and we'll get going."

"Sounds good."

The coffee wasn't as fresh as it was last night to Lucas's disappointment. The freshly made waffle more than made up for it. Lucas grabbed an apple for the road.

He and Darwin climbed in the Jeep, and Lucas entered the GPS coordinates for Bath. They stopped at a gas station to fill up on gas and get a cup of fresh coffee at the attached Dunkin Donuts. Satisfied with that pick-me-up, they set off towards Bath.

Now that it was daylight, they could get a better view of their surroundings. Lucas affirmed his initial impression of Chocowinity from when they arrived the previous evening: not much to it. It seemed like a place where hopeful entrepreneurs hoped to catch travelers as they passed through the intersection of Routes 17 and 33.

The four-lane Route 17 they were on crossed over the Pamlico River into the larger town of Washington. Founded the same year of the signing of the Declaration of Independence, the town's claim to fame was that it was the first to be named after the first President, George Washington. There appeared to be more to this town than the village they just left. Established older businesses lined the road.

They made a right onto US 264 soon after entering the town. Within a few miles, the town gave way to open land on either side of the road. Lucas figured cotton was the primary cash crop in the area. The fields held thousands of the small plants with fluffy, white buds peeking out of their tops.

A small green sign pointed to stay left for Nags Head and the Ocracoke Ferry, or to veer right for Bath. US 264 split and Lucas pointed the Jeep down NC 99. Ten minutes later, they entered Bath. In all, the trip from the motel to Bath took less than half an hour. It was just after 9 a.m. local time.

They passed over a small bridge into Bath. The town appeared to be untouched since the early 1900's. There were no big businesses, no fast-food chains, and no neon lights. The antebellum homes and churches made Lucas feel as though he stepped into a bygone era. He would not have been surprised for the paved roads to give way to dirt and to see the populace make their way around on horse and buggy.

"Do you see anyone?" Darwin asked, echoing Lucas's thoughts.

He shook his head. "No, I don't. You'd think that there'd at least be some movement."

They turned onto South Main Street towards the tip of town. As they moved down the street, to the left were many old stately white homes. On the right were more modest homes with private docks floating on Bath Creek.

The street ended less than two-hundred yards from their entry onto it. There they saw their first resident: an older gentleman wearing a gray hat on a golf cart in the process of picking up the newspaper from his driveway on the Bath Creek side of the street.

Darwin laughed. "Look at that old man. His front door is less than twenty feet away from the newspaper."

"Maybe he has a hard time walking," Lucas said. "Or he just likes driving his cart."

"I would," Darwin shrugged.

South Main terminated at Front Street, looking out over the harbor. They passed a home with a hand-painted sign in the yard advertising "The Lost Treasure Gift Shop." A small, red home and a large, white house on the corner followed.

On the opposite side of Front Street, there was a small parking lot near a small park named Bonner's Point. The park was a small strip of grass fifty feet wide, that made up most of the park. Tall trees dotted the grassy area terminating at the water's edge. Several picnic tables sat at the right end of the park with a great view of the water. Three park benches faced the water. It was warm enough for them to wear short-sleeved shirts, although not an appropriate temperature for them to be comfortable wearing shorts.

An older couple sat close together on one of the benches. A middle-aged woman in a jogging outfit ran along the tree-lined street with a pint-size, white dog at the end of a leash.

When Darwin joined Lucas at the side of the Jeep, in an almost awed whisper said, "Man, its quiet here."

Lucas took a moment to get a better sense of their surroundings. Aside from an occasional yelp from the dog, the only sound they heard was the lapping of the small waves against the wooden retaining wall at the water's edge. Missing were the sounds of automobiles and trucks and the hustle-bustle of modern America.

"It is," Lucas agreed. "Like we stepped back in time."

They walked down the embankment to the water's edge. The remnants of a tropical storm lingered off the coast, casting a gloomy pall over the bay. Although they had seen many boats tied up along the docks on Bath Creek, they did not see any out on the water. A dead tree rose from the water and pointed vaguely to the left in the direction of where Blackbeard's home once stood across the water.

"Yep. What do you want to do?"

Lucas looked back along the street they had just traveled down, and pointed, "Let's walk back that way. It looks like that treasure shop was open."

In the fifty yards between the park and the treasure stop stood two historical markers: one black, one white.

The black one read:

### *John Lawson*
### *1674–1711*

**Naturalist, explorer, and surveyor general for the Lords Proprietors, John Lawson traveled the interior of the Carolina colony in 1700-01. He described the 550-mile journey in *A New Voyage to Carolina*, published in 1709. Lawson was killed by Tuscarora Indians while exploring the Neuse River in 1711.**

**His house stood nearby.**

Beyond that marker and the next was a tiny red house with a stone chimney. The next marker was the reason they came to Bath. It read simply:

**Edward Teach**

**Notorious pirate called "Blackbeard." Lived in Bath while Charles Eden was governor. Killed at Ocracoke, 1718.**

"What do you think?" Lucas asked Darwin.

"Looks promising," he said.

"I know. Let's check out this treasure store."

The store sat in a regal colonial home with white siding and black shutters. It appeared recently renovated. Two large oak trees sat in the front yard straddling a concrete walkway. Neatly manicured bushes sat in well-kept flowerbeds at the foot of a wraparound porch. The porch had a two-person swing on the corner and several seating group arrangements. It was a perfect place for locals to congregate on warm summer evenings, sip sweet tea, and mint juleps.

They walked to the door and knocked. The house, similar to the rest of the area, was quiet. The sign in the window advertised the place as being open, and after a minute passed by, they almost decided to continue their search elsewhere.

As they began to turn to walk away, they heard a rattling from behind the green door. It opened, and a short, elderly woman opened the door. She seemed startled to see two tall—especially compared to her—men standing before her. She might also be surprised to see two customers this early in the morning on a weekday, Lucas thought.

She looked unsure at first and after a beat, smiled, and opened the glass door for them. "Good morning, gentlemen," she said with a voice Lucas suspected would fit right in narrating children's stories for Disney.

"Good morning to you as well, ma'am," Lucas said.

"I'm sorry it took me a minute to get to the door," she said. "My husband and I were out back digging in the garden."

"That's okay. We understand," Lucas said.

She smiled. "Well, come in. Come in. Have a look around."

She stood aside to let Lucas and Darwin pass. Darwin had to duck his head as he entered to keep from banging it on the oak doorframe.

The home was built in the early 1900's, although to Lucas it looked in good shape. There was a small foyer with a hallway going all of the way to the rear of the house, passing between two stairway landings on its way to a screen door. Hardwood floors shined with wax. To the left and right were two large rooms. Merchandise filled both areas.

"Over here to the left," the woman said, "is our pirate treasure room. And here on the right is our Christmas room, which we just opened this week."

Lucas peeked into the Christmas room first. Once he started looking in the pirate treasure room he'd forget about this one, and he wanted to show his respect to the woman whom he'd disturbed from her morning gardening. A decorated Christmas tree sat in the middle of the room, with tables around it. The perimeter of the room was filled with displays of various holiday decorations and ornaments.

He stepped to the first table and regarded a stand of ornaments made from seashells into the shape of a bi-wing plane – a well-recognized shape out here near Kitty Hawk where Charles and Orville Wright made the first flight. The next display had ornaments also made from seashells of differing shapes into the form of turtles.

The lady stood in the corner and watched as Lucas and Darwin made their way around the room.

"Are these homemade?" Darwin asked.

She smiled. "Yes, I make all of them myself."

Lucas figured that there were hundreds of different individual ornaments in the room. "That's impressive," he said.

"Thank you, sir," she replied. "I made most of the other decorations here as well."

"That's quite an accomplishment."

She told them about how she went about making the seashell ornaments, and Lucas was quickly lost. Arts and Crafts were not his area of expertise. They listened as the woman described at length how she made them. Lucas couldn't imagine how much time it took, and it gave him a huge amount of respect for her.

Lucas took a quick glance at Darwin. "Want to take a look at the other room?"

"Absolutely," he said. He looked down at the woman as he passed her by and waved at the handmade ornaments. "Ma'am, I'd like to see how you do that sometime."

"Well," she said in her fairytale voice oozing with a Southern twang, "I've already finished for the year. If you come back in the spring, well, that's when I get started."

"I'll do that," he said.

The group entered the treasure room. It wasn't really filled with "treasure," although there was a wooden chest filled with plastic gold doubloons. That was as close as it got to treasure. The room was filled with small gifts, jewelry, pictures, and anything having to do with pirates or the ocean.

A large glass display sat in the center of the room. It had jewelry, gift boxes, and porcelain bells. In one corner on the top sat several wooden boxes. Lucas stepped over, picked one up, and opened it.

Inside was a brass bosun's whistle. These were used aboard ships at sea by boatswains and quartermasters to pass commands to their crew when their voices could not be heard over the sounds of the sea. The pitch of the whistle was changed by placing a finger over a hole in the top. Because of its high pitch, commands and messages could be passed to the crew over the roiling sounds of the sea.

He thought it interesting and held on to it.

The lady stood patiently at the side of the room. "What brings you boys to Bath so early this morning?"

"Blackbeard," Lucas replied.

She smiled again. "Well, you've come to the right place. I have all sorts of stuff about Blackbeard. He used to live here. You know. In Bath."

"Yes, ma'am," Lucas said. "You have a lovely place here."

"Definitely," Darwin agreed.

"Why, thank you boys. What are your names?"

"I'm Lucas, and this is my friend Darwin. Pleasure to meet you."

"Yes, you as well. My name is Alethia. What is it about Blackbeard that interests you?"

"His treasure," Darwin said.

She gazed up at Darwin for a moment. She seemed to be deciding whether to take him seriously. "Well, we get that a lot around here."

"Treasure hunters?"

"Oh, yes. Every couple of years there's always someone who comes here trying to find his treasure." She pointed out the front door in the general direction of the sound. "They go out there to Teach's Point and dig around."

"Anyone ever find anything?"

She shook her head and gave a gentle laugh. "No boys. They go out there and dig holes in hopes of finding it, although I don't believe anyone ever will."

"Why is that?" Lucas asked.

"Because now that whole area is now privately owned and gated off, unless you live out there. One of the locals retired, passed his shipping business onto his son, and bought the whole thing."

"The whole thing?"

"Yes, he put a gated community out there. He'd wanted to do that for years." She stopped suddenly and furrowed her brow. "You know, someone did find something out there one time, long ago."

Lucas and Darwin shared a look. "When was this?"

She scratched her chin. "Probably about thirty years ago. The early eighties, maybe."

"Sounds about right. I don't know, it wasn't Teach's Point, though," Darwin said.

"What sounds about right?" she asked.

"Ma'am—,"

"Please call me Alethia," she said, cutting Darwin off.

Darwin cleared his throat and continued, "Alethia, I work for the North Carolina Museum of History in Raleigh as an archivist, and I was going through old storage rooms and found a box labeled *Plum Point Dig – Bath, North Carolina*. Is Plum Point anywhere near here?"

She smiled. "Why yes. Teach's Point is also sometimes called by that name, Plum Point."

# CHAPTER TEN

L UCAS AND DARWIN SHARED a look.

"Do you remember what it was they found?"

She gazed out the window, searching her memory. "I'm not sure, really. They unearthed several things such as stoneware, pots, and utensils if I recall. You know, it might have just been one person out there. Usually they come in groups."

"Do you remember anything about a diary or journal being discovered?" Darwin asked.

She shook her head. "No. No I don't. What sort of journal?"

Darwin hesitated before answering. "The diary of Mary Ormond."

"That would be quite a find," Alethia said.

"Well, there was one in the box," Darwin said.

She covered her hand with her mouth in surprise. "Oh, my. That's amazing."

Darwin told her the circumstances of what he found and a few details of what the book contained.

"I don't believe anyone has ever uncovered anything written or created by her or Teach," she said, referring to Blackbeard's real surname. "Why was it in the box?"

"I don't know ma'am."

"Alethia," she corrected.

"I'm sorry. Alethia. I'm not sure. The museum had a lot of field research going on during that time, and maybe it just got overlooked. I don't know why though. The person conducting the dig should've known the enormity of the find."

"I've lived here my entire life," she said, "and I can't once remember anyone finding something such as that. They've found various doodads and knick-knacks. Nothing of any importance. You're here for the treasure, right?" They nodded. "Does she talk about it in her diary?"

"I didn't get a chance to read all of it, but not that I saw," Darwin said. "There was a map."

"A map! How wonderful. So, where's his treasure?" she asked.

"We don't know."

"You don't know?" she repeated. "Isn't that what the map is for?"

Lucas smiled. "Well, that's the thing. The map is vague. It looks as though it was drawn by Blackbeard, however he didn't have any place names or landmarks besides a big oak tree written on it that tells what area is represented."

"Can I see it?" she asked. "Maybe I can tell you. I'm familiar with the waters around here."

"Yes, absolutely," Darwin said. "I have a copy of it out in our car."

"Where is it? Your car?"

"Just right out there at Bonner's Point."

She smiled again. "Well, if you'll escort me out there big fella, I'll take a look at it."

"I can just go get it and bring it back here if you'd like."

"No," she said. "It'll do me good to get out in the neighborhood every once in a while."

When they got out on the street, Alethia reached up and took Darwin's arm as they walked down the sidewalk towards the end of the street to the calm waters of Bath Harbor. Lucas lingered a few steps behind.

"Alethia?" Lucas asked.

"Yes, dear."

"I'm sure since you've lived here for so long and you have the Pirate Treasure Gift Shop, you probably know a thing or two about Blackbeard."

"I suppose I know a few things. There are others who know more. Is there something you want to know?"

"Well, there are many things I'd like to know," Lucas said. "One thing I was wondering was if he was born around here? Some say he's not from England, but from here."

She turned to look at him. "No, I've heard those rumors. They've been batted around here for three-hundred years. They're not true. He's from Bristol, England."

She made the statement in such a way that prevented any further discussion on the matter. Lucas believed her.

They made it to Bonner's Point, and Darwin passed her to Lucas while he dug in the Jeep for a copy of the treasure map. While he did that, Alethia and Lucas stared out over the calm water. The small amount of fog rolling over the water had dissipated, and the sun was trying to peek out from behind the clouds.

"It's beautiful, isn't it?" Alethia asked. "I've lived in that house almost my entire life, and I used to come out here every day and sit and read on the bank. I like watching the sailboats pass by; the seagulls fly overhead; the sounds of the water lapping against the bank always kept me calm. I can't imagine anywhere I would have rather lived."

"Hawaii?"

She considered it for a moment. Then in her fairytale voice said, "No. Not even there. It's just so peaceful here, Lucas. You young people get so wrapped up in school, your careers, and your family – although family is okay – that you fail to take the time to enjoy some of the nicer things outdoors. You look out over that water, Lucas, and tell me the last time you spent more than a day enjoying something like that."

Lucas winced. The last time he went to the beach, he was with Kristen. He didn't want to bring that up, so instead he said, "When I was a teenager, my family and I would go to Emerald Isle every summer."

"That's near here. I love that island just across the sound from Morehead City. You should take the time to get outside and enjoy things like this. You'll live longer."

"I appreciate the advice," Lucas smiled, reflecting on where he was in life. "I should."

"You should," she said in a tone that reminded him of his mother.

Darwin retrieved the map and walked back to Alethia. He handed it to her.

"Oh, my. This is extraordinary," she said. She traced her finger over the lines and mumbled to herself.

"What do you think?" Darwin asked.

"And this came out of Mary Ormond's diary?" she said. Darwin nodded his head. "If this is something she got from Teach, then I bet you could find his treasure if you found the X." This encouraged the two young men for a second until her next statement. "The problem is that this isn't from here. In Bath, that is."

Darwin's shoulders visibly drooped. "Where do you believe it is?"

"I don't know. Could be anywhere." She pointed at the X on the part of land resembling a kidney. "You see here where he's drawn these squiggly lines that look like they're streams or creeks?"

"Yeah."

"Bath doesn't have anything such as that. And this line here," she pointed at the shoreline drawn to the left of the kidney island, and then pointed out to the land on the left side of the water from Bonner's Point. "They're different. If he drew this from his ship, he wouldn't have drawn it that way." She handed the map back to Darwin. "No, this map isn't of Bath."

Darwin's shoulders sagged. Lucas let him know it wasn't the end of the world. "Well, we figured there was a possibility this wasn't from here, although there are similarities. We were just hopeful we could come here and find it quickly."

"I'm sorry boys," Alethia said. She watched the waves pass by. "You should go see Hugo."

"Who is Hugo?" Lucas asked.

"He's the son of the man who bought Teach's Point."

"Why him?"

She regarded Lucas as though she was trying to explain something complex to a five-year-old. "Well, he now owns the shipping company and knows the waters along the East Coast very well. He could let you look at the ruins and help you with the map."

"That would be nice of you and him."

She laughed. "Oh, and he's our foremost expert on Blackbeard."

That perked up Darwin. "Hey, that'd be great. How does he know so much about Blackbeard? Did he study him in school or something?"

"He may have, I don't know where he got his knowledge. All I know is that if people have a question about the pirate, they go to him."

"Sounds perfect," Darwin said.

They walked back to her house. There, she picked up an old, corded phone and dialed a number. After ten seconds she said, "Hello, Hugo . . . Yes. It's Alethia . . . I am well. Thank you. Are you nearby this morning? . . . Ok. I have two gentlemen here who would like to talk to you. . .. About Blackbeard. . .. Okay. Great. Are you over at your usual spot? . . . Thanks. I'll send them over. Goodbye."

She put the phone back in its cradle on the wall. "That Hugo is such a nice man."

"That's good," Lucas said. "So, he'll see us?"

"Yes, he said he wasn't doing anything except sitting out on the deck, trying to catch dinner."

"Sounds nice," Darwin said. "To have a house close enough to the water that you could catch your dinner on the back porch would be very convenient."

She gave him an odd look. "Oh, it's not quite his back porch. You'll see."

She gave them directions to find this Hugo. Lucas selected a small statue of Blackbeard from a shelf near the front door. The figure was posing with the barrel of a musket in his right hand and the stock of the gun going all of the way to the wood on a portion of what was meant to be wooden post on a pier and his left hand on his hip. To Lucas, it reminded him of the famous rum icon Captain Morgan. The figure in his hands wore a black long-coat, a tri-point hat, and brown boots that came to his knee. Three pistols in separate holsters were in a gun sling wrapped across his midriff. Another gun was stashed in his belt and sword hung from his right side.

The most striking feature was, of course, the full black beard. The coarse hair was tied off into five sections, bundled at each end with a red ribbon.

Lucas thought of the period in which Blackbeard lived. At six-foot one inches tall; he was well above average height for that era. Lucas remembered that the dreaded pirate lit long hemp fuses hanging from his hat before going into battle. The pall of the intoxicating dark smoke cast an intimidating figure.

"Good choice," Alethia said when Lucas handed it to her for purchase. "This is a close representation of what he probably looked like. Except for one thing."

"What's that?"

"His hat."

"What about his hat?"

"He wore a fur hat," she said.

"A fur hat? In this climate? I bet he had to stay hot," Darwin said.

She looked up at him. "He probably did, and everyone else during that day knew that too. I figure he wore it to show he was much tougher than everyone else was. That he could take it."

Lucas handed her the doubloon and picked up a small black flag with the famous skull and crossbones.

"Now you know," she said, "this flag is called the 'Jolly Roger.' Everyone knows this as a pirate flag."

"Yeah, Blackbeard used it didn't he?" Lucas asked.

She shook her head. "Some pirates did, although Teach had one of his own design."

"What did it look like?"

"Hold on," she said. She went into the depths of her house and returned with an old leather-bound book. She flipped though the book for a few seconds before finding what she wanted. "Here it is," she said and handed the book to Lucas.

At the top of the right-hand page was a black flag. It had a skeleton with horns holding a spear in one hand and an hourglass in the other. The spear pointed to a heart dripping three drops of blood.

"Quite a dread inspiring flag," she said. "The skeleton is the devil. The hourglass told ocean travelers that their time for living is running out. The heart pierced by the spear symbolizes a merciless death while the spear itself shows a violent death. The leaking heart represents a drawn out and torturous death."

The two men stared at the flag, taking in its many meanings.

"So basically," Darwin said, "when pirates put up their flags near other vessels, it signaled to them to surrender or die?"

She agreed. "Yeah, that's about it. Blackbeard's incorporated several elements to inspire terror. Hugo can tell you more about that though."

They thanked her for the information. She wrapped the statue for Lucas and placed it in a cardboard box before putting it in a plastic bag. She tucked the flag in along the side. Lucas took the doubloon and stuffed it in his pocket.

They thanked the elderly woman for the information and her time and then walked out to the sidewalk. Hugo's place was on the other end of the street, right where they arrived in Bath. Lucas took his package to the Jeep while Darwin waited on the sidewalk. They decided they would take advantage of the weather and walk to Hugo's place. It wasn't far.

When Lucas returned, Darwin was coming out of Alethia's house.

"Forget something?" Lucas asked.

"Oh, nothing. I just asked her if it'd be okay if I came back next spring and helped her. We exchanged phone numbers and said we'd keep in touch."

"She was nice," Lucas said.

They walked along the sidewalk to the start of the street. Alethia told them they could find Hugo at the end of the last driveway on the left-hand side. She said they couldn't miss him. He was in the big one at the end—whatever that meant.

The driveway at the end of the street had a house on the left side and a white speedboat with a "FOR SALE" sign taped to its side. The driveway was about twenty yards long, terminating at the water. At the end, they saw the bridge they crossed to get to Bath on the right and a small shack was next to the water on the left. It had a gas pump at the end of a small dock.

In between the bridge and the shack was a marina. The marina had eighteen slips that accommodated thirty-six ships. It stuck out in the water like a trident: a long dock split off into three prongs with slips spaced evenly apart. A fifty-four-foot-long gleaming white yacht occupied the slip at the end near the bridge.

"Well, she said we wouldn't have any trouble figuring out which boat was his," Darwin said.

There was a middle-aged man readying himself to cast off in a small fishing boat tied up in a slip on the left side. Other than that, there was no one else present. Just another quiet day in Bath, Lucas supposed.

They made their way to the yacht but saw no one above deck. They stepped aboard, the boat rocked with Lucas and Darwin's weight. Lucas rapped on the cabin door.

From within, they heard a voice say something unintelligible. They waited patiently for a minute, satisfied that someone was coming.

When the door opened, Lucas and Darwin found themselves looking into the eyes of Blackbeard himself.

# CHAPTER ELEVEN

THE MAN WHO ANSWERED the door obviously wasn't Blackbeard. The figure Lucas had just purchased from the Treasure Shop wasn't cast from this man, although it might have been. This man was about six-feet tall and had long, dark hair. He wore a long blue coat and had leather boots that came to his knees.

Blackbeard's most striking feature, his beard, was present on this man, although it wasn't as menacing. It hung, Lucas figured, about four inches from the bottom of the man's chin. It was full and black. Not grown to strike terror in the hearts of men.

His piercing blue eyes, on the other hand, did. They seemed to penetrate through the tall duo standing at his door, as though they were carving knives stabbing into an inanimate object. They pierced through the surface and into the core, doing their best to intimidate Lucas and Darwin.

"Yes," the man said in a sonorous, gravelly voice, "what can I do for ya?"

Lucas imagined the real Blackbeard possessing that voice and those eyes. If he had lived into his fifties. Lucas hesitated. "Good morning, sir. The woman at the gift shop called ahead."

The man smiled. It was unnerving. "Yes, dear Alethia. How was she this morning? Was she having trouble getting around?"

"No," Lucas said. "It took her a moment to get to the door, but she explained she was in her backyard tending to the garden."

"Good, good," the man said. "She is a fine woman, that Alethia. A pillar of our small community here," he said with a wave of the hand. Lucas noted frilled sleeves showing from the cuff of the jacket. "She said you boys wanted to ask questions about Blackbeard?"

Lucas felt a small slight at being referred to as a *boy*. He was in his early thirties. He replied, "Yes, sir. I drove up from Concord and picked up Darwin here in Raleigh. We were interested in finding out more about Blackbeard, and wanted to speak to someone who might be able to shed light on his life, maybe things that aren't written about him."

The man stood back at the question, his eyes boring into Lucas and Darwin. "It's odd that a couple of young pups such as yourselves would come all of the way out here out of the blue, on a weekday, with interest in Teach. Why is that?"

Lucas and Darwin glanced at each other. "I am an archivist at the Natural History Museum in Raleigh," Darwin said, "and I may have stumbled across something pointing to Blackbeard's lost treasure."

The man's eyes went blank as he tried to process what Darwin said. "Oh, my," he said. "We've had treasure seekers coming through here literally since the day Blackbeard died. Most were hopeful spelunkers, but it was rare that they had anything to go on."

The man regarded Lucas and Darwin for a moment before standing aside and saying, "Well come in, come in. You've piqued my interest. Let's all go up to the top deck and chat for a bit about pirates and scallywags."

Lucas had spent time on fishing boats at Summersville Lake growing up in West Virginia and been on outings on Lake Norman near Charlotte. Nothing he had been on compared to the yacht he and Darwin were now standing on.

They entered a companionway with walls made of glossy, light cherry wood and matching wood floors. A small galley with stainless steel appliances was on their left and a breakfast nook was on their right. A seating area with white leather seating was just past the dining room. A cockpit blended seamlessly with the galley.

Lucas assumed the deck below contained much of the same opulence. Probably Hugo's sleeping quarters.

They climbed a small stairway to a flybridge mirroring the instrumentation from the cockpit below. The space had seating for passengers to bask in the sun—when it was out. Two fishing poles lay against a short wall on the port side. A red case holding bait and other fishing accessories sat nearby. An open cooler on the starboard side of the flybridge had three long neck bottles of beer poking their heads from packed ice.

From the looks of the discarded bottles in a trashcan, Lucas thought that Mr. Riddick had gotten a head start on the day.

He reached into the cooler and offered Lucas and Darwin a beer. Darwin abstained. Lucas wanted to show his graciousness to their host and accepted the proffered light beer. He winced. He didn't care for light beers and preferred a fuller body offering. Life was too short to drink beers of inferior quality. Casting his aversions aside, he cracked the beer open and held it up to the one Riddick had already half-downed and tapped the necks together in a toast.

"Salud!" Riddick said.

Lucas returned the salute and took a long pull from the bottle. It was early in the day here in Bath, he thought, but it was five o'clock somewhere in the world.

They took seats around the bridge. Riddick pointed with his bottle towards the open water where the sun was still trying to shine. "Looks like this tropical storm is starting to clear. Been a miserable couple of days."

"Did you get a lot of rain here?" Darwin asked. "We got drenched in Raleigh."

"Yeah, we did," Riddick replied. "It was steady enough to wash out a couple roads."

"That must be what happened over in Chocowinity," Lucas said.

"Yeah, heard there were roads over that way that got flooded. They'll open them back up once the water abates," Riddick said.

"So, are you a Blackbeard impersonator or something?" Darwin asked.

The bearded man nodded. "That I am, son. I've been a Blackbeard impersonator for over thirty years."

"What got you into that?"

He had a long drink on his beer before answering. "Well, just after college I joined my father in his shipping business. I'd guess you'd say I was clean cut up until then. Then I spent time at sea and cultivated this beard. Didn't have much time to take care of my personal appearance while I was at sea."

"How long would you be out there?"

"It varied. We shipped up and down the eastern seaboard, sometimes going to ports in South America. Although rarely. Mostly, we delivered to Charleston, New Orleans, Philadelphia, and New York. We'd be gone for days at a time. Many days, I'd just scrub toothpaste across my teeth with my finger and spray on deodorant – for little good that did.

"Anyway," he continued, "I grew up here in Bath and was always around the legend of Blackbeard and the pirates that frequented the area. That's only a small part of the town's history, although even three hundred years later, the man continues to captivate people. Young and old alike.

"As a child, I was fascinated by Blackbeard's story. People around here think he was native to Bath, although from all of the research I did, I agree with the popular opinion that he is from Bristol, England. Though to be fair, no one knows either way." Riddick took a sip of beer and then continued, "So, I went to a Halloween party in the mid

1980's during the time I was helping my dad with his shipping business. I already had this beard going," he stroked it for effect, "and decided to get a pirate coat and matching hat and go as Blackbeard."

"I take it that it went well," Darwin said.

Riddick's bushy brows arched. "Yes, it did. Thought I looked good. Others did as well. Someone approached me after the show and asked if I could appear at a town parade the next month as Blackbeard."

"And the rest is history," Darwin said.

"Pretty much," Riddick said, taking a long pull on his beer. "I studied old pirate movies and worked on a West Country accent to try to make it sound as though my pirate persona grew up in England."

Lucas sat off to the side listening to Riddick as he went through his narrative. He sounded intelligent and spoke with an accent developed from an Ivy League school with a bit of a British inflection mixed in. His distinctive voice no doubt stood out in a crowd.

"So, do you add in phrases such as walk the plank, yaargh, keel haul, shiver me timbers and other pirate lingo?" Darwin asked.

Riddick waived his hand dismissively. "No, pirates didn't talk like that."

"They didn't?" Darwin said.

"No," Riddick said. "Those are nothing more than a theatrical construct. There was a movie in the early fifties called *Blackbeard the Pirate*. An actor by the name of Robert Newton portrayed Blackbeard in that movie. He added the pirate speak to make his character more endearing and stand out."

"Really?"

"Yeah, other writers, actors and impersonators saw how well that came across, and it didn't take long for "pirate talk" to be adopted everywhere. I try to be as accurate as I can, and therefore abstain from the use of it. I want for the people who see when I make appearances to get a performance as close to the real Blackbeard as I can."

"So, in your own way, while you're there to entertain, you're also trying to educate at the same time?" Lucas asked.

Hugo made another salute with his now near empty bottle of beer. "Exactly. I feel as though I'd be doing a disservice otherwise. Been doing it ever since."

"That's cool," Darwin said. "Did you continue with the shipping business?"

"Oh, yes," Hugo laughed. "Being an impersonator pays in peanuts compared with shipping. There's no way I could earn a decent wage being Blackbeard exclusively. So, the business grew enough that after my dad retired, we were able to hire people to take over the day-to-day operations while I worked at growing our influence."

"How is that working out for you?"

A satisfied smile crept across his face. "Quite well, actually."

"Are you married?" Darwin asked.

"That is one subject where the real Blackbeard and I differ. While he had at least fourteen wives, with our local Mary Ormond being the last, I have never been married," he smiled. "I've had my fun, although I never had a woman who would tolerate me for very long."

"Why is that?" Darwin asked.

Riddick leaned away from Darwin, as though taken aback by the question. "Well, because I'm a pirate."

"You mean you act like a pirate sometimes."

Riddick gave the bigger Darwin a frank look. "If you want to believe that, go ahead."

There were no threats in what he said. No menace. The man owned a successful shipping business and built it to the point that he was able to let others take the reins. Then, he became a Blackbeard impersonator. Lucas and Darwin had just met him and had never seen him take on that alter ego. To play a role such as Blackbeard, even if it were a PG version of a cutthroat pirate, Lucas imagined Riddick would have to get into character like any good actor beforehand. To be a good actor, a person had to try to get inside the mind of the persona they were playing as best they could.

How far did Riddick take it? How far into Blackbeard's personality did he delve? When Lucas and Darwin stepped onto Riddick's boat, the man appeared as though he was almost ready to attend an event as Blackbeard.

Over the years, how difficult had it become for Riddick to break character?

Riddick was giving the much bigger Darwin his most intimidating stare. Not being intimidated, the much younger man returned the gaze. Lucas's eyes swept to and from the two as they locked glares.

Riddick grew a crooked grin and gave a deep belly laugh. He clapped Darwin on the knee and said, "Had you going there for a minute, didn't I lad?"

Darwin returned the smile. "You did."

Sensing the conversation was off course, Lucas tried to get the conversation back to the topic at hand. "Okay, Mr. Riddick, we don't want to take up too much of your time today. Tell us about the real Blackbeard. Where did he come from? What led to him becoming a pirate?"

Riddick sat back and said, "Edward Teach, a.k.a. Blackbeard, has a background shrouded in mystery. Not much is known of his origins before his rise to infamy. While most believe he hailed from Bristol, England, there have been others claiming he came from Accomack County, Virginia and even here in Bath. I believe he came from Bristol."

"Alethia agreed with that," Darwin said.

Riddick nodded. "Yes, there are those from the old guard around here who hold on to the claim he was born here. There are still several families in Bath who have resided here since before the founding of the town. Since Blackbeard was a resident here just before his death is one thing that brings attention to this town. The old-timers want him to have grown up here, gone abroad, made a name for himself being a scourge of the seas, and come home for his final days.

"It's worth pointing out," Riddick continued, "that his birthplace has never been proven, although I believe based upon what we know, he was from England."

"Okay, so he came from England," Lucas said. "How did he get into pirating?"

"I figure he began his career in the Caribbean as a privateer in the early 18th century."

"What is a privateer?" Darwin asked.

Riddick waived his hand dismissively. "Bah, they were nothing more than officially sanctioned pirates. During the late 1600's and early 1700's, European nations were busy trying to colonize America. Explorers would arrive over here and claim a piece of land in the name of whatever nation they represented. The English, Dutch, and Spanish were constantly skirmishing with each other during this land-grab. Independent ship owners or captains could request a "letter of marque" from their government allowing them to attack enemies of the state on the high seas during times of war. Any cargoes or treasure won during these battles got split between the ship captains and the government."

"So, basically they were pirates who paid their taxes?"

"More or less," Riddick said. "Then over the years, the different factions of privateers from the different nations went to war amongst themselves. The battles raged from Europe to South America. This is likely where Teach learned his pirating ways. There is belief that Blackbeard's father was a privateer captain himself."

"Really?"

"Yes," Riddick answered. "Nothing substantiated though. They say the father returned to Bristol following the Dutch Wars around 1680. This was about the time many believe Teach was born."

"Teach was carrying on the family tradition?" Darwin asked.

"Maybe. Bristol was a big, busy port. Being from there, he would have been well educated—an advantage he would have over many he came across during his days of piracy. He likely saw and heard many stories as a youth of adventure from sailors returning from the Caribbean. There are stories that his stepfather beat him as a youth. When Blackbeard was in his early teens, a tale came from Bristol stating he nearly beat his stepfather to death during one such confrontation. Teach fled and went down to the docks and signed on with the first ship he could as a cabin boy."

"So, violence was a part of his life even at an early age?"

"Aye, it was," Riddick said. "Life was brutal back then in the region where he grew up. He was likely accustomed to seeing all sorts of brutality and treachery even at an early age."

"If he signed on with a ship headed out of Bristol," Lucas ventured, "wouldn't there have been a record of which ship he left on?"

"Not necessarily," Riddick answered. "Back in those days, there wasn't much paperwork done. Most of the sailors were either semi-literate or illiterate. They'd sign their names with an X or just shake the captain or quartermaster's hand. So, if Teach did leave from there, he wouldn't have necessarily had to fill out paperwork to do so."

"Gotcha," Lucas said. "So, Blackbeard got his start in the Caribbean?"

"Possibly. He could have sailed to the South Seas and around Cape Horn at the southern tip of Africa first. Then, sometime about 1697 he arrived in Port Royal, Jamaica. The slave market opened up in western Africa the following year. That kept ships busy as they made a triangle with slaves loaded in their holds between the African coast, Europe and North America."

"That's interesting," Darwin said. "I wouldn't have thought slavery would be involved in piracy."

"It's not an element of history spoken about much. Actually, many pirates, when they captured a ship with slaves on board, took the slaves to their next port and set them free," Riddick said. "Some of Blackbeard's most trusted crewmen were black."

"Wow," Darwin said.

"Yeah, they say that when he crashed his flagship, the *Queen Anne's Revenge*, half of his crew at that time was black. As he captured ships, he sometimes gave selected slaves the opportunity to remain on board with him. They weren't treated as well as their white peers, although it was a better life than what waited for them on the cotton plantations."

"That's true," Darwin said with him being the only black person in the group. The topic of slavery created a momentary uncomfortable silence.

Riddick and Lucas took a couple drinks from their slowly emptying bottles. Riddick twisted the cap off another beer. Lucas peered out over the water and saw a flock of seagulls making their way out to the Outer Banks. He asked, "Why did he wreck it? The *Queen Anne's Revenge*?"

"He wanted to seek a pardon from Governor Eden," Riddick answered. "If he didn't have the *Revenge* that would have shown the world he truly wanted out of pirating. There were only a few of his crew who knew this, including fellow pirate captain Stede Bonnet. He was past the date the king had given pirates in which to surrender or be hanged. Blackbeard, as it turned out, felt he had the means to persuade Eden to let him and his crew live, although they had not met at that point. Blackbeard had just laid siege to Charleston, and the Royal Navy wanted him dead.

"In June of 1718, I believe, Blackbeard and his flotilla of four ships entered the area around Beaufort, North Carolina. Three sloops and the *Revenge*. They all sailed into the narrow Topsail Inlet. It wasn't much wider than a couple football fields across and not very deep either. They carried more sail than they needed to, meaning they were going too fast for that stretch of water. The helmsman, without warning, turned the ship sharply to starboard and hit a sandbar."

"Did that sink it?" Darwin asked.

"No, it could have probably been salvaged at that point."

"What happened?"

"Blackbeard hailed Israel Hands, who captained the *Adventure*, one of the other sloops, and had him toss over a tow rope."

"So, Hands tried to pull the ship off the sandbar?"

Riddick shook his head. "Nope. The opposite in fact. The *Adventure* managed to drag the *Revenge* further onto the sandbar, damaging the keel and lower hull. This was after the main mast was broken during the initial crash. By then, the *Revenge* was dead. The *Adventure* ran on shore in the maneuver, crashing it beyond repair."

"What happened to the other two ships?"

"Blackbeard sent Stede Bonnet, to Bath Town in a longboat to meet with Eden and ask for pardon. Blackbeard intended to use the failed pirate captain as a guinea pig of sorts. Eden did pardon Bonnet and his crew, although that took about a week. At the time, it took about three days to sail from the crash site to Bath. A six-day round-trip. He ended up being gone about two weeks before returning.

"While Bonnet was gone, Blackbeard and his men set up camp on a small island away from civilization and had all of the remaining plunder transferred to the smaller of the two ships. He had promised the other sloop, the *Revenge*, to go back to Bonnet upon his return. Blackbeard had that ship stripped of anything useful: guns, ammo, plunder—you name it—while Bonnet was gone. He chose about forty men to crew the small sloop. They set sail, abandoning two-hundred or so pirates."

Lucas and Darwin shared a surprised look. "Just left them there. On an island?"

"That he did," Riddick said. "Look, he was a cunning, vicious, intelligent pirate. If he had to sacrifice two hundred or two thousand men to see to it that his plans came to fruition, he wouldn't have batted an eyelash before giving the order. I mean, if he *really* wanted everyone dead, he could have blasted the camp with cannon fire. At least he wasn't that brutal."

Although there were other pirates in the water, none was as notorious and as feared as Blackbeard. There were pirates more successful than the iconic pirate was. Bartholomew Roberts—also known as Black Bart—earned far more money, capturing five times more bounty than any other pirate did. Henry Every had the single biggest conquest when he captured a ship filled with the treasures of an Indian prince.

When most people think of pirate treasure, they imagine gold, silver, and jewels. It was rare, however, that pirates would take a ship with such lucrative spoils. Cargoes were often made up of items for trade such as coffee, tea, rum, medicine, rice, indigo, and sugar. For the sailors aboard pirate ships, rum was often their favorite find. For obvious reasons.

With that on his mind, Lucas decided it was time to get down to the subject that brought him and Darwin to Bath. The subject of treasure.

"Do you suppose his treasure was aboard when he crashed the *Revenge* into the sandbar?"

"I have no idea," Riddick responded. "Could've been. That's what many people like to believe. That is why we get people up here all the time, poking and digging around, trying to find it."

"And yet, it's never been found," Lucas said.

"Yeah," Riddick said. "It's just that every other person who comes to Bath to learn about Blackbeard is here trying to find his treasure. This whole town, Plum Point and every nook and cranny of the surrounding area has had someone crawling over it, trying to find gold."

"That's a shame," Darwin said.

Riddick gave him a cross look. "What's a shame?"

"It's a lovely town," Darwin explained.

The gruffness Riddick displayed over the treasure subject seemed to melt as his shoulders sagged.

"I'm an unpretentious guy," Darwin continued. "I like keeping things in my life simple. When we crossed the bridge here into Bath," he jerked a thumb at the bridge off to their right, "it seemed as though we entered a different world. A simpler time. A simpler place. This place is quiet and feels comfortable."

Riddick reached over and grasped Darwin's meaty shoulder. "Aye, my boy here gets it."

"And you get annoyed," Darwin continued, "when people don't take the time to appreciate Bath for what it is. Right?"

"That's right," Riddick said with a wicked grin. "I get tired of the treasure seekers. They are a blight on this town."

"Mr. Riddick," Lucas said in as soothing of a tone as he could, "we didn't come to Bath to dig up treasure. In fact, now we're reasonably sure it was never here."

The older man turned to regard Lucas and pointed at Darwin. "Which brings us to what your friend here discovered."

"He was sorting through old files and came across the diary of Mary Ormond," Lucas revealed.

Riddick gasped. Shook his head. "No way."

"He found it with other artifacts from a dig at Plum Point in – when was that, Darwin?"

Lucas kept his eyes on Riddick who stared at Darwin, surprised to be asked a question. "Uh, 1982," he stammered.

Riddick's gaze wandered out over the water, a distant look in his eyes. The sun began to dominate the sky. This thick shroud of clouds was breaking up. What started as a gloomy morning was giving way to a perfect fall day.

"I would have been about twenty-years old at the time. Don't know if I remember it."

"It wouldn't have been a large excavation," Darwin added. "The journal was in a box about the size that copy paper comes in." He used his hands to mimic an imaginary box in the air. "The box was tucked away in a storeroom we're clearing out. A man named Travis Cole was the person named as the person responsible."

Riddick's gaze traveled back out to the water for a moment before coming back to Darwin. "Well son, I hate to sound condescending, but did you ask this Mr. Cole about it?"

Darwin shook his head. "He doesn't work at the museum anymore, and I haven't had the chance to look him up."

Riddick kept his eyes locked on Darwin. "Oh. Well, you might not need to find him. I mean, he must not have thought it was too important just to throw it in a storeroom and forget about it. Is there something in that book pointing you in the direction of the treasure? Otherwise, why come out this way? Right?"

Darwin started to speak before Lucas jumped in. "There's a single entry that hints at the treasure."

Riddick cocked an eyebrow. "Really? History says no one knows where the treasure is besides Teach and the Devil," Riddick said. "I don't believe he would have told Mrs. Ormond. He barely knew her. She was fifteen when he married her. What does the passage say?"

"It's short," Lucas fibbed. "She said Teach came home late one night, completely drunk, and started boasting about his greatness. About how he was the toughest, greatest pirate in the world, and how he felt invincible. Then she said he got quiet and muttered something about no one ever finding "it" buried beside a huge tree underneath the falling sun in the cove to the south. She said he was smug about it."

Riddick looked from Lucas to Darwin and back again. He was trying to ascertain whether to believe what he just heard or throw the young men off his ship.

"If that is true," Riddick said, "then you might be on to something. Do you have it with you? Can I see it?"

"Couldn't take it from the museum," Darwin said, running with Lucas's deception. "I just jotted down what I could on a piece of paper and stuck it in my back pocket on the way out. This isn't strictly a sanctioned excursion. I happened to have a week off and asked Lucas if he wanted to come out here to check it out."

"You've sailed up and down the coast," Lucas said to Riddick, "do you know of anywhere that sounds like this?"

"Oh, that could be any number of places," the pirate impersonator said. "It just depends upon the shape of the coast and Teach's viewpoint when he described where the treasure lies. If he were out at sea, then that might be anywhere, although calling the area a cove narrows it down. It just depends on what his definition of a cove was. May well be a bay, an inlet, or any number of places."

"Anywhere like that around here? I imagine he'd place the treasure somewhere near where he frequented so he could get to it quickly if he needed to."

Riddick thought for a second. "That's probably true. The coast from here to Florida is like other coastlines, made hugely complex by all the inlets and island-shadowed estuaries, bays and peninsulas, rocks and reefs. But yeah, there are several places that might fit that description nearby."

"Like where? If he did have the treasure on board the *Queen Anne's Revenge* when he sank it, then it might close by."

"There are all kinds of bays and other areas like that near the coast here: Wyesocking Bay, Middle Bay, Jones Bay, Rose Bay, where the Long Shoal River lets out, Thorofare Bay, Jarrett Bay, and West Bay which runs into Long Bay. Just a bunch, really."

Darwin took out a small notebook and started writing those names down. He asked Riddick to repeat several of them before he completed his list.

"Well, look Mr. Riddick," Lucas said, "we appreciate the information you gave us, and we don't want to take up any more of your time today."

"No, no problem at all. I don't see how come you boys," Lucas grimaced at the slight, "couldn't have been more up front about the journal entry that brought you out here. Although you're treasure hunters, thanks for telling me about Mary Ormond's diary. I wish I could see it."

"I wish I could've had more time to study it," Darwin said. "They're strict about who gets extended access to the artifacts. I'm not one of those, yet."

"Maybe someday," Riddick assured him.

He collected their empty beer bottles before they made their way below deck. Riddick gave Darwin and Lucas his business card. Darwin gave the pirate his cell number. Lucas didn't, explaining he was just the driver on this expedition. In truth, he didn't want Riddick to have a way to reach him directly. If he had Lucas's number, he'd be able to look up his personal information.

When Darwin and Lucas had stepped off the yacht, Riddick asked, "Where do you think you boys are going to head next?"

"We might go out and check those bays out you told us about," Lucas said.

Riddick smiled. "Well, I've got a perfectly good vessel here that could take you where you want to go, and as you can tell, I've got some free time in which to take you."

Lucas returned the smile with a forced one of his own. "We appreciate that, Mr. Riddick. We'll let you know."

The pirate thought for a moment. "Another place you could go is out to the North Carolina Maritime Museum in Beaufort. They do a lot with the wreckage of the *Queen Anne's Revenge*. Might not help you in your quest, although you might get some useful information from there too."

"Thanks," Darwin and Lucas said in unison. They shook hands, and the duo began the short walk back to Lucas's Jeep.

"What was that about?" Darwin asked as they returned to the street. "What?"

"That game or whatever you were playing. Why were you holding back information from him? He could have been a bigger help, I think."

Lucas kicked a small rock on the pavement. "There was something about him I didn't like. I just couldn't trust him completely."

"Why? Because he was dressed like a pirate?"

"Well, not only that, but there was also something else there. Something in his eyes. His demeanor. I just had this feeling that I shouldn't tell him everything. Just an instinct."

Darwin sighed. "Listen, I suspected that you were leaving details out, and I trusted you enough to follow your lead. I just hope that by you not completely trusting him, it won't screw this up."

"If so, I'm sorry," Lucas said. He glanced back to the docks and saw Riddick standing on his deck, watching he and Darwin walk away. Their eyes met. "I get the feeling we'll see him again. Let's go find somewhere for lunch."

The pair would end up seeing much more of Hugo Riddick. Very soon.

# CHAPTER TWELVE

T HEY FOUND A PIZZA place on the water for lunch at a place appropriately named Blackbeard's Slices and Ices. Lucas ordered a couple slices of pepperoni pizza. Darwin had trouble wrapping his huge hands around a monstrous meatball sub. They got a seat at a table on the deck looking out over the water of Bath Creek.

"It was interesting," Lucas said.

"What's that?" Darwin replied after chomping down on a juicy meatball.

"I mean, we learned a little bit from the old lady, and pointed us to Riddick. He gave us a good idea to look at some of the surrounding areas. Don't have a way to do that just yet though."

"We could take up Riddick on his offer."

Lucas folded his greasy slice of pepperoni pizza and took a bite. The spiciness of the meat jumped out at first, and then the freshness of the cheese and the subtle seasoning of the crust crept in. *Pretty good*, he thought.

"Don't know if I trust him, although it would be free. Chartering someone might cost hundreds of dollars."

"I don't have that," Darwin said.

"I do. I'd rather save it if I could."

"What about checking out the Maritime Museum as he mentioned?"

"I don't know. Maybe." Lucas took a sip of sweet tea. Southerners loved their sweet tea. This was overly sweet even by their standards. "I just imagine that if when he wrecked the *Queen Anne's Revenge* and divided the crew, he took that treasure with him. If it's not in Bath, it must be in one of those places Riddick mentioned, right?"

"I would think so."

As they made progress on their lunches, Lucas thought back to something that was glossed over during their conversation with Riddick that should have been a bigger issue but wasn't.

"What do you imagine happened to this Travis Cole guy who discovered the journal?" Lucas said.

"I don't know."

"Should we look him up? See if we can talk to him?"

"Yeah, but as I said, I already looked him up in the staff directory. He's not with us anymore."

"Did you Google him?"

Darwin shook his head. "No. Didn't think about that. Has to be a bunch of Travis Coles."

"You can narrow that down, though. Add in different keywords."

"Hmm." Darwin reached down to the chair beside him and placed his tablet on the table. A sticker on the window beside the front door advertised free Wi-Fi in the facility, and he was soon online.

He first did a search for **Travis Cole**. The results displayed several Travis Coles. One of them was a former Arena Football League quarterback. Many of the results were of different Travis Coles on Twitter. Darwin clicked on several, and all of them were men under thirty-years-old. He flipped two more pages before adjusting his search. This time he typed **"Travis Cole" North Carolina State**. The results here were even worse.

"Not finding anything?" Lucas asked, finishing his second slice of pizza.

"Nope," Darwin said. "Just too common of a name. I tried his name by itself first and then tried adding North Carolina State. Still nothing."

"Try adding 'Raleigh' to your search. See if something pops up from the area where he lived."

Darwin grunted and tried the suggested search terms. He found more of the same on the first page of results: Facebook and Twitter links. He may have hit upon what they were looking for on the second page of results.

"Wow," he said.

"What is it?"

"Umm, well, here's an archived result from the Raleigh News and Observer."

Lucas felt his heart thump in his chest. "From when?"

"April 21st, 1982. A few days after the date on the Plum Point Dig."

"Cool," Lucas said. He thought Darwin would have been happier to find a result linked to Cole. He wasn't. If anything, he had the opposite reaction Lucas expected—the color drained from Darwin's face. "What is it?"

He tore his gaze away from the tablet and told Lucas, "He was murdered."

"What? Murdered?"

"Yes," Darwin said. "Here, take a look."

He turned the tablet around and pushed it across the table to Lucas.

*RALEIGH, N.C. — A researcher for the North Carolina Museum of History in Raleigh was discovered brutally slain in his apartment just off campus on Tuesday morning. Travis Aaron Cole was found alone after neighbors complained of a stench emanating from the apartment. The landlord gained entry and called the police.*

*Investigators say the body was in the late stages of decomposition in the living room of the residence located in the Heritage Trace apartment complex. They would not describe the state of the body, only to say it was gruesome. No signs of forced entry were found, and no motive or suspects are known at this time.*

*Police say the investigation is ongoing and will release further details as they become available.*

Lucas read the brief article three times before looking up. "Not much is it?"

"No, but dang. This was right after he completed his trip out here. Maybe that's why nothing was ever done with the artifacts. He never had the chance to do further research on what he uncovered."

"I wonder why no one else followed up on what he found."

Darwin shrugged. "Dunno. Maybe no one else knew about it or had time. With all that goes on at the museum, it may have just gotten lost in the shuffle without him there."

"Is there any way you could check? Ask some questions?"

"I can do that."

"Is there anyone you could call or email?"

Darwin thought about it as he looked out over the calm water. The sun was now alone in the sky overhead. It glittered on the lapping waves. "Yeah, maybe. I'm almost afraid I'd have to go back to Raleigh to be able to dig into it. A lot of those old records are still on paper. That's another facet of the updating project that I'm involved in. I'm going through old artifacts, while others are transferring the old paper files into the database. There is one girl I could call, though."

"Do you think they're up to 1982 yet on the paper end?"

"Not sure. They said they were close to that during the last staff meeting. That was last week."

Lucas tapped absentmindedly on the table. He wondered if Cole's death so soon after returning from Bath was a mere coincidence. What if there was a connection? "Do you see anything else about his murder?"

Darwin tapped at the tablet for a moment before shaking his head. "No. Nothing."

Lucas drained the last of his tea, and said, "Tell you what. I'm going to go out to the Jeep where I have my computer and grab it and make a call while I'm out there."

"Okay."

"Go ahead and do what you need to do—call, search or whatever. That'll give you an opportunity to talk to whomever you need to, and I want to see what, or if, I can dig up anything on Cole's murder. The timing of it seems strange."

"Do you suppose someone killed him over something that happened here?" Darwin said, pointing down at the table.

"I can't imagine one would have to do with the other, but you never know."

"You never know," Darwin echoed.

***

The knock came at the door a short while later. Just as Alethia expected it. Like clockwork. She could almost predict, word-for-word, exactly what she was about to hear.

That did not comfort her whatsoever.

She did not want to call Riddick earlier, although if she didn't and word got back to him that there were treasure seekers in town and they came to see her and she didn't tell him, she would be in serious trouble.

She feared him. Everyone did.

The entire town.

# CHAPTER THIRTEEN

Lucas exited the restaurant and crunched across the sandy parking lot to his truck. A few wisps of clouds hung in the sky. The sun felt warm and pure.

He didn't know anyone associated with the police department in Raleigh, although he did know someone who might be able to help him. Either by doing the research himself or by referring Lucas to someone who could help.

On the day of Trent Mahoney's murder and the day Lucas was himself a suspect, the name of the investigating officer was Greg Hanover. Lucas sometimes had to work with and against Hanover to clear his name that day. A respectful relationship developed between the two during the aftermath. They often got together for a cup of coffee.

He leaned against his Jeep and watched the seagulls fly over the rippling waters as he called Greg on his cell phone.

"Lucas, what's up?" Greg said when he came on the line. Although he was in his early fifties, his voice betrayed a youthful exuberance giving him a striking sense of humor for someone in his position. "It's been several months since I heard from you last. How's it going? Are you doing okay since . . . you know?"

"Uh, it's been tough to be honest," Lucas said.

Greg sensed the pending divorce wasn't a subject Lucas wanted to cover. "Well, you didn't call me to talk about feelings or any crap like that."

"No."

"Didn't think so. What's on your mind, Lucas?"

"I need to know the details of a police investigation that's over thirty years old."

Greg whistled. "Wow, if I'd known that's why you were calling, I would've never picked up the phone. Who was it?"

"Well, that's the tricky part," Lucas said. "His name was Travis Cole. He was murdered in Raleigh."

Greg cursed. "Jesus, Lucas. Raleigh? You know I work in Concord don't you?"

"Yeah, I know. I was just hoping you might be able to help me out."

Greg was quiet on the other end of the line for a moment. "Okay, I might be able to help. I'm old friends with a detective up there. I might be able to get in touch with him. He might've been around during that time. If he doesn't know anything about it, he might be able to point you in the right direction."

"Hey, anything you could do to help would be much appreciated."

"No problem. What is your interest in this?"

Lucas outlined, briefly, what Darwin found and what they knew of the circumstances around the finding of the diary of Mary Ormond.

"Okay Lucas. Let me wrap up what I'm doing here today. I'll reach out this evening or tomorrow and let you know what I find."

"Thanks Greg. Appreciate it," Lucas said and ended the call.

***

Darwin was four pages deep into search results on the museum mainframe back in the restaurant as Lucas ended his call with Greg Hanover.

As Darwin had mentioned to Lucas, the archivists at the museum were working their way back through the records, placing everything into a database. Their hope was that after cataloguing the documents, they would have a search program in place similar to Dewey Decimal System employed by libraries to keep their books in order. Paper records were located in file cabinets in a huge room in an upper floor of the museum. The actual artifacts were stored deep underground.

As crates were sorted and documents revealed, the results were sent to the two members of the computer team. After the project began, it became apparent that the five archivists digging through file cabinets would get ahead of those in the basement. It was easier to open a file, have it scanned in and indexed than it was to sort the boxes and figure out what it was they were looking at. Because of that, as the two teams went in reverse chronological order, Darwin's team in the basement was behind the document diggers upstairs.

The thirteen researchers were divided into three teams: five for the crates in the basement, five to riffle through files upstairs, two who input the findings into the database and one overall project leader. Darwin was a crate digger and the youngest member of the project. The members of the project held bi-weekly meetings to discuss progress, coordinate efforts, answer any questions, and to forecast ahead.

Darwin had hoped some piece of information would already be in the database relating to the Plum Point dig. When he did a quick search the day before, he had seen nothing. Now, sitting in the corner of the pizza place, he took his time scanning the entries, hoping to find something he had missed. Still, he came up empty. He saw projects dating back before Travis Cole's journey to Bath, so at least Darwin knew the file diggers upstairs had been in the file cabinet containing the dates of the dig.

To this point, Darwin wasn't aware of any crate or box from the basement that didn't have a correlating file from upstairs. He pulled his phone out of his pocket, flipped it open, and dialed a number saved in the memory.

A squeaky voice answered, "Hello?"

Darwin cleared his throat. "Hey Lisa. How're you?"

"I'm fine. What's up? I thought you were on vacation?"

Of all the people associated with the cataloguing project, Lisa Kramer was the one Darwin most got along with. That could be due to the fact that they were the only introverts on the project and for some strange reason, stuck together when the team was assembled—both inside and outside work. They were in several classes together during their time at North Carolina State, so they were at least familiar with each other when the museum hired them for the project.

"I'm just hanging out here in Bath with a friend," he answered.

"Bath? What's in Bath?"

He didn't know how to broach the subject without taking several minutes to set it up. He called her in particular because he knew he could trust her. She knew he wouldn't make a social call without good reason, and might be more inclined to help him because of that. So he got straight to the point.

"Look, I need to know if the people upstairs have come across any records pertaining to a dig in Bath from 1982. The project name was The Plum Point Dig and the person behind it was a guy named Travis Cole. I can't find anything in the database."

She thought for a moment. "Well, maybe they just haven't got to it yet."

"There are records in the database from before and after that period. Whatever file cabinet the records should have been in would have already been cleared. Right?"

"Well, yeah. What in particular are you after?" When Darwin didn't answer right away, she connected the dots. The already high pitch of her voice increased. "Wait, you said the Plum Point dig was from Bath, and now you're in Bath. What are you up to, Darwin?"

He panicked just a little. The mousy colleague could be intimidating when she wanted to be.

"Okay," he said. "When I was working the other day, I found a box from this dig. It was on the bottom shelf in a corner of the room I was in. It was weird. It wasn't organized the way it should be. Just a piece of paper saying where it came from, when it was done, and who did it. Nothing written about what they hoped to accomplish and no manifest of the findings."

"That is weird. So what was in the box?"

Darwin hesitated. He might get in serious trouble if she said something to project coordinator.

"Among other things, a journal," he said.

"Ooo. What sort of journal?"

"Um, more of a diary. It belonged to Mary Ormond."

"Who is that?"

"Not is. Was. She was Blackbeard's wife at the time he died."

"That's interesting." She was quiet a moment. "What was in this journal that caused you to go out there? Wait, how did you get out there? You didn't take your moped did you?"

"No. Had a friend from Concord come pick me up and take me."

"That's good. It would take you a couple days to get out there on your moped. Be dangerous as hell too."

"I know. I know. A guy I used to work for at a restaurant had an interest in pirate history. Called him up. Said I had a couple days to check it out. He owns his own business, so he took a leave and picked me up yesterday."

"What made you call him? Why would you of all people take a trip such as that on the spur of the moment? That's not like you, Darwin."

"I know. I just . . . I just was tired of sitting around doing nothing, you know? I was forced to take this week off and finding this map made me want to get out and do something about it."

"Wait . . . what map?"

Darwin squeezed his eyes shut in frustration. He'd let the cat out of the bag. "Oh, there was a treasure map in the journal."

He heard her gasp on the other end. "A treasure map? A real pirate treasure map?" she repeated in one rushed breath. "I thought those were made up. That they just existed in fiction"

"Well," Darwin said, "whether that's true or not isn't important. I have one."

"How do you know it was a map from Blackbeard and not this Ormond lady?"

The question brought Darwin up short. He didn't know for sure this was a map from Blackbeard. The circumstantial evidence favored that assumption. "Well, it was tucked away in this diary belonging to the woman who was Blackbeard's wife at the time of his death. The note scrawled on it is in a different, bolder style of handwriting than the rest of the journal. Can I say with one-hundred percent conviction that this is Blackbeard's treasure map? No. Although I'm confident enough that it is that I came out this way to dig into it."

He sensed her processing this. Determining whether she should help him or not. She reached a decision. "I'll look into it. Give me a couple hours. May not even be today, but I'll see what I can find."

Relief washed over Darwin. Another hurdle crossed.

"Have you tried finding this Cole guy?" she asked.

"Yes. He's dead."

"Dead? That's sad."

"Apparently he was murdered in his apartment after coming back from Bath." He heard her squeak in surprise. He continued, "That's probably why the box was still sitting in the archives. No one followed up on it. There should still be something in the file cabinets of the project. When he requested permission to do it, who approved it, etc."

"Good Lord. That's awful. Who killed him?"

"Don't know. Couldn't find anything online," Darwin said.

"Well, I'll see what I can find on our end Darwin."

"Thank you so much, Lisa. I appreciate this."

"You're welcome. Gotta' run. I'll call you when I find something," she said and broke the connection.

***

"So what now?" Lucas asked after he sat back down and they shared what they learned with each other.

Darwin looked out the window, then back to Lucas and shrugged. "I hate to say it; I think we should go back and speak to Riddick."

Lucas shook his head. "I don't trust him."

Darwin held out a meaty palm. "Be that as it may, the lone scrap of information we have is the map. Here's a guy who owns a shipping company, spent time on these waters and, by the way, seems to know everything about Blackbeard. If there's someone who can help us find this treasure, it's him."

"I know. I just think that," Lucas exhaled, "I just feel that somehow he'll try to screw us. You saw the look in his eye. What about going to the Maritime Museum as he suggested?"

"How far away is that?"

"In Beaufort. A couple hours away."

"Well, we're already here. Once we leave Bath, there's not much of a reason to come back. We have a couple days before we have to head home, no need to rush. Riddick told us he'll close by today. What if we need to catch him tomorrow or a couple days from now? Do we know that he will be available?"

"Probably not." Lucas clinched a fist on the table. Another thought occurred to him. "Wonder if we can rent our own boat?"

"You can drive a boat?" Darwin asked, giving his partner a surprised look.

"Yeah. I'm no expert," Lucas said. "I spent part of my adolescence on a lake, going fishing, and drinking beers, whatever. I piloted every once in a while. Usually when my friends were too drunk to steer."

"Think you could drive one around here?"

Lucas shrugged. "I'll give it a shot."

Darwin gazed at his friend for a long second. "If you say so. I feel that we should give Riddick a chance, but I'll trust you."

"Thanks. Tell you what, if I get out there and can't do it, we'll come back and catch Riddick. Deal?"

# CHAPTER FOURTEEN

T HEY DROVE THE SHORT distance back across town and parked at the same parking spot on Bonner's Point overlooking the sound. They saw Riddick leaving The Treasure Shop on their way back to the marina.

He greeted them on the sidewalk with a broad smile. "Ah, lads. You came back. I was just thanking Alethia for sending you my way. How can I help you?"

Lucas thought the bearded man was being a bit presumptive. "We're going to see if we can rent a boat for a while from that marina."

The smile on Riddick's face disappeared. "Oh, if you say so lads. I can speak with the owner and get you a deal."

"Thanks, Riddick. Appreciate it," Darwin said.

"The least I can do, lad." He started walking towards the marina. "Say, you don't happen to have any nautical charts of the area, do you?"

"We don't," Lucas admitted.

"You'll need one. If you're going to go cruising these different bays and inlets, many are surrounded with sandbars and rocks. Wouldn't want you to run aground or hit something and sink."

"No, wouldn't want to do that," Lucas agreed. The man had a point. "You wouldn't have one we could borrow?"

From behind, Lucas saw Riddick's chin dip. He didn't know if that meant the pirate was thinking or sad that Lucas didn't take him up on his offer.

He turned around, focused Lucas with a stare in mid-stride, and said, "I can scrounge something up for you boys."

"Thanks," Darwin said. "We had some time before both of us had to head home, and we thought if we headed to Beaufort to the Maritime Museum, we might not make it back here. We have our rooms at the motel reserved just through tonight. So tomorrow, we were headed to points unknown anyway."

"Good, good," Riddick said. "If you lads need anything, don't hesitate to give me a call."

The owner of the marina had a small building on the water at the foot of the docks. A single diesel gas pump collecting rust stood off to the right of the building entrance. Boats could pull up, gas up, and head for deeper waters.

The three men went inside the small building. A counter with a dingy Formica top took up most of the space. Two old coolers containing drinks, beer, and bait stood on the wall to their right. Two small aisles of retail shelving with various boat supplies and additional sundries were on the opposite side of the room. Souvenir shirts and navigational charts hung on the wall behind an impish ancient man with a thick, curly white beard smoking a large cigar. He reminded Lucas of a foul-smelling Grumpy from Snow White, although with a saltier disposition.

He gave Lucas and Darwin a sour look and blew a cloud of smoke over his right shoulder. Lucas glanced at the ceiling and saw a defined brown patina of cigar smoke staining the tiles above the man's head. This diminutive fellow must spend a lot of time standing behind that counter smoking those fat stogies, Lucas thought.

The man glared at their companion, nodded, and said, "Mr. Riddick."

"Sal," Riddick returned. "How are things?"

A nod. "'Bout the same. What can I do for you . . . folks?"

Lucas gathered that Riddick must spend a good deal of time around the marina. A regular. He thought the standoffish way in which the man greeted Riddick seemed odd. Like the way a fast-food manager greets an unruly regular.

"Yes," Riddick said, "these young lads need a boat to cruise these local waters. That green Tracker jon boat you rent out wouldn't be available right now, would it?"

The man, Sal, gave Riddick a suspicious look. "I do. Why that one? There are—"

"It's a fine vessel, and just what these two could use," Riddick interrupted.

Sal squinted and did a quick appraisal of Lucas and Darwin. "If you say so. It's out there."

"How much?" Lucas asked. He was familiar enough with a jon boat back from his days of cruising around Summersville Lake. Good vessels to cruise and on which to fish, however not built for speed. That was fine with Lucas.

Sal started to open his mouth, snuck a quick glance at Riddick, and quoted Lucas a price that seemed low, although he wasn't going to question it.

"We'll take it," Lucas said.

After filling out forms, providing payment and getting a cooler of drinks and sandwiches, Lucas, Darwin and Riddick stood on the dock before a small, drab olive boat. It was a twenty-footer with two seats side-by-side near the outboard motor. A weather-beaten captain's chair was on the right and an equally shabby passenger seat sat beside it. It was made of sturdy all-aluminum construction, had a couple rings

Lucas assumed was for holding fishing rods. A utility shelf sat behind the seats.

Darwin had grabbed a backpack from the Jeep containing a couple garden trowels to clear away any loose dirt from a possible burial location, a compact hoe and cultivator to break up any hard surfaces, Ziploc bags, a couple of toothbrushes and a small, folded metal detector.

"Come on back to my yacht," Riddick said, "and we'll take a look at our surroundings and see if we can eyeball some spots for you to focus on based upon what was in that journal."

Lucas jumped over the gunwale and Darwin handed him the cooler, which he stored in the space behind the seats. He rejoined them on the dock and then walked across to Riddick's boat.

***

Once on board, Riddick spread a nautical chart of the Outer Banks over the galley table on his yacht. It showed the many inlets, bays, creeks, streams, and small islands spread from the Pamlico Sound to the Neuse River to the south and on down to Morehead City. The map displayed the region as far east as Hatteras Island and the thin islands of the Outer Banks.

"Now, tell me again what the entry said in the journal," Riddick said.

Darwin had to try to recall what he had told the man earlier. There was no journal entry. Lucas had just made that up on the spot rather than letting Riddick know that he and Lucas had a crudely drawn map. Darwin thought it would help them all if he showed the pirate the map, although he trusted Lucas's judgment.

"Um, the entry said the treasure was beside a huge tree underneath the falling sun in the cove to the south."

"Right," Riddick said. "Let's say Blackbeard took the treasure off the *Queen Anne's Revenge* when it wrecked. That's about here," he said, stabbing his finger at a point in the water near Beaufort Inlet. The exact spot lay just off the shore near Fort Macon, at the eastern end of a skinny island home to Atlantic Beach and another narrow island named Shackleford Banks.

"This site was discovered in 1995," Riddick continued. "It wasn't proven to be the actual wreckage of the *Queen Anne's Revenge* until 2011. What's crazy is, is that this spot is in shallow water and within eyesight of where the major shipping lane runs through Beaufort Inlet to gain access to the Inner Banks."

"It was there for almost three-hundred years before anyone knew about it?" Darwin asked.

Riddick nodded and moved on. "Blackbeard made for Bath in a sloop after he marooned the rest of his crew. This was near the beginning of June in 1718. Records show he didn't meet with Governor Eden until sometime in the last two weeks of June. There's a fuzzy period there where they could have hidden the treasure.

"Many of these parts were just starting to be settled, and these coves or inlets were probably uninhabited. He may well have picked about any spot between the crash site and here to place the treasure."

"Where should we start?"

Riddick considered for a moment and jabbed at a blue section about twenty-five miles from Bath. "I'd say this area here. Rose Bay and Bell Bay. The sun sets over the west side of the small peninsulas."

Lucas studied the spot and spoke for the first time. Bell Bay didn't look right. "Let's try Rose Bay."

Riddick raised his eyebrows. "Why not the Bell?"

"It doesn't feel right."

"It doesn't feel right," Riddick repeated. "What makes you say that?"

Lucas shrugged, meeting the pirate's gaze. "I trust my instincts."

They held each other's stare for three full heartbeats before Riddick smiled. "If you say so, lad. Then head out Rose Bay first."

Darwin looked back and forth between the two men. The makings of a power struggle just occurred, and he was determined to keep the peace. He needed for both men to be cooperative. He trusted Lucas when he said he didn't trust Riddick, although the man seemed to be the person best suited to help them on their quest.

Darwin knew from the drawing that Lucas was probably right. Rose Bay didn't look anything like the lines sketched on the ancient sheet of paper. "I agree with Lucas here, Mr. Riddick. Something doesn't seem right with Bell Bay."

"As you wish Mr. Trickett," Riddick said and then plotted a course to several other bays or inlets in the area that looked the part.

"You know Mr. Riddick . . .," Darwin started to say.

"Please young man. Call me Hugo. I insist," the pirate impersonator said to the much larger, although much younger man. "I will not accept that formality. If I share my beer and rum with you, you are not to call me 'mister.'"

Two rows of white teeth appeared in the middle of Darwin's thick, black beard. "Thank you . . . Hugo."

"You were saying?" Riddick said to Darwin.

"I was going to say, that this is my first time on a boat."

Riddick regarded Darwin in disbelief. "You don't say?" He clapped Darwin on the shoulder. "Well, my friend, you're going to be in for a good time out there."

Lucas agreed. "Absolutely, just sit back. I'll do the piloting. Enjoy the voyage."

Darwin wasn't used to having a good time in this way. Growing up in that environment, being able to find a quiet corner and read a book was considered ideal. No one at school ever asked him to do anything with them. He was ashamed to ask anyone to visit him in the squalid conditions in which he lived.

Getting outside—with people—was a rarity. This was his vacation. He didn't think about it at the time he first called Lucas, although the goal of this trip resembled the career goals he had—going out on archaeological expeditions similar to Indiana Jones and having adventures all in the name of science and history.

Lucas interrupted his thoughts by asking Riddick, "How long will it take to get out to Rose Bay?"

Riddick looked out a window at the sparkling water and stroked his beard while contemplating the answer. "In the jon boat? An hour, hour and a half. Not too far."

Lucas picked up the chart and he and Darwin made to leave the yacht.

"Thanks for helping us out," Darwin said to Riddick.

"You're welcome," he replied. "Least I could do for you lads. You have my card. Give me a call should you need anything. You boys be careful out there."

Lucas squinted. He didn't know if the man was being helpful or . . . something else. "Thanks," he said, and he and Darwin left the large ship and walked back across the dock to their boat.

"How much do you think that yacht cost?" Darwin asked as they crossed the dock to their chartered boat.

"I don't know. Couple million?"

Darwin let out a long whistle. "It was definitely nice. That's for sure. Mr. Riddick—Hugo—must have a lot of money. Shipping business must be good."

"Must be," Lucas agreed.

They reached their boat. Lucas hopped in and then extended a hand and helped Darwin climb aboard. Darwin's bulk caused the boat to dip and the water to slosh on either side. Ripples of water disturbed the otherwise still creek.

"Whoa!" he shouted.

Lucas smiled and kept a hold of Darwin's hand and arm to help balance him and pull him towards the center of the boat. "Easy there big guy."

Darwin managed to laugh before taking an uneasy step to the passenger chair. He sat down with relief and said to Lucas who went to the rear to prep the outboard motor. "I must admit, I'm a little nervous."

Lucas stopped for a moment and turned. "Why? Because of this boat?" Darwin nodded. Lucas smiled. "Nah, don't be. It'll be fun. You'll see. Won't take long to get you your sea legs."

Darwin nodded again and faced forward. "Hope so," the big man said in a tiny voice.

# CHAPTER FIFTEEN

T HE PAMLICO SOUND WAS a perfect host for Darwin and Lucas. The water was calm. The breeze was just right. Vessels of varying sizes littered the waterway, on their way to catch fish, carrying freight, or—like Lucas and Darwin—just out cruising.

They made their way at a good pace that didn't make Darwin feel too nervous. At first, he held on with white knuckles to the green naugahyde of his seat. When they reached the open waters of the sound, he no longer feared for his life.

"This isn't so bad," he said to Lucas.

"Told ya. Just sit back and enjoy the ride."

Darwin settled in and basked in the sun.

Lucas wanted to enjoy the ride himself. After what he'd endured with Kristen leaving him, he needed this trip to get his mind off things. Being near water always had a purifying effect on him. The sound of the waves, the feel of the breeze, and the smell of the air brought him a sense of tranquility. When it seemed the world around him was too much to bear, the ocean let him clear his mind.

Navigating the small boat along the shore of the Pamlico Sound was exactly what Lucas needed, when he needed it.

When Darwin, Riddick, and Lucas studied a map of the surrounding area, looking for candidates that matched the map they had, Rose

Bay appeared to be a strong contender. The one discrepancy between what he saw on the treasure map and navigation chart was that the entrance to Deep Bay to the eastern side of Rose Bay flowed diagonally southeast rather than in a northeasterly line of the mainland as depicted on the old map.

When they were about halfway to their first destination and came around a bend, they saw what resembled a large speedboat with red racing stripes streaking across the water leaving plumes of water spraying into the air behind coming from the direction of where they assumed Ocracoke Island lay. At first, it seemed they would cross paths. Then the fast boat veered to its right, toward the mainland before disappearing around a finger of land jutting out into the sound.

"Man!" Darwin shouted over the growl of the small engine. "I didn't know boats went that fast!"

"That was a fast one," Lucas agreed. To him, it seemed the speedboat was headed in the direction of Rose Bay, their first destination. He figured there must be a great fishing spot somewhere in there they wanted to find. Although, that didn't explain why they'd be in such a hurry.

Lucas consulted his map as they came to an open expanse of water about three miles wide. This was the mouth to a section containing three small bays: Spencer Bay on the left, Deep Bay on the right, and their target, Rose Bay back in the middle. They rounded a small, rocky island less than two-hundred and fifty feet long that had tall clumps of sea grass making purchase among hardscrabble. Hundreds of small fiddler crabs scurried over the island in search of food.

Once past that, they entered a large open space. The water seemed darker here. More ominous in a subliminal way.

They motored towards the middle of the region. Lucas picked up the speed. Darwin didn't notice. His thoughts were on what might lie ahead.

"This is it!" he said, grabbing Lucas's arm. "We might find treasure here!"

For a second, Lucas shared his friend's enthusiasm. Then he saw the speedboat.

Dead ahead.

***

The speedboat floated in the middle of Rose Bay a mile deep into its mouth. The inlet was about a mile and a half wide from point to point. Lucas couldn't make out any defined details of who was on board, although he saw a glint reflected off something made of glass.

Lucas cut back on their speed and coasted past a small area marked on the chart as Striking Bay and clung to the shoreline of a small peninsula on the west side of Rose Bay. He wanted to keep as much water between them and the speedboat as he could. They then idled past a crease in the shore known as Lightwood Snag Bay that was just over half a mile wide.

Now, they were close enough to make out details of the men aboard the speedboat. There were two men with fishing lines disappearing into the water on either side of the boat. Another man stood in the middle, holding a pair of binoculars to his eyes, staring directly at Lucas and Darwin. From this distance, they looked like a rough crew. All wore doo-rags emblematic of what people imagine pirate crewmembers wearing. The two men with the fishing rods had thick, bushy beards. The roughneck with the field glasses was shorter and slighter in build. He wore a pair of thick framed glasses, had a Van Dyke beard, and wore a leather vest over a bare chest.

Lucas had the impression that the man with the binoculars was the leader of the crew. When the man saw that Lucas had seen him, he set down the binoculars and picked up a fishing pole in one swift motion.

Darwin was checking them out as well. "Looks shady," he said.

Lucas grunted. "Sure does. Keep your eye on them. I'm going to see if I can spot a place near where X would mark the spot on the map."

According to the notation made by Blackbeard on the back of the map, they were looking for a large oak, about fifty paces from the water's edge. The first problem, Lucas saw, was a complete absence of trees near the shore. There was a line of birch trees, however, two hundred yards inland. It was currently low tide, so the "shore" was acres and acres of mud flats. Even during high tide, these waters remained shallow. Not deep enough for a heavy boat, one perhaps laden with treasure, to float.

He tried to imagine if there could have been trees on this stretch of land three hundred years ago but doubted it. Recent tides shaped the headland between the water and the trees. This ground consisted of thick, muddy brown sand. Simply not enough soil to harbor root systems needed by trees. He pointed this out to Darwin.

The archivist thought about it for a moment, and said, "It might be that a hurricane, or multiple hurricanes, blew through bringing strong tides that washed all of the soil and fauna away."

"You think?" Lucas inquired. His friend was more well versed about geology than he.

Darwin's eyes narrowed. "No, not really. The shoreline could've changed over the course of the years, although I don't believe this is the right place."

"Should we try to pick out an area where we think the treasure might be if this were in fact the spot? I'd hate to leave out of here without checking, just in case."

"Yeah. Won't hurt."

"Alright then." Lucas picked a spot a half mile past the northern edge of the Lightwood Snag Bay and grounded the small craft on the narrow beach.

"This looks fine," Darwin said, getting to his unsteady feet and pulling on his heavy backpack. "See any dolphins?"

"Nah., I see a lot of birds. I assume the land on the east side of this Rose Bay is part of the Swan Quarter Wildlife Preserve."

Lucas looked towards the three rough characters on the speedboat who were doing their best to look convincingly oblivious with three separate fishing lines in the water. He wondered if they had any bait at the ends of the lines. The leader glanced their way, then turned and said something to one of his partners when he saw Lucas returning his stare.

*Don't look too obvious*, Lucas thought. He looked to Darwin who was surveying the land. "Hey, when is high tide?"

Darwin consulted a tide chart given to him by the marina master for a moment and said, "It's not supposed to come in for several hours."

"Good," said Lucas. He slowed the boat to a crawl and grounded it into the wet sand bar, bringing them to a halt.

They climbed off the boat and their shoes sunk in the muck an inch. If they were in the correct place, then any treasure buried by Blackbeard might have been washed away long ago. They explored the muddy area for about twenty minutes, looking for any sign it used to be covered in a maritime forest.

"See anything?" Lucas called to Darwin, who was kneeling, looking at an oddly shaped rock outcropping ten feet away. "No. Don't think there would be a way to bury treasure here anyway. The bedrock is only a couple inches below the sand."

"Good point."

"If it was ever here, then it would have washed away with the rest of the soil."

"That would suck," Lucas winced at the thought. He pointed to the solitary line of birch trees more than a hundred yards inland. "Let's go back there. Maybe the water has receded and that was the original shoreline."

Darwin agreed that this line of thought was worth investigating. Just before they plodded back to the tree line, they saw where the farthest point the tide reached. The trees sat up a bank from where the water's edge would be. The trees were spaced close together. The line of them was no more than fifteen feet wide. Tightly knit branches in the canopy helped the trees to withstand hurricane force winds. Lucas imagined the lonely group hugging close together when the next Hurricane Hugo roared through.

Beyond that was a vast salt marsh as far as the eye could see, with a sparse handful of single trees scattered like small clumpy islands. Currently, it looked like a wasteland. When high tide came in, this section would flood.

On the other side of the trees, coming from the bay, they heard the growl of an engine start. Lucas said, "Sounds as though our friends are leaving."

Darwin agreed as they stood side-by-side at the edge of the marsh. "I feel that we should move on. We're wasting our time," he said.

Lucas agreed and they began the walk back to their boat. As they stepped out from the trees and back on the muddy ground, several seagulls who had been standing nearby enjoying the soft breeze took flight in alarm. They flew off towards the opposite shore over the heads of the mystery men on the speedboat.

The speedboat was now next to their boat. The engine sound they heard wasn't for the three men leaving the bay. The sound came from them idling closer to their boat.

"Hey!" Lucas shouted, waving his arms at the men. "Get away from our boat!"

They were two hundred yards away from the two boats. The speedboat idled in the water just behind their boat. Although the men couldn't hear Lucas's exact words, they caught the meaning and ignored him.

He and Darwin took off running in the direction of the boats. It was slow going as their shoes sunk into the soil with each stride. There were no obstacles between them, just open ground. Lucas thought of this at the halfway point, just before the leader pulled out a gun and pointed it at him and Darwin. Without hesitation, the man fired.

"Get down!" Lucas shouted at his friend.

They both hit the ground as several bullets zoomed through the space they had just occupied. The muddy sand made for a soft landing at least.

Lucas thought they were just beyond the range for a pistol to be accurate, although he didn't want to test that theory. He scrutinized their immediate vicinity for anything that might help them. He and Darwin had no projectile weapons. If it came to hand-to-hand combat, at least they had sharp spades and the cultivator that could double as an insidious weapon, if need be, in Darwin's backpack.

He looked up to see one man jump from the speedboat onto the jon boat. Another tossed him rope with a hook attached.

Lucas heard Darwin huffing and puffing to his right. He sounded as though he was having a panic attack. Lucas had been in situations where he had had a gun pointed at him and lived to tell about it. He was determined that this would be another one of those events.

"Stay calm," Lucas assured him. "We'll get out of this."

Darwin couldn't answer verbally but nodded his head emphatically. While Lucas was looking Darwin's way, he saw that off to their right and behind them fifteen feet was the rock outcropping Darwin had investigated earlier. If they reached that and lay flat, it might provide enough protection to shield them from any bullets.

Of course, they had to make it there without getting hit first.

A bullet *thwocked* off the ground three feet away from Lucas, sending up splatters of mud. The shot jolted Darwin and Lucas reached out to grab his left wrist.

"Look at me Darwin," he said. Darwin gawked at the men on the boats in terror and then to Lucas. "I'll get you through this, but you have to listen to me."

Darwin's green eyes were as wide as flying saucers. He broke eye contact with Lucas and glanced at the man with the gun eighty yards away, mustered up some courage and then looked back to Lucas. "What do you want me to do?" he whispered.

Lucas took a deep breath. "Do you see those rocks behind you and to your right?"

Darwin chanced to look back. "Yes," he said, returning to Lucas.

Another bullet deflected off the surface near Darwin. A spray of mud hit him in the face. He coughed, spat, and brushed the sandy sludge away.

"Listen, when I say go, get up, duck, and run to those rocks as fast as you can and get down. Can you do that?" Darwin indicated he could. "Great, leave your backpack here. You don't need the extra weight on you."

"Okay," Darwin said and shrugged off the backpack.

Lucas looked back to the men in the boats. The man in their boat apparently finished whatever he was doing to the jon boat and reached out his hand for help to get back across to the speedboat. The leader took the gun down enough to reach out and grab his friend's hand.

Lucas saw their chance. "Go!"

Darwin stumbled to his feet and ran as fast as his six foot eight, three hundred plus pound frame would allow to the outcropping. Lucas was right behind. With the nature of ground, the going was slow, but within seconds, they were lying flat on their stomachs on the other side of the rocks.

Lucas realized that the man in the speedboat didn't fire a single shot at them as they ran for safety. He had counted seven shots fired and thought he remembered that a typical 9mm handgun holds fifteen bullets. The man shouldn't have had to reload yet. Then Lucas grasped the reason.

"We're safe," he said.

Darwin was lying in front of him in the crease with his size fourteen feet at Lucas's head. "Are you sure?"

"Yeah, they stopped firing."

Darwin came to that realization, turned, and raised his head above the rocks to look in the direction of the shore. He saw the man with the gun give them one last look before he hopped down from the gunwale and went to the controls.

A moment later, the speedboat roared and raced away with Darwin and Lucas's jon boat in tow.

# CHAPTER SIXTEEN

"WELL," DARWIN HUFFED, "WHAT are we supposed to do now?"

Lucas thought for a moment about their situation as they stood at the water's edge. He had run back to the spot where their boat had been to see it trailing behind the swiftly moving speedboat. The irony that modern day pirates had just hijacked their boat while they were looking for a three-century-old pirate treasure near the final home of that pirate was not lost on him.

He checked Google Earth on his phone. The internet connection he had out here was slow. Their current location had them far from civilization. The large bay before them and the marshland behind them cut them off without a boat. It was the middle of the afternoon. All the clouds trailing the tropical storm from earlier in the week had moved out to sea, leaving behind a glowing sun, baking the rocks and them under its harsh glare.

"Have any food or drink in that backpack?"

Darwin thought about it, started to unsling the pack, and stopped. "Nope. Everything we had was underneath the seats."

Lucas cursed to himself. "I hate to say it, but do you still have Riddick's card? We're stranded, and he might be the person who can get us out of here the quickest."

Darwin was aware of Lucas's feelings for the man and wouldn't have mentioned him unless he thought they were out of options. Darwin fished in his pocket and handed Lucas the card.

"Thanks," he said and dialed the number on the card.

Riddick picked up after half a ring. He must have had his cell phone in his hand. "Hello?"

"Hugo? This is Lucas from earlier."

"Yes! How are you lad? Find the treasure yet?" Riddick sounded delighted to hear from them.

"No, not exactly. Do you remember your offer from earlier to transport us around the Pamlico Sound?"

"Yes. Yes, I do."

Lucas glanced at Darwin who met his eye. "We'd like to take you up on your offer."

***

While they waited for Riddick to rescue them, Lucas thought that it almost seemed as though Riddick was awaiting their call.

They sat on the same weather-beaten, eroded group of rocks that gave them cover while they were being shot at. Lucas noted that their surface was somehow clean of bird droppings. Unless the water washed over these rocks every day, it was a remarkable feat in this wildlife sanctuary.

Several different species of seabirds played about the bay, either soaring, floating on the calm water or circling high above before diving into the bay, trying to catch a fish. They saw a few successful attempts. An occasional ship passed by the opening to the trio of bays, but none of them entered the area. They were too far away from the main boat lanes for anyone to see them. This was a quiet place. Lucas now understood why pirates hid in these bays.

Darwin's phone rang. "Hello?"

"Darwin! Hey, it's Lisa." Then, without allowing Darwin to get a word in edgewise, she launched into what she'd found. "I asked Walt. You know Walt? Been here forever. I asked Walt if he remembered a guy by the name of Travis Cole. You know what he told me?"

Again, she didn't wait for a response from Darwin before continuing. "He told me this Cole guy was a real nice kid. Came from a family of academics. He was shocked when Cole was murdered. Said Cole kinda reminded him of you: a young guy who wanted to do big things in fieldwork. Hated being stuck in a lab.

"Anyway, Cole liked to take trips on the side—kinda like you're doing right now—to research his own projects. Said he couldn't remember Cole ever finding anything. Then, a couple days before he was killed, Cole told Walt he was going to the coast for the weekend to look into something. At the time, Walt worked at the information desk up front. He said a couple days later, Cole came in with a box tucked under his arm, said hi to Walt and explained he was in a hurry before heading downstairs into the basement."

She continued, not allowing Darwin to speak. "Walt said he got off work while Cole was downstairs. That was the last time he saw Cole alive."

"Dang. That's terrible. Did he say anything else about the box Cole had?"

"No," Lisa answered. "Said he never thought about it again until I asked him about Cole just now. It wasn't an area he worked in, and he assumed Cole would have let someone else know about it. He said the police questioned him later, although he never mentioned the box. It was something he saw all of fifteen seconds and forgot about it until now."

"Hard to believe he recalled that after thirty years."

"Well, you know Walt. He's sharp as a tack when he wants to be. A dim bulb when he doesn't."

"True," Darwin agreed. "Do you think you could go down and grab the journal?"

Lisa hesitated. "Me? Go downstairs? I don't like that place. Not enough sunlight. It's depressing."

"Come on. For me?"

Darwin heard what seemed like an audible smile on the other end. "Okay, Darwin, I'll do it for you. Where can I find it? What am I looking for once I find it?"

He told her where it was located. "I'm hoping she wrote about the treasure in the book somewhere. Blackbeard may have told her something about it that she wrote down. Or maybe, he told her something she didn't know related to the treasure."

"Cryptic, you mean?"

"Yes, cryptic. That's the word. See if you can find something similar. How late do you work tonight?"

"Supposed to be five, but I'll stay over if I find anything interesting."

An hour later, Riddick's large yacht rounded the bend and into the mouth of Rose Bay.

# CHAPTER SEVENTEEN

RIDDICK GREETED DARWIN AND Lucas with a pair of cold beers pulled from a cooler in the galley. "So, they just took your boat, huh?"

"Yup," Darwin answered. "Just like that. It's as though they watched us go into the trees and saw their chance. Lucas said one of the guys had been watching us since we arrived in the bay."

"Before that," Lucas added. "The same guy had a pair of binoculars trained on us."

"Could have been that he was just birdwatching while his buddies fished," Riddick said and added, "This is a big natural sanctuary for dozens of different types of birds."

"Yeah," Lucas halfway agreed. "Except they shot at us and stole our boat. The dude didn't look like a birdwatcher either."

"What?" Riddick said. An angry look crossed his face. "They pulled a gun on you?"

"Yeah, when we started running towards them, the short leader guy pulled out a pistol and just started shooting at us."

"My goodness, lad. I'm sorry to hear that. I hope this doesn't alter your perception of Outer Banks hospitality. Are either of you injured? Did they hit you?"

"No," Darwin said. "Came close, but damn that was scary."

"I bet."

"Anything we can do to them? Have them arrested?"

"Did you get a good look at them?"

Darwin and Lucas shared a look. "Not very well. Two bigger, rough looking guys with bandannas and another smaller guy with glasses."

"Hmm," Riddick rubbed his chin. "What about the boat? What kind was it? What color?"

"It was red. That's all I know," Darwin said. "I'd never been on a boat until today."

Lucas scratched his head. "Yeah, I'm not sure of the exact make and model. All I know is that it was a speedboat."

"Well, the Coast Guard will need to know details such as that," Riddick said. "There are a lot of rough characters around here and even more red speedboats. The color of choice for that type of person."

"My question is," Lucas said, "is why were they even shooting at us? If they were out just having fun, then why not just forget the jon boat when they saw us and left? It's not as though our boat could have caught them."

"Good question," Riddick answered. "I'd say since you caught them in the act, they had a choice—as you said—of either hightailing it out of there or getting what they wanted. They chose the latter and needed to buy time while the guy secured your boat."

Begrudgingly, Lucas agreed. "Yeah, but why bother to begin with? They could sell the thing, for what, a thousand bucks? I mean, what if they got caught? Would taking our boat have been worth it?"

Riddick shrugged. "I get your point. There's another thing here to keep in mind."

"What is that?"

He leaned in towards Lucas and smiled, "They might have just been imbeciles."

Lucas couldn't help but laugh, nor could Darwin.

As crazy as the whole situation was, that the trio of roughnecks may have just been dumb and wanted to do something to get their blood pumping. Why not? They were the only two boats in sight, tucked away back in a remote inlet. Darwin and Lucas were the only people nearby. From the distance they'd been, they didn't get close enough to get a good enough of a look at the marauders to pick them out of a lineup.

After the moment of levity died down, Darwin asked, "So, what are we supposed to do about the boat? Let them get away with it?"

Riddick stared back across the bay and arched his bushy eyebrows. "Honestly, from my experience, I'd wait before reporting it. There are many not so endearing characters—probably idiots in this case—around the Outer Banks who like to believe they have pirate blood in them. They come out here, get drunk, do stupid things such as marooning a couple guys by stealing their boat. My guess is, once these guys get it back to wherever they're going, they'll find where the boat is registered, and then take it back to Bath next time they're around."

Darwin and Lucas gave each other a look communicating that what Riddick said did make sense. They weren't native to this part of the state but believed the tale of pirate blood in the area.

"What do we tell the harbormaster?" Lucas asked. "Didn't seem like a forgiving guy."

"Let me talk to Sal," Riddick said, putting a hand on Lucas's shoulder. "See if we can come to an arrangement. We've known each other for years. We each have our secrets we'd rather not get out if you know what I mean."

Darwin nodded happily, while Lucas wondered what Riddick's secrets entailed.

*****

They decided since the afternoon was winding down, instead of going further out and covering more ground, they'd return to Bath and their motel for the evening. Lucas wanted to get a bite to eat, take a long, hot shower, try to forget that they had been shot at today, and study more on Blackbeard. Darwin had the same thoughts and wanted to explore the neighborhood near the Baymont Inn if enough daylight remained.

Riddick said he would take them out for dinner at a favorite local seafood establishment—his treat—if Darwin and Lucas were up for it. They declined, although they agreed to let Riddick take them out on his yacht the next day. After spending a couple hours on the jon boat, Darwin and Lucas agreed that in the future they would much rather sail from the extravagance of a luxury yacht after spending their first ten minutes aboard Riddick's. They agreed to meet at first light the next morning.

On the return trip to Bath, Riddick regaled Darwin and Lucas with several tales of moronic events he remembered having to do with people in and around the Outer Banks. Such as the old unemployed crab boat worker who broke into a house and stole some jewelry. He got caught because he dropped his own unemployment check on the bedroom floor.

He said that while there are fewer savory sorts of characters in the area, even the worst seemed to have a partially working moral compass. He told a story about a young hooligan who found an old woman's purse left behind on a small tour boat. He looked inside; it had hundreds of dollars in cash and credit cards. He went to a K-Mart over in Nags Head and spent over $3,000 on videogames. Also in the purse was an envelope containing a power bill that was due soon. The man was caught when he paid the bill for her using one of her credit cards.

Riddick's most unfortunate story was about a man who stole a car from a marina parking lot out at Lake Mattamuskeet. The cops located him and chased him for several miles north along Route 94. The thief eventually drove the car over an embankment near the Pocosin Lakes National Wildlife Preserve. The man climbed from car before the police could get to him and fled on foot over the cotton fields until he reached an inlet named The Frying Pan.

What the man forgot—or didn't know—was that The Frying Pan, so named because of its shape, emptied out into the Alligator River National Wildlife Refuge. Darwin nearly got sick as Riddick described the police finding what remained of the man amidst a feeding frenzy of gators.

"There are just a lot of dumb people out this way," he explained, gesturing over his shoulder to where they had just come from, "who will lie, cheat, and steal just for the hell of it. That's probably all it was with your boys and boat back there."

It was almost six when they returned to the Bath Marina. They said thanks and goodbye to Riddick, and then returned down South Main Street to Lucas's Jeep. While on Route 99 heading west towards Washington, Darwin used a restaurant review app to find them a place to eat. There was one seafood and steak eatery near the waterfront that came highly rated, touting "traditional Southern Style cooking with a modern and fun twist."

Once inside, the atmosphere was easy and relaxed. The clientele was a mixture between families with a couple of kids to couples on dates to men just returned to shore from a long day at sea. Island music consisting of Jimmy Buffet and Zac Brown Band tunes resonated softly from hidden speakers.

The place smelled amazing: a mixture of seafood, burgers, smoky pulled-pork barbecue, and mouth-watering steak. Lucas hoped the food tasted as good as it smelled. He studied the prices on the menu and suspected that his friend came out here on a shoestring budget. He saw Darwin flipping back and forth between the pages on the menu, possibly figuring out what he could afford.

"You know," Lucas said. Darwin looked up. "You were right about Riddick. I should have listened to you to begin with. Let me make it up to you by buying you dinner. My treat."

"You sure?"

"Absolutely," Lucas said. "Don't worry about it. My way of saying "I'm sorry.""

"Well . . . thanks," Darwin said, and flipped back to the front of his menu where the pricier options were.

Lucas saw a look of relief flash across his friend's face. Lucas was glad he could do something good for Darwin.

The server came, smiled, took their orders, and departed.

"Did you hear back from your detective friend?" Darwin asked.

"No, not yet. I'm sure Greg will get back to me when and if he finds out something. What about your girl? Anything?"

"Nah. She'll call."

After a short wait, the aroma of their food preceded the server by several steps. Lucas didn't know how famished he was until she set down a platter of fried shrimp and a sirloin steak in front of him. Mashed potatoes with gravy and melty macaroni and cheese were the sides. He thought of what Kristen would say had she seen that he hadn't ordered a single veggie. He smiled at what would have been an outright rebellion, but knew he'd regret the starchy dinner later.

On his side of the table, Darwin didn't know where to start. He likewise had a skewer of shrimp—coconut for him—and had a thick slab of ribs sitting atop seasonal veggies and rice.

They thoroughly enjoyed their dinner, paid the bill, and left as a small band trio of Jimmy Buffett lookalikes was setting up on a compact stage in the corner. Lucas considered staying for the live music, but remembered they had an early morning coming and he had research to do.

When they returned to the hotel, Darwin said he was going to go for a walk. Clear his mind from the day's events, he said. Lucas, for his part, was beat. He was tired and had a full stomach. All he wanted to do was to retire to his room, wash the accumulated grime off, climb in bed, and fire up his laptop.

Once back at the Baymont Inn in Chocowinity, they parted ways and agreed to meet by Lucas's Jeep sharply at 7 a.m. the next morning.

Lucas went to his room, peeled out of his still damp and odorous clothes and took a long, hot shower. He did his best thinking in the shower. He hatched his idea for the bookstore in the shower one morning, if memory served him correctly.

As the steamy, slightly salty water poured over him, he thought about their quest. Was it a quest, or just something to do to take his mind off Kristen? Sure, he was serious about trying to find the treasure. He was relieved that his travels and ordeal on this day kept his mind occupied. The only slow times he had where her betrayal could have crept into his mind were on the boat ride out to Rose Bay, waiting for Riddick to arrive while stranded on the mud flats, and then the return trip on the water to Bath. During all three of those times, he still found his attention taken by conversations with Darwin and Riddick and replaying the events of the bandits who stole their boat and fired shots at them.

Now that he thought about it afterward, the idle times from today weren't all that idle. It was a refreshing change of pace from the chaos since Kristen left.

So, if the plan for tomorrow was to almost randomly search the bays and inlets that came close to drawing Blackbeard's drawing on the map, would it be a monumental waste of time if their search came to nothing? At Rose Bay, they realized that much might happen to coastal shores over the course of three hundred years. Erosion, shifting of sands and waters could have changed the environment of where the treasure hid, if it hadn't washed away.

Everyone assumed Blackbeard had his treasure with him after he sunk the *Queen Anne's Revenge*. What if he hid it before then? What if he hid it *long* before then? If that was the case, then the map could represent any place between here and Cuba.

He rinsed out the foamy shampoo and reached for the travel-sized bottle of conditioner.

As he massaged the white cream into his scalp, he didn't feel they were in real danger from the man shooting at them today. Lucas figured the man was just trying to keep him and Darwin at bay while they stole the jon boat.

As he rinsed out the conditioner, the thing that stuck out the most was learning of Travis Cole's death. The man who discovered the journal. His unsolved murder seemed even more mysterious when you take into account that he had just come from Bath that previous weekend.

What reason would someone have to kill a young researcher in cold blood like that?

Lucas grabbed his fluffy, green loofah—he didn't travel without a loofah—and squirted body wash on it and worked it into a lather. As he went through the process of cleaning the sand, dirt, grime and stink off his body it occurred to him that if Riddick were the owner of a large shipping company, there should be news about him online.

Changing his stream of thinking, he reflected again on the treasure. What would he do if he located it? Would it change his life? Could he keep it? Did it exist, or was it a myth? With so many people over the centuries coming to Bath to try to find the treasure, including himself, had anyone ever figured out where the treasure may well have come from?

He enjoyed the final step of the shower. That was to rinse the suds off his body. He enjoyed this perhaps the most.

Then, considering all the people who came before him in search, he remembered the California Gold Rush in the 1800s and how it affected those people. They would do anything to find gold, even resorting to murder. He figured the treasure hunters in search of Blackbeard's gold resort to similar tactics.

He turned the water off with the squeak of the dull, silver knob. As he reached for the white motel towel hanging from a silver painted bar, the thought struck him: what if someone murdered Travis Cole over the journal?

# CHAPTER EIGHTEEN

Darwin soon understood why Chocowinity was so small. There was nothing here.

The name Chocowinity came from an old Tuscarora Indian word meaning "fish from many waters" stemming from the Pamlico River, Chocowinity Creek and Chocowinity Bay nearby. The town had a population of less than a thousand. Its location made it a crossroads for people traveling about the eastern part of North Carolina. In the early 1900s, the town was a hub for the Norfolk Southern Railway. Conductors sometimes called the town "Marsden" because it was easier to spell on a telegraph than "Chocowinity."

The sidewalk in front of the motel ran along Business 17. The "business" part of it consisted of two fast-food restaurants, a shady drug store, an even shadier service station, and one halfway decent truck stop.

He crested a small hill walking north and saw nothing worth investigating in that direction. As he turned around and started walking back towards the motel, his cell phone rang in his pocket. He pulled it out, checked the screen, and saw it was Lisa Kramer.

He smiled and answered. "Hey Lisa. What's up?"

"Hey, they're making me go home," she said.

Darwin checked his watch. It was just after seven. She had already been there two hours past when her shift was supposed to have ended. The sun was on its descent to the horizon. Splotches of pinks, reds, and yellows glowed through the sparse cloud cover. He said, "Oh, well, thanks for staying."

"My pleasure. I have to tell you, this thing is incredible, Darwin."

"What? Did you find the journal?"

"Yes!" she shouted. Darwin had to pull the phone away from his ear to keep the drum from bursting. She continued, sounding out of breath, "This is incredible. Mary Ormond was what, sixteen when she married Edward Teach, er, Blackbeard?"

"Something like that."

"She was a farmer's daughter, and it's astounding that she was so well written."

"I thought the same thing in reading over what little bit of the journal I could before I had to leave."

"I don't know where she got her education, but I'm amazed by the level of writing. This is a great find."

"Have you learned anything?"

She cleared her throat. "About the treasure, 1600s or just in general?"

"Well, both. Any clues on treasure are what I'm looking for."

"I haven't read anything about treasure as of yet, but man, she had a weird life."

"I'm sure. How so?"

She cleared her throat again. Darwin had noticed she did that a lot. He wondered if she had allergies from the musty old artifacts in the museum.

"First, she wholeheartedly loved him. She rarely referred to him by name because when she did, she called him "my love.""

"Aww. How sweet," Darwin said.

"Not really," Lisa replied. "As I said, I haven't a chance to dig too deep, but she's graphic and frank in her description of life with him."

"How so?"

"First, let me backtrack. I don't know if "loved" was the right word to say. I'd say more like she was infatuated with him. By the time he landed in Bath, he was known the whole world over."

"His reputation preceded him," Darwin said.

"Exactly. Everyone knew who he was, and his reputation, aside from being a bloodthirsty pirate, was as a ladies' man."

"Right, he'd quote, unquote married several other women before Mary Ormond for no reason than to sleep with them. It's like the bad boy in the corner of the bar with all the girls hanging off him. Some women are attracted to rogues and scoundrels. That's why you see women who move from abusive relationship to abusive relationship, because that's just the type of guy they're attracted to."

"True," Lisa said. "I don't know if at sixteen years of age how many, if any, relationships Mary had before she met Blackbeard, but from some of the accounts in here, the man was extremely abusive—both physically and sexually. However, in a few of the entries from the days when he was at sea, she described how much she missed him and how she hoped he would return safely.

"There are several accounts of the times he did return with presents. I've counted three occasions where Blackbeard brought several men with him and allow the other men to have their way with her." Darwin grimaced at the thought. Lisa continued, "She wrote of being struck and even knocked unconscious by him in drunken fits of rage."

Darwin shook his head. "She was a bright young woman, apparently. I wonder why she put up with the abuse."

"Again, he was her Sugar Daddy. Just the realities of life back then. He brought her jewelry and other valuable baubles when he returned home."

"I'd read one passage saying that."

"So, here comes this larger-than-life figure into her life, known to be extremely charismatic and may have had a hidden romantic side. He may have seen her at a gathering and been taken with her and she with him. As you said, his reputation preceded him. She knew what she was getting into." She paused. "As I said, this journal is fascinating in every way. I can't believe it is in such good shape. I can't believe Cole found it and it's been sitting in the basement here for over thirty years."

"Me neither," Darwin said. "So, no mention of treasure?"

She was silent for a moment. "Not that I've seen."

Darwin grew disappointed, until Lisa said, "Wait a minute. She said he mentioned a war chest. You don't think that'd be the treasure, would you?"

The statement gave Darwin goosebumps. "Possibly. In what context did he or she mention war chest?"

She thought about it for a moment. "Remember what he had done just before that. He crashed the *Queen Anne's Revenge* and *Adventure* and sailed up the Pamlico Sound and to Bath to essentially swear off his pirating ways to Governor Eden and be granted a King's pardon for his sins."

"I think that was just a formality," Darwin said. "They had to go through the process of having Teach sign that form so he would no longer be wanted by the English crown. Blackbeard kept a low profile for a couple months, setting up house in Bath and staying out of trouble so the British authorities would believe he had retired to civilian life. Then, when he resumed attacking ships a couple months later, he gave Eden a cut of the profits."

"A neat arrangement if you can get it."

"Right. There are tunnels that were supposed to be under Eden's estate, across the water from Blackbeard's estate, for him to take the plunder."

"Tunnels?"

"Yeah, from what I read, there was a tunnel cut from the river to the governor's house to smuggle goods."

"Very interesting."

"I mean, it's a legend. No one has ever found them, but during the late 1600s and early 1700s, people who lived near rivers carved out tunnels to escape any possible hostile Indians. There's also no actual evidence that Eden and Blackbeard were in cahoots. Although, after Blackbeard's death, they located part of his loot behind Knight's house in a barn."

"That's fascinating," she said, paused a moment, and continued her train of thought, "So, here he was, looking at the backside of his career as a pirate. He knew that although he'd sworn off piracy, there were others out there who still wanted him dead. He probably tired of having to give Eden a cut of his work."

"So..." Darwin said, "What did she say about a 'war chest?'"

"Oh, right," she said, "Sorry. Got off track. Anyway, she said he was drunk most of the time he was home and was always mumbling something to himself."

"Interesting."

"Right. He still had pirate fever. He wanted that booty."

"Old habits die hard."

"So, he had this grand plan to sink his flagship, take whatever he could that was on board, make an arrangement with Eden, and try to live a quiet life."

"Except it wasn't so quiet."

"Apparently. Perhaps Blackbeard had to go out, attack and rob other vessels and give a portion of it to Eden as part of the arrangement. He's stuck paying taxes."

"Might be," Darwin said. "So, what about the war chest?"

"Hold on, I'm getting to it. Blackbeard might have retired just to find himself working for the man. He had already decided he wanted to retire to civilian life, but the circumstances of that retirement kept him from doing what he wanted to do." She cleared her throat and continued. "So, Mary wrote that he would get drunk and depressed and talk about how if he had his war chest that he and she could find a tropical island somewhere and set up a new life away from the dangers of the British and Spanish governments. He said he just had to get away from everyone, including his crew, to go get it."

"That's interesting. Did he happen to mention where it was?"

"Not that I've read yet."

"Dang."

"Look, don't tell anyone this," she said. Darwin's pulse quickened. He liked secrets. "I photocopied as much of the journal as I could before I left. I was going to continue reading it when I got home. After I stop to get something to eat first. I'm famished."

Darwin couldn't fathom being hungry at present, after just having had one of the most delicious meals of his life. "Oh, that'd be great," he said. "Hey, do you have a scanner at home?"

"I do."

Darwin smiled. Jackpot. "Would there be any way you could scan those pages and send them to me as a PDF? I need some reading material tonight. How much of it were you able to get?"

"A good chunk. I can do that for you."

Darwin was relieved. "Thanks. I'll buy you dinner sometime."

The words were out of his mouth before he realized he said them. He'd never asked another woman out on a date before.

Without hesitation, she said, "Sounds like a plan."

Darwin stood beside the road after the connection broke, looking down the long hill at miles of spreading cotton fields and the sun going down beyond them.

He let out a heavy breath. An eventful day, indeed.

# CHAPTER NINETEEN

After the shower, Lucas lay in his bed with his laptop open. He had the television tuned to a college football game on ESPN with the sound turned most of the way down. When the network showed a game on a Tuesday night, it typically pitted two decent teams from small schools together. You never saw a big school such as Texas or Ohio State during the week. Teams of their ilk played on Saturdays where they were going to get network coverage and huge crowds.

For these two teams who came from schools with small budgets, the payout from this game could pay for their athletic department budget for the entire year. The stands might be empty, but at least the checks would be fat. Lucas applauded that. Sometimes, these small school teams ended up playing an entertaining game.

This game may have been enjoyable, but Lucas wouldn't have noticed. He was absorbed in his research, trying to learn everything he could about Blackbeard and his influence on the shaping of the New World.

For years, piracy was considered a spreading cancer, slowing and even eliminating economies of Britain's American colonies in North

Carolina and the Caribbean. Importers were afraid to send supplies, materials, and people to America for fear of being captured by pirates. In the early 1700's, the growth of the colonies stalled while pirates roamed the waters along the coast from Philadelphia to Charleston—the main route ships traveled when sailing from England.

After Blackbeard's death, the authorities captured and executed other well-known pirates such as Charles Vane, Stede Bonnet, and Jack Rackham. These events and increasing anti-piracy patrols in American waters helped stem the pirate scourge.

Just before his death, Blackbeard had been in talks with Vane and presumably others about joining forces. They would have had almost fifteen hundred men at their disposal and a fleet that may well rival anything the British Navy might throw against them.

Blackbeard would have been the influential leader of this group. With the number of men and the type of firepower they would have had, not only could Blackbeard have repeated his blockade of Charleston, but he may also have done that anywhere along the North American coast. Landing, attacking and taking a major settlement such as Baltimore, Williamsburg, or New York was a possibility. He could have sailed to the Caribbean and drove out the governor of the Bahamas, Woodes Rogers. Blackbeard and his merry men would have controlled the waters from Florida to South America.

This is what scared everyone from potential settlers, traders, and governments. It wasn't his piratical attacks; it was the potential of what he could do.

Lucas considered this. When Governor Alexander Spotswood commissioned Blackbeard's death, he didn't know he was changing world history. Spotswood believed it had to be done. King's pardon or not. If it weren't for that event, colonists may have never wrested control of America from the British Empire. A world superpower may have never been born. If that hadn't happened, would the Wright brothers have invented flight? Would Benjamin Franklin discover electricity?

Would Bell have invented the telephone? Would we have landed on the moon?

Those thoughts were too deep for Lucas to consider now. He'd had a long day. He was physically and mentally tired.

He had one more thing he wanted to look up before going to sleep. Other would-be treasure hunters had traveled to Bath. He wanted to see if they had ever found anything.

He ran a Google search for "Blackbeard", "Bath, North Carolina" and "Treasure hunters" and hit Search.

The first link at the top of the search results was from the Smithsonian. Lucas clicked it, and soon saw it dealt with the finding of the *Queen Anne's Revenge* off Morehead City. Another article showed that many have made their way through the marshy surroundings to the property to search for buried treasure, leaving many unfilled holes behind. Another showed the last official dig was about thirty years ago, which, Lucas surmised, was after Travis Cole had done his solo gig out there. That dig, the article read, said they'd uncovered shards of pottery and other relics of civilization that may or may not have been related to Blackbeard.

It had been decades since someone had organized a search. Part of Lucas wondered if that was because, after three hundred years, the trail had gone cold. Was there a trail to begin with? He went back to Blackbeard saying the night before his death that "only himself and the Devil" knew where the treasure lies. Was that a clue in itself?

He shook his head and tried a different search. This time he typed "Hugo Riddick" on a whim.

When the results appeared, Lucas went "hmm" to himself. The top half of the first page was of a "Hugo Riddick" who was a registered sex offender in Virginia Beach. Not too far away from here, Lucas thought. He disregarded that group of results. That Hugo Riddick was twenty-three years old.

Below was a link to a company website for Salty Pirate Shipping Services. Must be Riddick's company, Lucas thought. He clicked on the link, and it took him to a page with a profile of Riddick and a tasteful portrait. He had his hair tied back, beard groomed, wearing an expensive looking black suit with cornflower blue tie.

The bio was short. It read:

*Hugo Riddick is the only son of Salty Pirate Shipping's founder, Zachary Riddick.*

*Hugo obtained an Economics degree from North Carolina State University with a minor in Marine Sciences in 1981. After graduation, he stayed close to home and went right to work for his father, helping to streamline ship management protocols and improve cash flow routines.*

*He took over Salty Pirate Shipping following his father's passing in 1997 and has led the company into a new era with exponential growth.*

*In his spare time, you can see him at various coastal festivals, dressed as the pirate Blackbeard.*

The most interesting part to Lucas was the fact he graduated from the same school as Travis Cole. He wondered if they knew each other.

***

On the opposite side of the wall, Darwin stared intently at a PDF of the journal pages Lisa had sent earlier. They were waiting in his inbox for him after he took a shower of his own where, unlike Lucas who thought of the events of the day, thought about Lisa.

They first met during their sophomore wyear at North Carolina State in a Geology class. They sat near the back of the large room in a corner beside each other. They both were the types to shun attention and felt comfortable to do their work where classmates had to turn around to see either of them. They didn't communicate this to each other. In fact, it was something they didn't ponder. It was just the way they were.

Though they came from different backgrounds—Darwin mired in poverty, Lisa's parent's successful entrepreneurs—they had similar personalities. They kept to themselves, shared a love for Harry Potter and board games and couldn't go anywhere without a book tucked under their arms or noses.

There was never any thought of romance. Since they shared the same major, they worked side-by-side in the classroom and on projects. They both began working at the museum at the same time and sat, of course, in the back corner together of the same orientation. Love and companionship were the farthest things from their minds for the four plus years they'd known each other.

Darwin still shook his head thinking about him blurting out a dinner proposal to her earlier. It was something he had never thought about, for anyone, in his life. Sure, there were girls who caught his eye over the years, although he lacked the confidence to say anything to someone.

Except for one time. And that ended in humiliation. The event lasted for twenty seconds.

In seventh grade, Renata Wilson stole his heart. Puberty hit her early, and when she was thirteen, she had more gifts and curves than any of the other girls. Darwin's male classmates of course noticed that fact. The problem for Renata was that, at that time, she wasn't very pretty. His peers weren't interested, but he was. Renata knew she was further along than the other girls were and did not lack for confidence.

He approached her one day after gym class with the other kids who were waiting for the bell. Darwin towered over her as he did everyone else in school. He had never said a word to her until then. He thought he'd seen her looking at him from time to time during workouts in class. He hoped that perhaps she was interested. So, he mustered up as much courage as he could.

"Hi," he said, still sweaty from gym class.

She glanced up at him from playing with her fingernails, chomping fast on pink bubble gum, and gave him a once-over. She rolled her eyes, "Whatchyou want Darwin?"

"I just, I just wanted to say hi. Tell you that you looked pretty."

Her lips drew up like a duckbill and went *pfft*. "Whatever Mongo." She gave him a lazy dismissive wave before returning her attention to her fingernails. "Now go back to your cave or cardboard box or wherever it is you live and bother someone else."

He didn't remember what happened immediately after that. The next thing he recalled was that he left school and was running down the sidewalk to his house in hopes that his mom might give him some words of wisdom, to provide comfort. He burst through the door to find her naked and as high as a kite with a homeless looking dude doing that thing adults do—in his living room. Where he played his video games.

That series of events left him scarred. He'd seen his mother in compromising positions more times than he cared to remember, but Renata tore his heart out and stomped on it. In front of his classmates.

Not until earlier while talking to Lisa had he said anything to a girl—a woman—with even remote romantic undertones. He didn't know where it came from. Maybe his experiences this day made him feel like a different man. He'd had to step outside his comfort zone several times and do things he had never done before.

Maybe this treasure hunt would benefit him in more than one way.

He did his best to wash that escapade aside to focus on the tablet's screen. The syntax and grammar used by Mary Ormond was somewhat archaic and difficult to decipher on occasion. For most of the entries, Darwin could figure out the subject matter and/or the intent. He had the impression that she was a simple young woman.

She caught the eye of Edward Teach at a community gathering. Her father was one of Bath's most successful farmers, and in those days, a man such as he carried an air of prestige about him and ran in more influential circles. Were it not for the farmers of that day, many early colonists would have starved.

Ormond described her courtship with Blackbeard as torrid and quick. She was the only known wife of Blackbeard's to come from a legal marriage. He also lived with her until the day he died. Although that was just for three months, if his history served as a guide to his behavior, he must have cared for Ormond in a way he had not cared for a woman before—the gang rapes aside.

Darwin believed that after reading her journal that when it was made public, it would provide an exclusive and only known account of Blackbeard's last days. It would also serve as a window into the lives of those who lived in the colonies during the early eighteenth century. She wrote of the everyday concerns and tasks that went along with life during that period: having to hand wash clothes out at Bath Creek, being afraid of Indian attacks to her relationship with her husband and family on the farm. Darwin imagined that she was a good wife, and her farm upbringing gave her the knowledge and skillset to be a supporting wife despite her young age.

He did not see her refer to Teach as 'Blackbeard' or as a pirate, only as 'Edward' or 'my love.' After getting accustomed to her writing style and seeing that she wrote mostly of her daily life (which didn't seem all that noteworthy in itself), and because it was getting late, he decided to scan for any mentions of the buccaneer.

He found the entry Lisa said contained mention of his war chest. Ormond described one night during July that Teach came home from the only pub in Bath:

**October 2, 1718**

*He was so sloshed I had to drive to his side and holp him to a chair after he flung open their front door to keep him from falling embarrassingly on his visage. Usually, he has a short temper at that* hour. After he partakes of the rum, I grow afeard. Violence is his normal recourse.

Although this time, peradventure he had drunk something different. His breath didn't carry the usual aroma of rum & he had an odd demeanor. I guided him to a chair & rushed outside to retrieve him water from the cistern.

When I had returned, I gave him the glass & sat at his side, stroking his arm.

"The fools. The fools," he had said, almost in a stupor. "All anyone wants to ask me is where the treasure is buried. None of the bastards has't a clue. The only ones who did are dead now. "

His statement made me frightened. I asked him what he meant.

He laughed. "All of the men who were with me when we raided that ship off Trench's Island. I marooned them after I sunk the Annie. They knew where to find my war chest."

"Did you mean for them to die?"

"I did. I couldn't bear to kill them myself. They were good men. I just didn't want anyone left to get to the gold before I could return."

I was thoroughly confused. The townsfolk often asked me if I knew where to find his treasure. That surely Edward would confide its location with me. Its location is all anyone wants to know. This was the first time I can recall him speaking of it. I had hoped he would continue before sobering up or passing out.

Unfortunately, I had no such luck.

He stopped speaking, looking off into a distance only he knew how far it stretched. He seemed eternlly depress'd for a moment before looking at me. "Then I came here and met you."

As he always did, he managed to make my heart grow big. I loved this man.

I sat there for a few minutes at his side while he stroked my hair. "Do you think you'll go back & get it? Your war chest?"

*He stopped in mid-stroke, and I was momentarily frightened that he would strike me. But he did not. Lost in thought he was.*

*He said that he would like to, but didn't know the time in which he could.*

*He went silent & the soft petting of my hair ceased. He had fallen asleep.*

***

The entry ended there. Darwin studied the next several entries to see if she elaborated anymore on that conversation but learned nothing. He went back and re-read the passage again, this time jotting sloppy notes in a beaten spiral notebook.

After the destruction of the *Queen Anne's Revenge* and *Adventure* at Topsail Inlet, Blackbeard selected about forty of his most trusted men to transfer whatever plunder he had aboard the two flagships to cram whatever they could aboard a long boat. The remainder he on the shore of a small island near Beaufort. Some two-hundred and fifty men.

Most people thought he would have kept the big treasure near him. His war chest. That's why so many came to the Outer Banks, hoping to find it. Could it be that everyone was looking in the wrong location for almost three hundred years?

The entry came from a month and a half before Blackbeard's death. Darwin wondered if he found time between this event and his death to go to wherever this Trench's Island was. Careful study of the known events between the second day in October and November 22nd should shed light on that. The problem, however, was that Darwin didn't have time for careful study now. He would ask Riddick while they were on the water tomorrow.

The biggest clue, Darwin thought, was the mention of Trench's Island. Darwin had not heard of it, and if that island was anywhere along the eastern seaboard or in the Caribbean, he figured he would have learned of it during his college studies.

He brought up Google Maps and searched for the island. He gave the screen a funny look when, after hitting ENTER, the screen immediately zoomed in on a place named the Heritage Library. He saw nothing relating this library to anything called Trench's Island.

He hummed to himself while doing the same search, this time on the web. The top result read **Trench's Island Heritage Library Foundation**. He clicked. Sat back. Read several paragraphs. Hummed some more.

Now he understood the connection to Trench's Island. But that brought a bigger question to Darwin's mind. How did *that* place have a substantial treasure during the early eighteenth century?

Back then, there was nothing there.

# CHAPTER TWENTY

D ARWIN AND LUCAS GRABBED two cups of coffee to go just as the last drops of the first pot of the morning finished brewing in the lobby. Lucas tasted it first, and thought it was better than the previous morning. They grabbed a couple apples and bananas, stuck them in their pockets, checked out of the motel, threw their bags in the back, and climbed into the Jeep.

As they crossed over the bridge into Washington, the first rays of light streaked across a cloudless October sky above. The morning breeze felt cool in the open cabin of the Jeep, and despite the season, they were due for a muggy day.

"Did you hear from your friend?" Darwin asked, meaning Greg.

Lucas took a sip of coffee from a travel thermos bearing the West Virginia University logo on the side. "Nah. Not a peep. All I did was research treasure hunting in Bath and the surrounding areas and investigate Riddick."

"Find anything?"

Lucas shrugged. "Well, beyond being rich, I learned that he and Travis Cole both graduated from North Carolina State at the same time."

"Think they knew each other?"

"Dunno. It's a possibility. They had the same majors."

"That is interesting. I'm not a strong believer in coincidences."

"Me neither." Lucas paused as the Jeep's tires thumped from the concrete of the bridge to the asphalt of the main drag in Washington. "What about you? You hear back from your girl?"

"I did." Darwin left him hanging.

Lucas took his eyes from the glow of the headlights pointing their way between the pre-dawn streets and looked at Darwin, smiled, and said, "Come on. What is it?"

Darwin thought how to best frame his answer. "I believe we're searching in the wrong place."

"What makes you think that?"

Darwin related the passage of Mary Ormond's from the journal and the mention of Trench's Island.

Lucas was speechless while they navigated out of Washington proper in the direction of Bath. "Do you suppose he ever went back?"

"I don't know. The entry was dated about a month and a half before his death. Don't know if he would've had the time to do so. That period of his life is well documented from what I remember. Perhaps more was known of his whereabouts during the last month of his life than the previous thirty-eight years."

"Hmm. So, where is this Trench's Island? I've never heard of it."

"I hadn't until last night, but that's the most interesting part."

"Why do you say that?"

"Because the island no longer exists."

# CHAPTER TWENTY-ONE

As Lucas cruised through coastal town after coastal town after breezing through Jacksonville and Camp Lejeune, he missed having someone in the vehicle to talk with. To keep him distracted. Despite the reason he was in this part of the state, he couldn't get his mind off what Kristen did to him. He couldn't understand if she made the decision to leave him because of the issue with having kids or for something else.

He may never know the answer and that bothered him to no end.

Round and round those thoughts swirled in his head, amid the forty-mile stretch from Surf City to Topsail to Ogden. When he reached Wilmington, he found his knuckles turning white from gripping the steering wheel. His blood pressure had to be through the roof.

*Stand strong,* he thought to himself. *It won't be long before it's over and finalized.*

It was something he tried to keep his mind from wandering to, but he thought about having to get back into the dating game. Single life. He didn't enjoy it before. Since he'd gotten married, his hairline had receded while his waist had expanded. Not by much either way thankfully. He didn't know how, or if, he'd appeal to another woman. Any woman. He didn't even know where to go to find a single woman. He imagined he'd have to join a gym. Maybe buy new clothes. He hadn't bought a new outfit for himself in five years.

Maybe he should just stay on the road forever. Get away from it all. Go somewhere tropical. Where the ocean and the sky blended into each other. Float on a raft in blue waters while the breeze whistled off the bottle in his hand. He was sure he'd find women there.

He stopped and got gas in a town called Woodburn. He went inside the station, used the restroom, washed his hands, and then got a cup of coffee and a donut out of a plastic case.

As he climbed into the Jeep, he got out his cell phone and dialed Greg Hanover.

He made a right turn back onto Route 17 as a groggy sounding Greg answered, "Hello?"

"Hey Greg. Lucas here. Figure anything out?"

The detective cleared his throat. "Hold on. A little. Let me get my notebook." Lucas heard shuffling, amplified by the Bluetooth sound streaming over the speakers in the Jeep. "Okay. I haven't spoken to anyone yet. I got to the station late last night and did a search on our computers. All of this is over thirty years old and sketchy anyway."

"Oh."

"First, the subject was discovered in his apartment. The person who wrote the report said there was blood all over the place. From where they found the body, to the walls near him, to a chair in the living room and in the bathroom."

"Oh," Lucas repeated.

Greg cleared his throat again. "Someone shot him in the back of the head with presumably a large caliber bullet."

Lucas cringed.

"There's more," Greg said. "It looks as though he was tortured before being shot."

"Goodness."

"Yeah, he was missing a couple fingers and toes. He was probably strapped to a chair while the killer dismembered him."

Now Lucas understood why the newspaper referred to the state of Cole's body as "gruesome."

"Wouldn't he have bled out before the guy could shoot him?"

"Maybe. Maybe not. Depends on how fast it all went down."

Lucas didn't want to imagine what Travis Cole must have persevered during the last moments of his life.

Greg continued. "His apartment was in an old turn-of-the-century home that had been divided into four units. At the time, only one other was occupied, and that person was out of town on vacation. The entrance to Cole's apartment, the report read, wasn't visible from the main road. He lived on the bottom floor in a studio apartment accessed from the rear of the building."

"So, barring a neighbor being in the building, no one would have known what was going on."

"Presumably. Until the stench reached the surrounding area," Greg said.

Lucas's nose crinkled at the thought of the stink. "What else did the report say?"

"There was no real sign of struggle from the victim. They didn't find any skin under his remaining fingernails from where he may have scratched the killer while trying to defend himself." Lucas heard Greg shuffle some papers. "Let's see here. No known motive at the time the report was filed, nor were there any suspects.

"They questioned his family, friends, and coworkers and couldn't find anyone who didn't have good things to say about Mr. Cole. He came to work on time. Stayed after when allowed. Didn't have much of a social life it would appear. No known girlfriend."

"Dedicated to his job, then," Lucas said.

"That seems the case. A young guy trying to make a name for himself at his chosen career is the picture I got."

After taking a moment to digest Greg's report, one thing kept tugging at Lucas's mind. "Was there any mention of a journal?"

"What?" Greg asked.

"You know. A journal. A notebook. This one would have been very old."

"Not that I remembered reading," Greg said. "Why?"

"Well, Cole was killed after spending the weekend in Bath where he presumably found this journal that led us out here."

"You think someone killed him over that?"

"I don't know. Seems like a strange coincidence that he located it and got murdered soon thereafter. I mean, if he was missing fingers and toes, it's as though someone was trying to make him talk."

"I dunno. Over a journal? Seems farfetched," Greg said.

Lucas shook his head, although he knew Greg couldn't see him do that. "No. I believe you're missing the point. Someone may have thought that journal held the key to unlocking one of the world's biggest mysteries. If that was what was driving this person, then a dead body wouldn't be but a small speedbump in the way of reaching that goal."

"But—," Greg started and then paused. "But how would anyone know that Cole found it if he had just returned home? It's not as though they had cell phones or email back then."

"He might have used someone else's phone, or a payphone."

"Yeah, I'll concede that."

"Did you find anything else?"

"No, that was about it," Greg said. "I'm going to call the guy I know and see if he recalls anything about this Cole guy later today. I have to leave soon. Just got a call that a guy was killed on Cabarrus Avenue near downtown Concord. So, I'll be busy with that for a while."

"Ok. Thanks Greg." Lucas told him about where he was and what he was doing. "Call me when you find out something."

Greg said he would and ended the connection.

At least the call got Lucas's mind off Kristen. He spent the rest of the drive to Hilton Head wondering if a mutilated corpse from over thirty years ago would come back to haunt him and Darwin.

# CHAPTER TWENTY-TWO

MOVING AT A MORE relaxed pace south than his friend was, Darwin sat in the top of the yacht, watching hundreds of seagulls swarm over a shrimp boat they were passing by just off the coast of Morehead City.

The ocean swells were calm. Sun glittered in a million points of light off the water. The smell of sea salt carried on the breeze, buffeting his bushy, curly hair and beard. A handful of wispy clouds dotted the sky overhead. Darwin decided he couldn't have picked a better time to spend his first full day at sea.

Unfortunately, it wasn't all for pleasure. He listened to Lucas's admonition not to spend too much time on the phone with Lisa. He wanted to wait until she was at lunch before calling her. They were close enough to land that he still had two bars of cell phone reception. He hoped it remained that way for a couple of hours before noon.

Riddick set the autopilot and joined Darwin topside. He had two bottles of Corona trapped between the fingers on his left hand. He offered one to Darwin. He abstained. Riddick seemed unaffected by the decline of his offer and set the extra bottle at his feet as he sat down.

He popped the cap, took a pull, and surveyed the waters ahead of them. "Beautiful day, don't you think?"

"Definitely."

"So, tell me why we're going to Hilton Head? Why don't you believe the treasure is around here?"

"Well, that might not be our final destination."

"Why is that?"

"I feel that Hilton Head is where Blackbeard gained this treasure."

"What makes you say that?"

Darwin didn't know how he should answer that. He imagined Lucas wanted him to keep his mouth shut and just to tell Riddick to captain the boat. Darwin couldn't ask a man to gas up a boat and head south on such a trip at a moment's notice without giving him a better reason.

"My friend at the museum emailed me a couple pages of the journal she had scanned. In one entry, Ormond recounted a time Blackbeard came home completely drunk and blubbered on about how he wanted to go back to Trench's Island for the treasure everyone kept asking about."

"Trench's Island?" Riddick scratched his chin.

"Yeah, that's what Hilton Head was called back then."

"Ah. So why isn't the treasure closer to here?"

"Because in the passage, he referred to marooning all the men who knew about the treasure's location near where he sunk his ships. He wanted them all dead but didn't want to kill them."

"Dead men tell no tales," Riddick said, reciting the old pirate saying. "You know, there's no proof that Blackbeard killed anybody until the battle that took his life."

"Really?"

"Yeah. He gained his nasty reputation because of his appearance, meanness, and theatrics. When he approached vessels to attack, the other captain generally raised his white flag after seeing Blackbeard's flag. They wanted no part of him."

"Interesting."

"Do you know on what date Teach said this to Ormond?"

"Yeah, that was the other thing I wanted to ask you about. He said that to her around the middle of October."

"Then he died just over a month later."

"Right. Do you know what he did in the month just before he died?"

Riddick finished off the first Corona and opened the second, took the first sip, and said, "A short time before that, Blackbeard and the men he had remaining with him arrived in Bath, towing a French ship. When asked where the crew of the other ship was, Blackbeard responded that they just stumbled on the ship empty like that."

"Yeah right."

Riddick eyed Darwin. "Exactly. Eden convened a Vice-Admiralty Court in Bath in late September 1718. Blackbeard and four of his crew testified and signed affidavits to the effect that there had been no piracy. They just found an empty ship.

"Because there was no proof that they weren't being honest, Eden had no choice but to let Blackbeard and his crew go and declared the French ship a derelict vessel. Eden wrote that the verdict was made "as any other court must have done, and the cargo disposed of according to law.""

"What does that mean? Disposed of according to law?"

Riddick held up a finger. "That my friend is what caused the trouble. You see, normally a court awarded the cargo to those who discovered the ship, the salvors. The Crown took its portion. Then, the North Carolina authorities took theirs in the form of sixty barrels of sugar delivered to Eden's estate, followed by another twenty to his treasurer, Tobias Knight."

"Wait. So did Eden and Knight basically get a kickback from this?"

"More or less, yes. Later, Blackbeard took the French ship back out to Ocracoke and burned it, thereby eliminating any evidence. To the north, Governor Spotswood of Virginia caught wind of this. Normally, piracy was to be handled within individual colonies. Nevertheless, Spotswood believed the scourge named Blackbeard needed to be dealt with. He suspected that Blackbeard and Eden were in cahoots and wanted to put a stop to the piracy before it spread to his Chesapeake Bay."

"Blackbeard was dealing with all of this during the last month of his life?"

"You might say that. He spent much of his time at his base out at Ocracoke. That's where the men sent by Spotswood to kill Blackbeard located him November 22nd."

"You don't think he had time to run down to South Carolina for a few days and retrieve his treasure?"

Riddick thought about it for a moment and shook his head. "Nah. Not likely. I'd say wherever it was when he said that to Mrs. Ormond is where it still is, unless someone else stumbled upon it."

"If that were so, I'd imagine we'd have heard about it by now."

"That's probably true," Riddick said. "There's a big underground treasure market, although I don't recall hearing anything about artifacts from his main treasure."

Something in what Riddick just said sent a chill down Darwin's spine. "So, have you found anything left behind by Blackbeard?"

"Found? No. Acquired? Yes," Riddick answered.

"What does that mean?"

Riddick stood and leaned against the railing. The sea breeze caused the hair on his face to flutter back and forth. "It means that, no, I have never discovered anything myself. I have purchased things believed to come from the estate of Blackbeard's."

Darwin's eyebrows raised. He was impressed. "Like what?"

Riddick held up a finger. "Hold on a second." He disappeared below deck for a minute before reappearing holding an odd-looking gun. "This," he said, handing it to Darwin.

He hefted it in his big hand. It was made of iron and wood. It had weight to it. It felt old. Important. "What is it?"

"This," Riddick said, "is believed to be one of Blackbeard's flintlock pistols."

Darwin felt a shiver run over him. "Wow."

"I found it on eBay, believe it or not."

"Really? How do you know it's authentic?"

"There's no real way to be sure, but the seller was able to trace the chain of custody from 1717 to today. One of Blackbeard's crew members had it, gave it to his kid, who gave it to his kids and on down."

"So, it was a family heirloom that someone decided to sell?"

"That it was. The man who sold it to me lives down in Wilmington. I drove down and met him. He gave me the history behind it. I believed he told me the truth. So, I bought it. I have more items back at the house. I'll show you sometime."

"That'd be cool."

# CHAPTER TWENTY-THREE

L UCAS MADE IT TO Hilton Head just after noon. He picked up Route 278, which ran the length of the island. It was his first time in the area. If it weren't for the palm trees and many of the types of businesses operating close to shore, he wouldn't have known he was close to the ocean. Thick jungle, businesses, and resorts separated the four-lane highway from any views of the beaches or water.

He passed by the Heritage Library on his right. He was hungry and wanted to get lunch first. Beside the library was a diner advertising all-day breakfast. Lucas went down the street, made a U-turn, drove back, parked in the library parking lot, and walked over to the restaurant. Now that he was out in the open air, the atmosphere told Lucas he was near the water. He smelled the ocean breeze. The humidity clung to his skin like an extra layer of clothes.

He ordered a short stack, bacon, and coffee from the cute waitress with red hair who gave him a suggestive smile. He looked about and saw a couple of elderly couples sharing a late lunch and four uniformed cops at a table near the back. Three men and one woman. They were having coffee. That made Lucas happy. If this was a place where members of the local police force gathered for a cup of coffee, then it must be good.

The waitress returned less than five minutes later with a steaming mug of coffee and a plate of food. He drenched the pancakes in thick syrup he suspected was ninety-five percent sugar. He cut into the pancakes and thought about the smile from the pretty waitress. He wasn't used to having that happen to him. Perhaps he just hadn't noticed during the past five years of marriage. Perhaps she smiled that way at everyone.

Twenty minutes later, he finished, paid the check and left a bigger than normal tip. *She deserved it*, he thought.

The library sat behind two Carolina pines separated by short bushes and a marble sign with the library's name sandblasted into it. The library was in a white, concrete two-story building with a crow's nest peeking above the middle of a brown tin roof. Not a visually appealing structure, Lucas thought.

The interior's features matched the outside. It reminded Lucas of every other public library. There was maybe ten people in the building altogether. Workers and readers. A desk sat at the front for patrons to check out books. Rows of shelves packed full of books ran down the left and right sides of the room. The center of the room had tables and chairs where patrons sat, doing school research or flipping through a magazine or book. A full complement of computer kiosks sat in the back left corner.

Another desk spanned the back wall mirroring the one at the entrance. Lucas walked back to it. Two women and three men sat behind the desk; their eyes focused on computers. All wore lanyards around their necks, which had their names in bold print along with thumbnail pictures that resembled driver's license photos.

None looked up when Lucas approached the desk. He stepped to a straggly haired man in the middle of the desk.

"Help you?" the man asked, not taking his eyes away from the computer.

Lucas saw the man's name on the lanyard. "Hey Kyle, I'm looking for Ezra."

The man had the Pavlovian response to hearing someone say his first name and looked up. "Old man Ezra?"

Lucas shrugged. "I don't know. I guess. I was told to ask for him."

By this time, the other four people behind the desk stopped their work to listen to the conversation. Lucas saw two of them smiling.

The man pushed back from his desk, stood up and said, "Follow me."

He led Lucas behind the desk to an elevator that took them to the third level crow's nest. The elevator doors opened revealing a small naturally lit room with stacks of ancient books piled on two wooden tables in the center and on waist high bookshelves lining the perimeter of the room.

A diminutive old man with thick glasses and three strands of long gray hair falling from his scalp sat in a chair with his back to them at one table. His face was inches away from the yellowed parchment of a dusty book. He held a magnifying glass in the small gap between his glass's lenses and the letters on the page.

He did not seem to notice the two men's entry into the room.

Kyle cleared his throat. "Mr. Hefner?"

The man set the magnifying glass aside. Looked left. Looked right. Did not turn around. Shook his head. Picked up the magnifying glass. Went back to reading.

"Ezra," Kyle said, louder this time and tapped the man on the shoulder.

This time, the man turned around in surprise. "Oh, Kyle," he said with a voice that seemed to struggle to get the words out, although drenched in a thick Southern twang. "Didn't hear you come in." He squinted at Lucas. "Who's this?"

"He asked to see you," Kyle answered.

The man regarded Lucas and dismissed Kyle.

After the elevator door closed on the library assistant, Ezra said, "I don't get many visitors here." He gestured for Lucas to pull a chair out from the other table and sit. "What can I do for you?"

Lucas explained to him the events that brought him to Hilton Head. As he spoke, he noticed that while the man appeared to be two steps from the grave, his eyes followed everything Lucas said. If the rest of his senses were leaving him, Lucas hoped his mind was still intact. He figured the man opposite him must be in his nineties. Maybe pushing one hundred.

Lucas couldn't imagine still coming to work at that age.

"You're looking for anything pointing to where Blackbeard may have acquired a treasure when Hilton Head was known as Trench's Island?" Ezra said.

"Yes. Any help you could give me would be much appreciated."

The man stretched his neck to look over both of Lucas's shoulders. "What friend? I can't see him. Sorry, my eyesight isn't what it once was."

Lucas stifled a laugh. "No, he's coming separately."

"Oh," Ezra said, running a hand across his forehead. "That's a relief. Thought I was going crazy."

"No worries," Lucas said. "Does that ring a bell? Blackbeard?"

The man stroked his chin. "I don't recall any mention of him in the records," he gestured to all of the books in the room.

"What about pirates in general?"

Ezra pursed his lips and narrowed his eyes, making the million wrinkles in his face more defined. "No, not really."

Lucas was heartbroken. End of the trail.

He began to think about his next step when Ezra held up a small, crooked finger and said, "Hold on. Maybe. Give me a minute."

Lucas watched as he struggled to his feet. The man had a pronounced limp and reminded Lucas of a hobbit, as Ezra went straight for a bookshelf a third of the way back on the right side of the room. He kneeled, plucked a thin green book, and returned to where Lucas sat.

He handed the book to Lucas and said, "Turn it to page thirty-seven. Read the text beginning in the third paragraph down."

As soon as the man set the book in Lucas's hands, he knew that it was the oldest book he'd ever held. It was thin, no more than fifty pages in length, and had a distressed leather cover. It had a faded inscription on the front that Lucas couldn't make out. It also had an embossed design of a galley with three tall masts in faded silver on the right side of the cover. Lucas saw old smudges where dirt and dust had collected.

Lucas opened the book. The spine made cracking noises from decades of disuse. The interior emanated the strong, musty odor Lucas associated with old books. The paper had faded to a dingy brown over the centuries. The letters **Mrs. E. R. Barnes** were written in faded pencil inside the front cover in stilted lettering.

He flipped the page. It read:

### *MY INCREDIBLE JOURNEY TO THE NEW WORLD*

**By**

**IGNATIO AZEROLA**

**LONDON**

**John B. Alden, Publisher**

**1792**

Lucas closed the book and traced a finger along the faded inscription on the front. Those were the faded words, he thought.

He looked up at the small man still standing before him. The man was studying Lucas's expression closely.

He wrinkled a brow. "Who is this?"

With infinite patience, the old man wheezed again, "Page thirty-seven. Third paragraph. Read it aloud if you will."

Lucas leafed to the page with the utmost care not to damage the fragile pages. The spine was trying to come apart from the stack of thin paper. Although the paper had faded, the lettering still stood out.

He found the suggested paragraph, cleared his throat, and began reading aloud:

"A fierce storm separat'd us from the *Jeronimo*. At about four in the afternoon, a pirate vessel accosted our ship.

"They came with a fighting posture, hoisting a foul pirate flag before anchoring within musket-shot of our ship. Their cannons fired, disabling our ship.

"The group of pirates gathered on deck and shouted many curses at my men, waiving pistols and cutlasses in the air. Their captain appeared, sending all my men into a cower.

"He had a fierce countenance. His visage was obscured by a cloud of dark smoke and that he had a long, black beard with bundles of hair bound together with ribbons. He demanded all treasure in the holds. I feared for mine life if I disobeyed. I feared for mine life if I returned to Spain. In the end, I allowed the pirate to take what he wanted."

When Lucas finished the passage, Ezra rasped, "Mr...?"

"I'm sorry I didn't introduce myself when I came in. Caine. Lucas Caine."

The wrinkles on his face deepened as he smiled. "Mr. Caine, I have been the proprietor of the Trench's Island Commemorative Library since its inception over sixty years ago," he waved a hand, indicating the entire room, "and hand collected almost every volume here."

"Wow."

"It started as a single shelf in the little Hilton Head library that once stood near here," he drawled.

"The book you hold in your hands is one of the first, and oldest, in this collection. It is also one of only about fifty ever made and probably the last that hasn't been lost or destroyed."

Lucas stared down at the pages in his hand. "Incredible."

The man sat back in his chair and made himself comfortable. Lucas thought it was story time.

"Ignacio Azerola is a forgotten footnote in Spanish history." Ezra's voice was no longer a wheeze as he told his story.

Lucas imagined the man had become a skilled storyteller during his half-century or more of working in the library.

"He was a wanted man in Spain, this Azerola," Ezra said. "Persona non grata, if you will. The passage you read refers to a pirate attack on a ship named the *Nuestra Senora de Atocha*." He paused. "Are you familiar with the sinking of the Spanish treasure fleet off the coast of Florida in 1715?"

"Vaguely," Lucas said. "That was when a hurricane hit a bunch of ships carrying gold and additional treasure, right? They all sunk?"

"More or less," Ezra said, and then eased into a story. "The fleet was supposed to have carried the king's share of New World production in the form of taxes. Which, back then, was a fifth of everything. These fleets had been in service since 1526 if I recall correctly. By 1715, Spain had laid claim most of western South America all the way up to Mexico. They controlled all the gold, silver, and jewels both above and below ground."

"A substantial amount," Lucas said.

"Yes, a very substantial amount." Ezra wheezed, caught his breath, and continued, "Not only did the fleet carry what was intended for the Spanish crown, other people who made their wealth in the New World had private cargoes aboard. They were trying to send it home to their families."

"Wow."

He raised his bushy eyebrows. "Yes, wow. Anyway, the fleet was hit by what must have been a massive hurricane as they sailed up the Florida Straits. All ships, save one, sunk. Almost all that treasure came to rest in shallow waters. The Spanish sent out rescue parties. They saved about fifteen hundred sailors."

"That's good."

"They located many on a nearby beach. Others made it up to St. Augustine," Ezra said. "Almost immediately, Governor Corioles in Havana organized salvage expeditions to recover what they could of the treasure. They recovered a great deal of it, but everyone in the Caribbean, America, and Europe knew about it. They all wanted a piece. This is what kicked off the Golden Age of Piracy.

"Shortly thereafter, the waters along the East Coast and the Caribbean were thick with pirates. No doubt, your Blackbeard found his way there for that very reason."

"OK, so where does this Azerola come in?" Lucas asked, gesturing with the ancient tome in his hand.

"Azerola," Ezra said, "was the captain of the *Atocha*, a ship carrying a vast amount of the salvage from the wreckage on its way back to Spain."

# CHAPTER TWENTY-FOUR

THE IMPLICATIONS WERE STAGGERING. If the pirate with the "fierce countenance" and face obscured by smoke that attacked Azerola and the *Atocha* was Blackbeard, then his hidden treasure might be bigger than anyone ever imagined. In all the reading Lucas had done in the past on pirates, he hadn't come across one who used that particular brand of theatrics other than Blackbeard.

"Could this have been where Blackbeard got his treasure?"

Ezra shrugged. "I don't know." He saw Lucas's shoulders sag. "Now, that's not to mean it couldn't be. The attack on the *Atocha* occurred in February of 1717."

"Hmm. The earliest recorded event where someone described Teach as having a long, black beard wasn't until later that year. That meant that in February of that year, he wasn't well known yet. Azerola may not have known whom he was dealing with until afterward. What did Azerola do?"

"The man did as he was told," Ezra said. "He said he'd give the pirate everything they had aboard. Most of his crew jumped ship and went with whoever this pirate was. The *Atocha* had separated from the warship that was supposed to have been protecting it, the *San Jeronimo*. He wrote that when it came over the horizon, the pirate took what he could and high-tailed it out of there."

"Ah," Lucas said. "I know Blackbeard liked to hang around the various inlets and atolls near Savannah and pick off passing ships. He may have pursued the *Atocha* to near here, plundered it, and high-tailed it north."

"That's essentially what Azerola described as happening. Only five crewmembers chose to stay with him and the *Atocha*. The rest took off with the pirate. He wrote that the *Jeronimo* came within shouting distance of the *Atocha* to make sure everyone was fine before taking up the chase on the fleeing pirate ship."

"Did they come back?"

"Azerola wrote that the *Jeronimo* came back within half a day. The pirate sloop was too fast for them. They returned to get the story of what happened. The *Atocha* was basically dead in the water, so they took the remaining crew what treasure was left and sailed back to Spain."

"Did he say the name of the pirate ship? Did he notice?"

"He did. It should be near that passage you just read."

Lucas looked down and scanned the pages in the book. He flipped through several pages and saw it in a paragraph near the end of that chapter:

"I caught the pirate ship's name as it turned about and cast away from us: *Revenge.*"

Lucas gasped. That was the name of Blackbeard's first ship.

***

After taking a moment to process this, he asked, "What happened to Azerola?"

"He said he lived in fear for the rest of his life. The rest of his journey was the subject of that book. He realized his days were numbered. Letting that amount of treasure get stolen was an unforgivable offense. So, when the *Jeronimo* stopped in Philadelphia to take on supplies before crossing the Atlantic, Azerola snuck off and hitched a ride with another vessel to Britain."

"Man, that's rough."

"It was a tougher time back then. You did what it took to survive. No matter what. He hated the New World and wanted to go back to Europe. He knew a noose was waiting for him the instant he set foot on the shores of Spain. He settled into the English countryside and raised sheep. Near the end of his life, he published that memoir."

"Incredible," was all Lucas could say to that. "Any idea where the pirates may have gone?"

Ezra scratched his chin. "As far as I can recall, there wasn't a description of the *Jeronimo's* chase of the pirate ship except to say it disappeared."

Thinking back to Blackbeard's use of various land features to hide, Lucas asked, "So, do you think they could have waited until they were out of sight of the pirate ship and ducked into the mouth of a river or something and let the *Jeronimo* go past?"

"It's possible, yes."

"Do you feel that this could have been Blackbeard? The pirate ship has the right name, although there might have been others in the ocean with the same name at the time."

The old man rested his index finger on his lips and expelled a quick breath. "It certainly may have been. Many pirates during those days were known by reputation and could be identified on sight. By all accounts, Azerola was an intelligent man. I bet that he would have identified Blackbeard at the beginning of his account if he knew who the pirate was who boarded his ship."

"Makes sense," Lucas said. The untold riches taken from the holds of the *Atocha* could have been the war chest Blackbeard drunkenly mentioned to Mary Ormond.

Outside the windows, the tops of the palm trees swayed in the light ocean breeze. It wasn't definite, although there was an excellent chance the pirate described by Azerola was in fact Blackbeard. The ship had the right name. Twitter and the internet didn't exist back then for news to spread rapidly. Many events throughout history are lost in the mists of time because there wasn't someone nearby to document them. Unless someone came across a diary from the man himself, the world will never know everything Blackbeard did during his reign of terror in this part of the globe.

This could be one of those lost chapters.

He didn't know what else he could get from Ezra. He knew something he could look at that might bring them closer to finding the spot depicted on the map. Lucas thanked the man for his help and exited the empty library.

# CHAPTER TWENTY-FIVE

Right then, his phone rang. He regarded the Caller ID and answered, "Hey Greg. Find anything?"

"Yeah, I made a few calls, ended up talking to the guy who investigated the case. He said he's about a week from retirement and that was one of his first cases, so he remembers it vividly. It was a dead end case."

"How so?"

"The killer left no evidence behind besides the bullet recovered from the back of Cole's skull. It was the type that when it hit its target, it shattered into a million pieces. It didn't exit out the back of Cole's skull, just turned his brain to jelly."

Lucas winced. "Could they find a motive?"

"That's the thing. From all reports, Cole was one of the nicest guys you'd ever meet. He was an inquisitive sort, always asking everybody questions. His friends said he did that because all he wanted to do in life was learn—whether that be through archaeology and science or wanting to know what you had for lunch the previous day. Everybody liked him. Kept his nose clean."

"Huh. So, no suspects?"

Lucas heard Greg leafing through some papers. "Well, after they combed over his correspondence and phone records—remember, this was before email—they found just one person he'd had contact with during the previous couple of days before his death. An old classmate from North Carolina State." The hair on the back of Lucas's neck stood on end. Greg continued. "The police went out and talked to him. The guy said he didn't know anything. He didn't have a rock-solid alibi, but he lived a couple hours away from Raleigh at the time. They questioned him but couldn't connect the dots."

"Yeah? What's his name?"

Lucas heard the shuffle of more papers. "Here it is . . . a Hugo Riddick."

Lucas's heart stopped. *Darwin*.

When Lucas didn't respond, Greg said, "Lucas? Everything all right?"

"Uh, yeah. Maybe. I don't know. Listen, thanks. I'll call you back. I appreciate you digging into this for me."

"Yeah, no problem, Lucas. Let me know if I can do anything else for you," he said and ended the call.

After having time to reflect about what happened the previous day during his drive down here about the men stealing their boat, it seemed like an incredible coincidence that those guys seemed to be just hanging out, two guys fishing, and one guy watching birds through a pair of binoculars.

Like Darwin, Lucas didn't believe in coincidences. The different variables of how certain people came to be in certain places at the same time made every event an infinitely incalculable scenario. Such as Azerola saying a pirate ship named *Revenge* attacked them in 1717. It almost had to be Blackbeard.

Now Lucas knew the theft of their boat was a conspiracy. The pieces fell into place. Riddick was the only person in the world who was aware of his and Darwin's destination at that time. Riddick was a wealthy and powerful man. If he'd possibly killed a man before, what other dirty deeds for which he was responsible? Those guys on that speedboat were his cronies. Real life cronies. Had to be. They'd been in the area and Riddick called them.

Of course, Lucas thought, Riddick told them to take their boat if they got the chance. He was correct in thinking he would be the obvious choice for him and Darwin to contact if they ended up stranded somewhere. That type of cunning echoed something the real Blackbeard may have done had he been alive today.

Now, he had to figure out a way to get Darwin away from Riddick without drawing suspicion.

Lucas looked to his right across the lot at the dark car sitting in the shade. His sense that something was wrong with this scene started pinging. He'd bet money that these were Riddick's men and they would follow him when he left the parking lot.

What if he could get them to leave the lot before him?

He scanned to his left at the diner's parking lot. One of the police cruisers was still there.

He thought of another alternative to driving away: the frontal approach.

He turned off the ignition and walked back over to the pancake place. He went in. The pretty waitress with red hair stood at the register by the door, alone. Her nametag read "Lynn." He didn't see a ring on her finger.

That alluring smile was in place. She seemed delighted to see him again. He gave her his best smile. He ordered three large, sweet teas and had them loaded onto a drink caddy.

He peered at the back corner of the diner and saw two cops, the woman, and another man, still sitting at a table across from each other engaged in what appeared to be an intimate conversation.

"Here you go," she said, placing the drinks gently in Lucas's hands. "Anything else I can do for you?"

He continued smiling. "Actually, you can. Two things as a matter of fact."

***

He exited and walked back to the library parking lot carrying the drink tray, past his Jeep and right up to the Charger.

He saw the shapes sit straight behind the tinted windows and become alert as he approached. He walked up to the driver's side window and knocked on it with the knuckles of his left hand. The glass was hot enough to scorch his skin.

The person inside hit the button to roll down the window. Inside, two large men with thick beards, silver reflective sunglasses, and wearing bandanas sat in the two front seats. Another smaller guy was in the backseat. He had a goatee and thick, black-framed glasses.

The same three men who stole Lucas's boat the previous day.

That is why he ordered three teas.

When the window fully withdrew into the door casing, Lucas stuck the drink caddy through the window and before they could say anything, he said, "Hey, I saw you guys sitting over here. Thought you'd be hot. Thought you could use some refreshment."

The mongoloid sitting by the window took the tray without speaking. The man with the glasses, who seemed to be the brains of the outfit sitting in the back, did. "Thanks."

Lucas looked from him to the other two Neanderthals sitting in front. He squinted. "Have I seen you guys somewhere before? Recently?"

"Don't think so," the guy in the backseat said.

"Really? Hmm." Lucas stood up straight above the roof of the car. He felt three sets of eyes studying him from inside, wondering what he was up to. He peeped over and saw two people exit the diner. He smiled, leaned down. "I know. You're the guys who shot at me and stole my boat."

The driver's hand lashed out the window and tried to grab Lucas by the collar. He jumped back and the guy's meaty hand grabbed empty air. The other two men flung open their doors and jumped out of the car. The shorter guy with glasses was the closest. He tried to get face-to-face with Lucas, but the top of his head only came up to Lucas's shoulders.

"Hey!" a woman's voice yelled from across the lot. "Leave him alone!"

In unison, everyone turned to look at the person who yelled. It was the police officer running towards them, her partner a few paces behind.

The caveman who was halfway around the car from the passenger side turned and ran back into the car. The short guy facing Lucas gave him an intimidating stare, seemed to make a decision, and rejoined his associates in the car. The driver put it in gear, peeled out just missing Lucas, and jumped the curb exiting the lot, almost striking a passing vehicle.

"Are you okay?" the male officer asked as they came up to Lucas.

He saw the car at the edge of the horizon speeding away. It would disappear from view in a matter of seconds.

He turned to the officers. "Yeah. Thanks for that."

***

Lucas had wanted to keep the entire thing quiet. He knew how he had wanted that scene to play out. Walking up to the car the way he did placed himself in danger. He needed to do that for two reasons. The first was to confirm his suspicion of who the car's occupants were. The second was that he needed them to disappear. If Riddick was having them watch him, then he didn't want them tracking his movements.

One of the two things he had asked the waitress was to tell the officers two minutes after he left the diner that she suspected Lucas was acting weird and carrying drugs and where they could find him. He calculated that would give him just enough time to cross the lot and confront the roughnecks. He hoped the officers would come running from the diner looking for him. Thankfully, they did. He didn't know what he would have done had they not done that.

He figured that if the guys in the car were in fact the same ones from the previous day, they wouldn't want to talk to the cops.

When they asked him about drugs, he told them what he had arranged with the waitress. That he needed an excuse to get them out there quickly. They didn't like that. When Lucas told them he wouldn't tell anyone they were having an affair if they'd forget this entire thing happened. They told him to have a good day and to stay out of trouble.

Earlier, when he went and got the tea, he saw the two of them holding hands across the table. There was one squad car parked outside. They both wore wedding rings. He wasn't for sure, but he couldn't imagine a police force allowing a husband and wife cop to work together.

Back in his Jeep, he sent a text to Darwin: **Where are you?**

After a long couple of seconds, Darwin replied: **Getting close. Just passed by a place called Pritchard's Island. About an hour out. Sup? Find out anything?**

Lucas: **Yes. Text me just as you're pulling into the marina.**

Darwin: **Okay. Do you know where the treasure is?**

Lucas hesitated before responding: **No. But you've possibly already passed it.**

Darwin: **Interesting.**

Lucas: **Listen. Be ready to get off as soon as you get here. It's vital that you do. I'll have specific instructions. Have your things together. Be ready to get off fast.**

Darwin: **I can do that. Is everything OK?**

Lucas: **Just be ready**

Darwin: **Gotcha**

He didn't want to let Darwin know about Riddick just yet, although his texts may make Darwin suspicious. At this point, the pirate did not know what Lucas knew. His henchmen may call him with an update, although they didn't necessarily know what Lucas knew either. He also did not want Darwin to know where the treasure was. If Riddick was the type of man Lucas suspected he was, he might do something nasty to Darwin if he figured out the location.

He just hoped Riddick didn't do anything crazy.

Lucas sat the phone in the seat next to him and punched in the directions for the marina, where Riddick told him to meet them. He did not know what would happen once he got there. He had a feeling that trouble awaited him.

No matter. Darwin was in danger. It was up to Lucas to get him out of it.

# CHAPTER TWENTY-SIX

The Harbour Town Yacht Club was nestled in a small marina in the upscale Sea Pines section of Hilton Head. It is home to a pro level golf course, shopping, dining and recreation with a majestic lighthouse overlooking everything. For a boat to get to the area coming from the north, it has to traverse the length of the Hilton Head and sail around the southern tip.

For Lucas to get to it, all he had to do was turn right after leaving the library, go straight, and navigate an elaborate roundabout. He was there in fifteen minutes. It might have been ten had he not stopped at an ATM. He didn't think it would hurt to have cash in his pocket should he need to grease some palms.

He navigated the maze of palm tree-lined streets, following the signs pointing to the yacht club. He passed the clubhouse for the golf course and resisted the urge to go in and have a look around. The lavish homes gave way to a quaint shopping district as the road met the water. The pavement swept along a gradual curve along the riverbank leading to a marina where he saw dozens of ships of different makes and sizes. All looked luxurious.

There was a car park along the water's edge where Lucas backed his Jeep in. He wanted his Jeep to face the road leading away from the marina in case he needed to make a hasty retreat.

White and red-bricked buildings encircled the small bay. Berths ringed the edge of the marina with one prominent dock jutting out into middle the dark water. The red and white striped lighthouse towered over everything. The smell of salt water mixed with the aroma of fried seafood coming from a restaurant at the foot of the lighthouse. Lucas imagined getting fantastic water views while dining there. Unfortunately, he had more immediate things to do.

He hurried to a small building marked "Harbour Town Yacht Club." Two- and three-story luxury yachts drew Lucas's eyes to them. These vessels made Riddick's yacht look like a dinghy in comparison.

He went in and immediately felt out of place. A man with intense blue eyes, perfect silver hair wearing a navy blazer with elbow patches and gold buttons with an embroidered Harbour Town Yacht Club emblem on his left breast stood at attention behind the desk.

"Can I help you?" the man asked Lucas in an uppity accent with a hint of derision.

"Yes, I'm waiting for someone to come into the marina," Lucas answered, waiving a hand at the water behind them.

The man somehow raised an eyebrow without moving any other muscles on his face. Botox, Lucas thought. "And who might that be?"

"Hugo Riddick."

"One moment." The clerk looked down and leafed through the pages in a logbook. "Yes, Mr. Riddick is due in port here in about thirty minutes."

"Does he have an assigned slip? That way I could be waiting for him."

The man regarded Lucas with skepticism, eyebrow still cocked. "Yes. Number forty-three."

"Thank you."

"Anything else I can do for you . . . sir?"

"Yes, do you have a nautical chart of the surrounding area I can take a look at for a minute?"

For a moment, the man didn't answer, perhaps deciding whether Lucas was worth his while. "One moment," he said and disappeared through a door behind him. He returned a minute later with a two-sided laminated map and set it on a counter a distance away from his station. "Here you go . . . sir."

Lucas stepped over, thanked the man, and picked up the large chart. The key was in a white bar running down the right side and the title *Hilton Head – Beaufort, SC INSHORE FISHING CHART* was in the top-left corner. He reached into his back pocket and withdrew a printed copy of Blackbeard's map. He placed it on the chart, starting at the left edge and slowly moved it to the right—past Hilton Head, past Parris Island, past Prichard's and Hunting Islands and stopped. It was right there at the right edge of the chart.

Jackpot.

Now that he saw it, he could smack himself.

He knew that place. He knew it well.

Getting there would be the hard part.

***

Darwin's grip tightened on his phone. He couldn't take his eyes off the screen.

***Listen. Be ready to get off as soon as you get here. It's vital that you do. I'll have specific instructions. Have your things together. Be ready to get off fast.***

He knew Lucas had his suspicions of Riddick. During this voyage, the man seemed open. Congenial. Honest. He had told Darwin about his shipping business, his hobby as a Blackbeard impersonator, and the travels that came about as a result. He appeared at many pirate festivals along the eastern seaboard and down into the Caribbean.

Darwin stayed up top for most of the journey, taking in the sights, sounds, and smells of the ocean. As a child, his mom never took him on vacation. He went on field trips during elementary school, and rarely ventured far from his home near downtown Concord. Going to the beach never crossed his mind. The ocean existed in a world beyond his own.

Now that he was out here, he never wanted to leave it. At some point, as they cruised past Charleston, he made up his mind that his goal in life would be to become a maritime archaeologist. Before this trip with Lucas, he hadn't made any real personal goals. For most of his life, getting out of his rotten home in Concord was his only thought. What he'd do after that was wide open. He wanted to study archaeology. All history fascinated him.

After finding this map and journal and undergoing this adventure, this was what he wanted to do. He learned in his studies over the past few days that there were many unsolved mysteries regarding ships lost at sea during the formation of the New World. Spanish ships loaded with treasure never made their way to their destinations during the Golden Age of Piracy. Ships carrying hundreds of passengers in hopes of starting a new life in America never made it to shore. There was so much he could study. His mind swirled at the thought.

Lucas's text messages brought Darwin back to the present. He looked at the passing shore five hundred yards to his right. The first of the hotel complexes along Hilton Head's northern shore passed by.

Now Darwin had to figure out what he was going to do. It was mid-afternoon. The plan was for Lucas to get there first, see if he could dig anything up at the Heritage Library, then they'd meet up once Darwin and Riddick arrived and go from there. Apparently, Lucas had found something, but didn't want to reveal it yet.

If he was supposed to go see the man at the library to get background information on Trench's Island and find any possible clues about pirate attacks, why give Darwin the instruction to be ready to jump ship? It had to be something to do with Riddick. Had Lucas heard back from his police investigator friend?

Riddick navigated the yacht along the shallow waters of the Hilton Head coast in the captain's chair to Darwin's right. The pirate's beard fluttered in the breeze. He wore a Parrot Head baseball hat to keep the rest of his long hair from flapping everywhere.

The opening chords of "Margaritaville" suddenly blared from Riddick's shirt pocket. It was his cell phone ringing. He looked at the screen, pressed a button, and said, "Just a sec." He asked Darwin, "Can you take the wheel for a minute. I need to take this call."

Darwin looked ahead and saw clear waters. There were no other vessels in their line of sight. He had never been behind the wheel of a car, much less a million-dollar yacht. His only driving experience came via moped. The thought of the taking over for Riddick made him nervous.

The pirate saw Darwin's hesitation and said, "Look, there's nothing to it. Just keep the ship pointed straight ahead. This won't take but a minute."

Darwin let out a breath. "Okay. I'll give it a shot."

He stood up allowing Riddick to pass by, not before giving Darwin a reassuring pat on the shoulder. "You got this. Give me a minute on the phone with this guy and I'll be right back. If you need to slow down, just push this lever forward slowly."

Darwin climbed into the captain's chair and placed his hands on the controls. Without another word, Riddick disappeared through the stairway leading below.

Darwin settled in, and after a minute, found himself comfortable.

***

"You stupid morons!" Riddick screamed into his phone from his private cabin in the bottom deck of the yacht. There was an entire level between he and Darwin, and he figured with that buffer and the noise from the engines that the young man wouldn't be able to hear him. "You had one job. Keep your eyes on him!"

"We're sorry boss. Nothing we could do. He came up to us. He somehow figured out who we were. Then the cops came when the situation escalated."

"Does he know you're associated with me?" Riddick asked.

"Don't think so. He just said he knew we were the guys from yesterday."

Riddick paused to collect himself. Getting angry could lead to making the wrong decisions. He only resorted to violence as a last recourse. That had happened several times in his life. It never ended well for the person on the other end of his rage. He wouldn't go that far unless he was out of alternatives.

"Why were the police there?"

"I have no idea. We were at a library for Christ's sakes. What is a cop going to do at a library besides kick homeless men out of the bathrooms and arrest people for overdue library books?"

"Yeah. I wonder if Lucas somehow tipped them off."

"Don't know boss. I gotta tell ya. You were right about this Lucas guy. Couldn't tell much from him and his buddy yesterday besides that they were both tall. Up close, you can tell this guy is smart and looks as though he can defend himself."

"I know. That's why I called you."

"What do you want for us to do now, boss?"

"Where are you now?"

"I don't know," the man said. "Hold on. Let me look . . . we're sitting at some place called the Coligny Plaza Shopping Center."

"I know where that is. Okay, head out of there and meet me back at the marina. We should be there in twenty minutes or so."

"Gotcha boss. We're going to pick up a bite to eat real fast. Run through a McDonald's or something."

"That's fine."

"What will the kid say when he sees us?"

"Leave that to me," Riddick said and ended the call.

***

He climbed back to the bridge to find Darwin sitting back in the captain's chair, at ease piloting the yacht. When he saw Riddick emerge from the bowels of the ship, he started to get up, but the pirate placed a hand on his shoulder. "Nah. Stay there, lad. You're doing fine."

Darwin looked back, laughed, and said, "If you say so."

Riddick pointed at the green waters ahead. "Just watch out for any sandbars. You'll be okay." He reached into a cooler behind the passenger bench and withdrew two ice cold Coronas. He offered one to Darwin, who declined, and returned one to the melting ice in the cooler.

"Everything okay?" Darwin asked.

Riddick took a long pull on the Corona before answering. "Aye, it is. It is. All is well." He took another drink. A line of seagulls flew past overhead. Their squawks sounded like derisive laughter. One pooped on the deck, which didn't surprise Riddick. He was used to birds of all sorts using his yacht as a bullseye.

On this trip, Riddick had come to know the gentle giant piloting the ship. About his rough childhood. How they shared the same college alma mater. How Darwin was making his professional start as a lowly archivist at the Natural History Museum in Raleigh. While Darwin didn't say as much, Riddick gathered the young man led a lonely life. That he never fit in wherever he has been. He didn't seem to have a plan or many goals. Just takes things one day at a time.

"Do you like working at the museum?" Riddick asked.

"It's all right. I have to start somewhere."

"What do you ultimately want to do?"

"Honestly, I didn't know before this adventure. I was just now thinking that after this trip I'd love to get into marine archaeology, particularly searching for lost ships."

"If we find this treasure, lad, you'll be able to do anything you want in that field."

Darwin smiled. "That'd be good."

Riddick took a pull from the Corona and studied the young man as he navigated the ship. His posture and body language—the slump of his shoulders, early wrinkles around his eyes and brows—suggested a hard life. One not full of joy and good times.

"Darwin, my boy, are you happy with your life?"

The question was not one Darwin had ever considered. During his childhood, no one encouraged him to do anything with his life. His mom was always unhappy. Usually angry and didn't want to be bothered. She treated Darwin as more of a burden than anything else. His happiness was not at the top of her to-do list.

He just . . . existed.

He watched a line of about a dozen pelicans fly by and land together in the rolling tide off to their left.

He said, "You know, I'm not now, but I'm getting there."

Riddick placed a hand on his shoulder and squeezed. "I think you're a brave young man who has never had a decent shot." He took another drink of beer. "I'd like to give you that shot."

Darwin took his eyes off the waters ahead and turned to Riddick. "How do you mean?"

He removed his hand from Darwin's shoulder and sat back, took a sip of the cold beer and said, "What we are doing right now is one of my main hobbies outside my shipping company."

"What is that?"

"Treasure hunting."

"Oh."

"I became interested in it about thirty years ago. My father had a place on the shore out at Ocracoke where we used to stay on the weekends during the school year and then all summer. The summer before I graduated from college, four of my friends and I were there for a few days. We took a boat out along the shore and ducked into a small lagoon with clear waters. It wasn't very deep, maybe fifteen to twenty feet. We had a cooler of beer and a sack of sandwiches with us. We planned on being out for the afternoon. Just having fun."

"Sounds like a good time."

"It was. I dropped anchor and we hung out for a while there. We all got a good buzz going and went for a swim. My friends started arguing about who the best swimmer was for some reason. One suggested having a contest and seeing who could dive down the furthest. In our drunken reasoning, we didn't consider how we'd be able to judge who won.

"So, two of my friends went under before me. They were under maybe thirty seconds or so before resurfacing. I'd been around the water all my life and thought I was a good swimmer. I knew I could hold my breath for longer than those guys. I took a deep breath and went down, down, down."

"What happened?"

"Well, the lower I went, of course the water got darker. I touched the bottom. The light was dim, although I could still see what was there in my vicinity. Right at the very edge of my vision, I saw something sticking out of the sand that had a straight line to it."

"Oh man. Nature doesn't create straight lines."

Riddick winked and pointed a finger. "Exactly." He finished off the beer and continued, "By that time, I had to get back to the surface before I drowned. Knowing that, I kicked towards it. I couldn't believe my eyes, Darwin. There was a freaking wooden boat sitting down there."

"Wow. What did you do?"

"I kicked back to the surface as fast as I could. My friends were blown away that I'd been under so long. They thought I had drowned. One of my friends was sitting on the deck and I yelled for him to throw me a flashlight. I caught my breath and went back down. This time, I came straight down on it. It was small. It was a rowboat that may have come from a pirate vessel. The grotto we were in was the type of place, well hidden, that pirates might navigate into to make repairs to or careen a ship."

"That's incredible. You must have been excited."

"Oh yes, lad. More to the point, I was hooked. I was looking at a future ahead of me involving my father's business. I knew from being around the ocean in this part of the world that there were many old shipwrecks from the early stages of New World settlement that had never been found, many laden with riches beyond our imaginations."

"Have you located any?"

Riddick gave a pained expression. "A couple. Nothing big like the trail we're on now. I was close to finding the *Golden Fleece* that John Chatterton and John Mattera discovered in 2009 down in the Dominican Republic and another ship that Mel Fisher discovered in 1985 off Key West. That one was one of the first shipwrecks I went after. I came up short. I knew it was near there, although I couldn't pinpoint the exact spot. That one was worth half a billion dollars."

Darwin let out a long, low whistle. "Oh man. How much do you suppose Blackbeard's treasure might be worth?"

"That's difficult to say without knowing where he got it from."

"True."

"Which is one reason I wanted to talk to you. In college, I studied marine engineering. I don't have a research background. I do a good amount of digging while trying to track down these lost ships, although I don't know the first thing about using computers to track down leads or how to prize information from libraries or museums." He stopped for a moment as a pair of dolphins started jumping out of the water alongside the yacht. They followed for a couple hundred yards before disappearing. "Darwin, I must say I'm very impressed by what you've done here. Finding that map and tracing the treasure this far. We're so close, I can feel it."

"Thanks."

"So, my question is," Riddick said, "how would you like to do that for me? Full-time?"

Darwin's hand gripped tighter on the steering wheel as the possible implications of Riddick's question registered. "What? Do you mean you would pay me to look for treasure for you?"

"I would. I'd pay you a base salary of seventy-five thousand per year, plus travel expenses. I would also set you up with your own office and hire assistants for you if you need them. If you found something promising, I'd finance the operation for you."

Darwin didn't know what to say. He didn't know of anyone as he grew up—friends and family—who made much money. Except for the drug dealers, that is. Getting offered that kind of money was beyond his imagination. He recognized going into college that unless you hit it big, archaeologists were rarely rich. They often struggled to get funding for various projects.

This was the offer of his dreams. Riddick made the pot richer.

"Oh," he said, "you'd also keep ten percent of anything you found."

The numbers flashed through Darwin's head. One even halfway large find would make him rich beyond his wildest dreams.

"What do you say?" Riddick asked.

"I don't know what to say," Darwin stuttered.

"Just say yes," Riddick said, standing and holding out his hand to Riddick.

Riddick took it in a firm grip. "Yes, let's do it."

So happy was he at the offer, he forgot about Lucas's instructions.

# CHAPTER TWENTY-SEVEN

L ucas left the Yacht Club and walked into the blaring sunlight. He shielded his eyes so he could get his bearings in terms of the direction the numbers on the dock slips went. The wood planks spread outward from the shore of the harbor in the shape of a crescent. The yacht club sat at the apex of that crescent, halfway around the water's edge. Sandblasted plaques hanging on posts displayed the slip numbers prominently. Lucas observed that the first slip sat near his Jeep on the other end of the marina and counted to the number twenty-five slip which was closest to him.

He turned and circled in the opposite direction. The lighthouse now loomed above his head to his left. The eighteenth hole of the famous Harbour Town golf course lay beyond it. The marina was about half-full of vessels of various shapes and sizes. As he looked ahead at where he estimated Riddick's berth would be, he saw a familiar sight.

He stopped and blinked twice. It couldn't be.

A large red speedboat with red racing stripes sat tied to a post. It appeared to be the same one that stole the jon boat.

***

Lucas got as close as he dared before he ducked behind some bushes. He hadn't seen anyone come near the boat yet. If someone popped their head up, Lucas didn't want them to see him. He was certain it was the same boat. The odds that a similar speedboat would be here in the slip right next to where Riddick was supposed to come were too astronomical to comprehend.

Lucas pushed aside a branch from a fluffy azalea to survey the boat. He watched it bob up and down in the gentle surf of the harbor for five minutes. No one approached or left it. He didn't think anyone was aboard unless they were lying on the floor of the boat, perhaps taking an afternoon siesta.

Seeing this boat here at this time all but confirmed that Riddick was associated with the guys from the Charger earlier. He looked across the water into the marina parking lot, searching for that dark car. It wasn't there. Thank goodness for small favors. That would explain how those men got to Hilton Head so soon after Riddick learned of their changed destination.

If the thugs in the dark car spoke with Riddick after their encounter at the library, Darwin might be in trouble. Lucas cursed himself for splitting up with his younger friend. Darwin was big and smart. Not worldly. He'd lived a sheltered existence. Lucas hoped he could recognize that he was in danger.

He hoped Darwin would be ready to move from the boat when it arrived.

***

Darwin was happy. A rare feeling. He was so giddy he didn't know what to do with himself. Unlimited options now lie before him. He'd be able to afford a better apartment and clothes without holes. He could expand on his diet of cheap junk food and maybe, just maybe, trade in his moped for a car. A shiny, new red Camaro, perhaps?

What would the people who knew him back home in Concord think of that? Seeing Darwin roll back into town in a souped-up sports car. One that dishonest money didn't buy at that. He imagined the looks on their faces.

Riddick had taken over the controls as they rounded the curve of the island to steer through a higher concentration of vessels emerging from the mouth of the Harbor River. Daufuskie Island passed by to their left. He saw the perfect green grass from a golf course running along the water on the right. Several groups of golfers were playing. The tip of a lighthouse came into view.

The excitement of Riddick's generous job offer made Darwin momentarily forget why they were here to begin with. Blackbeard's lost treasure.

"Do you feel we're near it? The treasure?"

Riddick nodded. "I believe so lad. In the realm of the search for Blackbeard's treasure, we're in virgin territory. Many have come to Bath over the years with what they proclaim to be maps and proof of where Teach hid the treasure. Many dug holes all over Plum Point where X marked the spot. This, this is new."

"I hope so."

"And we wouldn't be here if it weren't for you. You uncovered something, recognized it as important, and guided us here. You, Darwin. You did his. You must be commended."

"Thanks," Darwin smiled.

"Of course, you'll be well rewarded if we find it."

"That'd be fantastic."

"Just need to bring it home."

Riddick cut back to idle speed as they entered the zone just outside the marina. The lighthouse was now in full view, majestic in appearance. They had passed several on their journey from Bath. Darwin thought this was the finest one he'd seen yet.

Changing the subject, Riddick asked, "Your friend is supposed to be here, right?"

All of the positive thoughts and hopefulness blinked out of Darwin's mind. What had Lucas's messages been about? He wished he'd given more details.

"Yeah, he sent me a message a little bit ago saying he would."

"Good. Good."

The golf course and lighthouse floated by. Riddick angled the yacht toward the entrance of the marina. Just then, Darwin's phone buzzed in his pocket.

He took it out. It was a message from Lucas: **I'm hiding in the bushes behind your boat slip. Riddick can't be trusted. I'll explain later. GET OFF as soon as it's safe.**

Darwin scanned their destination ahead. An empty slip sat on the left. A speedboat with red stripes was on the right. He glimpsed the top of Lucas's head protruding from a row of bushes behind the concrete pathway on the bank.

Everything clicked into place. The theft of their jon boat. The speedboat with red stripes. The same one before him now. Riddick's private calls. Lucas's veiled warnings.

Riddick had somehow engineered this entire scenario. Just after Lucas and Darwin met with Riddick at the marina in Bath and rented the jon boat, he had called his cronies to either scare Lucas and Darwin or maroon them somewhere. That forced the two to call on Riddick's services. This morning, once Darwin informed him they needed to go to Hilton Head, Riddick had suggested that Lucas and Darwin split up. Presumably to get the younger, more malleable Darwin alone on a long trip. Riddick did not call his secretary to say where he'd be. He called his henchmen, telling them to get here as fast as they could. Darwin saw the logic. Get his men here quickly so they could monitor Lucas while having a boat in the event they needed to be on the water to find the treasure.

Then, Riddick had buttered him up with the job offer too good to refuse.

Darwin fell for it. Hook, line, and sinker.

He felt like a fool.

Darwin stood and prepared to head below. He stopped. "Were you serious about that offer?"

Although they were within twenty yards of sidling into their dock slip, Riddick took his eyes off the water, looked Darwin straight in the eye, and said, "Absolutely."

Something about that look and that answer gave him away. It might have been the way his right eye twitched, the crow's feet becoming pronounced, causing the left eyebrow to raise by a fraction of a centimeter. It may have been the way the right corner of his mouth tugged upward in a half-smile that could also be read as a snarl. Or was it something in the tone of his voice. *AB-solutely*?

Trying not to let his voice betray his thoughts, Darwin said, "Awesome. I'm going to head down and see if I can spot Lucas anywhere."

"Great. Grab that rope when you get down there and tie it to the pier when I stop. That way I don't drift."

Darwin nodded. He ducked inside the gangway door as fast as he could. He needed to think, alone, and had a very short amount of time to make a life-altering decision.

Go with Lucas or stay with Riddick?

# CHAPTER TWENTY-EIGHT

Lucas watched the expensive yacht approach the dock and slide into the berth beside the familiar speedboat. There weren't many people nearby. The closest people were a couple of elderly women power walking in the shopping village beyond the yacht club. Lucas almost wished they would swing by in his direction.

Innocent bystanders had the potential to defuse a volatile situation.

He didn't know how Riddick would react when Darwin jumped off the boat and the two of them ran off with knowledge of where the treasure might lie. He did not know if the pirate was in possession of any firearms. He had seen several cutlasses hanging from the wall in the galley. He figured he could outrun the man twenty years his senior. Darwin too.

Lucas took a quick glance at the parking lot on the opposite side of the harbor. His Jeep sat alone in a spot at the water's edge. The black Charger of Riddick's crew wasn't in sight. They might appear at any time.

***

The yacht bumped against the dock as Darwin emerged at the door-way at the stern of the craft.

There was one choice he could make. He'd seen money make peo-ple do bad things in his life. Robberies, beatings, theft, even murder. People stopped at nothing to attain it. They thought that having money translated to security,later, while he often saw the opposite of that. The people who somehow scraped the money together to buy that luxury car were back to driving their old beat-up 1995 Mazda a few months later after their new Mercedes was repossessed. He knew people who had robbed convenience stores—and got away with it—to get the money to make a down payment on a McMansion in one of the ritzy new neighborhoods around Charlotte. He'd seen others spend time in prison for breaking into houses, selling drugs, assault, armed robbery, and worse.

They thought money bought them security. To Darwin, money didn't equate with happiness. Sure, he wanted to be comfortable. Not live paycheck-to-paycheck. Someday he will have his own car. That would come if he were patient. Despite what he'd seen in his upbringing, he held on to the hope that good things would happen to good people if they remained true to themselves and to others.

In the end. He stuck with Lucas. One of the rare people on this planet he could call "friend."

The boat came to an uneasy rest. Darwin reached down and picked up the thick piece of rope. As instructed. It had a loop already made one on end, like a lasso. The other end was attached to the yacht. He dropped it into the water—not as instructed—and watched the end disappear down into the dark green water.

The growl of the big twin-diesel engines died. He could hear himself think again. With Riddick killing the engines, he would be down shortly to see if Lucas had appeared.

Lucas did appear. He came around the azalea bushes. "Darwin. Come on. We've got to get out of here."

Darwin clutched at his backpack containing his digging gear and printouts from the diary of Mary Ormond. "I don't know what's going on, Lucas. But I trust you."

"Great," Lucas said, pointing across the harbor. "My Jeep is parked way over there."

"Let's go before Riddick comes down."

Too late.

Riddick appeared at the doorway. The sea breeze made his long beard flutter. "Ah, Lucas. There you are. What did you find out?"

The two younger men shared a look. Time to go.

"I'm not saying," Lucas said.

Riddick's face turned red. Then, trying to remain calm, he said "What?"

"I said, I'm not telling you. I did some research on you. I don't believe that you're as friendly and helpful as you've tried to pass yourself as."

Riddick stood up straight. The redness of his face faded. He held a hand to his chest. "Lucas, son, I have no idea what you're talking about?"

Darwin looked from Lucas to Riddick. Lucas had learned more than just the location of the treasure, Darwin thought.

He took a quick stock of his surroundings should they need to leave in a hurry. The walkway leading off to the left of them ended in another fifty yards. He thought the golf course was behind the azalea bushes and palm trees. To their right, the walkway circled past a large building and met another sidewalk coming from the row of shops forming a sharp V. Then past that was Lucas's Jeep.

If the harbor was as a circle drawn on a piece of paper, Darwin and Lucas were at the bottom. His Jeep was at the very top. A good distance away.

He turned his attention back to the standoff between Riddick and Lucas.

Lucas smiled. "Does the name Travis Cole ring a bell?"

Riddick blinked twice in rapid succession. Lucas knew he had him.

"I, I, I've never heard that name before."

Lucas smiled again. "Yes, you have. You met each other at North Carolina State. You were classmates."

"I don't—"

"C'mon. Travis Cole? You know. He was the researcher whose brains you blew out in 1982."

***

Lucas had played his hand. That didn't mean he didn't have more aces up his sleeve, though. He knew before he said the name of "Travis Cole" that the situation might escalate from there.

For his part, Riddick remained composed. "That's a serious accusation there. I assure you, I don't know what you're talking about."

Instead of responding to Riddick's comment, Lucas turned to Darwin, who had yet to say a word. "You ready to get out of here?"

Darwin's eyes were locked on Riddick. Lucas thought Darwin looked betrayed. He was angry. He feared for Riddick if Darwin got his hands on him. Well, maybe not. Still, he didn't want to cause a scene in broad daylight.

"Come on Darwin. Let's get out of here before he does something stupid. Like try to kill us."

Darwin hitched his backpack across his shoulder. "Absolutely," he said with determination.

"What about my offer?" Riddick pled.

"What about it?" Darwin said.

"I'll make you rich. All the money, cars, and women you'll ever need."

Darwin waved his hand. "You can keep it. Lucas was right, you can't be trusted."

"You don't believe him, do you?" Riddick said, looking at Darwin and pointing at Lucas.

"I don't know what all he knows," Darwin said. "I just know that a minute ago back there, when I asked you if you were serious about the job offer, although you said you were, there was something about the way you said it that I didn't like."

Riddick seemed as though he was about to blow.

"I'm ready Lucas," Darwin said, and before Riddick figured out what was going on, took his size sixteen foot, placed it on the hull of the yacht, and shoved as hard as he could. Without the boat being tied to the dock, and despite its massive weight, Darwin was still able with his enormous strength to make the huge craft float away from them.

Too far for Riddick to jump from the ship to the deck. He was helpless to watch as chasm developed on the water between dock and vessel.

Darwin and Lucas waved. Riddick flipped them off.

The two men rushed off to Lucas's Jeep.

***

As soon as he was back inside, Riddick called his men and climbed the stairs to the bridge up top while the phone rang.

"Yeah boss?" the man answered as Riddick climbed into the captain's chair and started the engines.

"Where the hell are you?"

"We're nearby. In Sea Pines. Getting ready to round the corner to the marina. What's up?"

Riddick let out a relieved breath. There was still a chance he could control the situation. He'd let whatever it was Cole found over thirty years ago get away from him once. He would not let that happen again.

"Okay. Perfect. Look, I just docked at the marina a second ago. Those two guys just took off."

"Why boss?"

"Never mind that. You're going to see the guy's Jeep parked right by the water as you come around the corner. They're hurrying that way. You can't let them get out of here."

"I read you loud and clear boss," the guy said and hung up.

Riddick stood. There wasn't much he could do while the boat drifted. Those two clowns were on foot and there was no way Riddick could catch up with them even if he tried. He had to depend on his guys. They had let him down twice in a twenty-four-hour period.

A third strike would come with severe consequences.

He tracked Darwin and Lucas as they passed from view behind the yacht club and reemerged three seconds later.

Just then, he saw the black car his guys would be driving round the corner of the village and move toward the parking lot. They had to stop Darwin and Lucas. Riddick was too close to the treasure to let it slip away now.

He stood and started waving his hands, trying to get the attention of the driver. Riddick thought he saw someone wave behind the tinted windows. Riddick pointed madly from Darwin and Lucas to the Jeep. They were almost there. No more than fifteen feet away.

In the next moment, everything slowed down to Riddick. He saw Lucas pull his keys from his pocket and hit a button on the key fob to disarm the alarm. The black Charger's wheels squealed on the blacktop. The brake lights on the Jeep blinked twice. Darwin and Lucas jerked at hearing the squealing tires.

Riddick looked on as the big, heavy car smashed into the front of the Jeep. Darwin and Lucas dived away to the ground to avoid the collision. Glass, aluminum, and metal shards exploded into the air as the momentum of the car pushed the bigger Jeep backward, over the concrete wheel stop, down the bank and into the water. The front half of the Charger followed it, submerging itself in water up to the door handles.

Riddick stood with his mouth hanging agape. He didn't hire these guys for their brains. He had them around to clean up messy situations in return for a decent salary and good weed. In their position, however, he did not see a better alternative than just running over Darwin and Lucas.

People were starting to swarm out from the village at the sounds of the calamity. Several men who ran out from the restaurant on the water were the first to arrive. He tried to keep track of Lucas and Darwin, but they disappeared into the mob. He saw several people with their phones out, some taking videos and pictures. Evidence, Riddick thought. Other onlookers had phones held up to their ears, presumably calling 911. Others were trying to get to the Charger to see if they could help the men trapped inside.

Riddick knew one thing. He didn't want to be anywhere near here when the authorities arrived.

He piloted the yacht back to the dock and cut the engines. He hurried below, pulled the length of rope from the water, and looped it around a post. He went back in and below to his cabin. He grabbed a few things and exited the yacht.

He heard the call of the first sirens in the distance.

He had to make himself scarce, and fast.

# CHAPTER TWENTY-NINE

Lucas took stock of himself, making sure all limbs were attached, that he had no broken bones or was bleeding freely from anywhere. Satisfied he'd live another day, he looked at Darwin who was taking a similar inventory of himself three feet away. He seemed fine except for a scrape on his forehead above his left eye.

Someone handed Darwin a tissue, which he applied to staunch the bleeding. Less than a minute after the crash, a dozen people were standing near the two, making sure they were okay. Lucas stood and surveyed the Charger half-submerged in the water. Several bystanders were there, trying to get to the men trapped inside. None of them seemed to be moving.

There was no sign of Lucas's Jeep.

There were now two things he loved that had been ripped away from him. His soon-to-be ex-wife and his Jeep. He loved that truck. It was his baby. He'd spent countless hours tinkering with it, making his own customizations, driving around town with the cabin cover off, cruising.

Now it was gone to the bottom of the harbor. He imagined his insurance company would pronounce it totaled and he'd have to start from scratch. He already had to pick up the broken pieces of his marriage. This was too much.

Lucas couldn't make out any of the faces near him, trying to help. They were all blanks. His mind was a swirl of what had just happened. He might have been killed.

Riddick.

He did this, Lucas told himself. The pirate may not have been the person behind the wheel of the Charger, but that car wouldn't have been here if it weren't for him.

Lucas wanted to confront the pirate, although he saw that would be a mistake. At this point, he didn't care about the legal consequences. He was aware enough of himself to recognize his safety.

He remembered Riddick had pirate cutlasses on board his yacht. Lucas was unarmed.

A roar came from across the water. Not from the yacht. The sound came from the big speedboat.

Lucas saw Riddick's black beard flap in the wind as he gunned the boat and zoomed away from the harbor.

***

Paramedics at the scene treated Darwin and Lucas. They put a thick piece of gauze over Darwin's eye. Lucas had a cut on his knee that required a Band-Aid to treat.

The mongoloid and Neanderthal in the car were unconscious. Both had several broken bones. The brains of the outfit had been sitting in the middle of the backseat, leaning forward with no seatbelt. At the moment of impact, he was flung headfirst into the windshield. He broke his neck and was pronounced dead at the scene.

Police questioned Darwin and Lucas at length. Having not committed any crimes, they were both released on their own recognizance, but were told they may need to make themselves available for further questioning in the future. Lucas then spent half an hour on the phone with the insurance company explaining his situation, taking care of the details that went with having a vehicle struck in a parking lot and then submerged in water. That wasn't fun.

Two large tow trucks came. One extricated the Charger from the water after an ambulance took the two remaining cronies to a hospital. A van from the Beaufort County Coroner's Office came and zipped up the ringleader in a body bag before taking him away.

Good riddance, Lucas thought.

The Jeep took more doing. Someone managed to dive in the water and hook a winch from a tow truck around the shaft of the drive train under Lucas's Jeep. Placing the hook on the front bumper would have been easier; however, there was no more front bumper. Its shattered remains floated away in the current.

Lucas watched with sadness as the thick cable of the winch retracted, pulling the Jeep up from the depths of the harbor and onto a flatbed truck. Water poured from the exposed engine compartment and around the door seams as it reemerged from the dark water. Lucas climbed up onto the truck's bed and extracted what he could from the Jeep that wasn't already ruined. There wasn't much. Everything he was able to salvage in a duffel bag full of soaked clothes. The Blackbeard figurine he purchased from Alethia in Bath was destroyed. Darwin had the same situation with his belongings. Fortunately, he took his backpack with his notes about the journal, tablet, and tools for digging and excavating with him when they separated back in Bath.

After all the curious onlookers and medics left, a police officer asked Darwin and Lucas if they needed a ride to anywhere. The two looked at each other with blank expressions on their faces.

"I wouldn't know where to go," Darwin said. "What do you think, Lucas?"

They needed to get to where the treasure was. Lucas didn't believe the friendly cop would take them on a two-hour trip. The problem for Darwin and Lucas was that Riddick could get there in less than an hour with the speedboat. Riddick's problem was that there was no way he could know where the treasure was. Lucas hadn't told Darwin where to go for just this reason. He didn't want any possibility of Riddick knowing.

The thought gave Lucas comfort. He hoped he would never see the pirate impersonator again.

Lucas didn't feel they needed to hurry, although he still didn't want to waste any time should the pirate somehow figure it out.

The sun was beginning to set across the Harbor River over Dafuskie Island. Considering what they'd just undergone, Lucas thought it was a beautiful thing. Breathtaking. Peaceful. His heart rate finally slowed. The ringing in his ears went away.

Lucas looked at his watch. 7:17. There was still time. He said to the officer, "You know, there's one place you can take us."

***

The police cruiser deposited Darwin and Lucas at the diner beside the library.

Darwin had a confused look on his face as he studied the restaurant's façade. "What are we doing here?"

Lucas smiled. "When entering a new location for the first time, it is best to find allies quickly."

Still puzzled, Darwin asked, "What is that supposed to mean?"

"I met someone while I was waiting for you all to get here who might be able to help."

"Oh, great." Darwin's tone dripped with sarcasm. "I want to remind you that we just got out of a car of someone who offered to do just that."

"I know. Their uniform limited them. We couldn't expect them to take us where we need to go."

"And where is that?"

"Edisto Island."

"Never heard of it."

Lucas placed a hand on Darwin's shoulder, guiding him towards the door. "I didn't expect you to have."

***

Lynn was still there. Her shift wasn't supposed to end for another fifteen minutes. She appeared more tired than she did earlier that afternoon. The day for her was winding down. Lucas figured she had already mentally prepared her evening. He was about to throw a wrench into those plans.

She stood behind the register, cashing out a group of disorganized teenagers, a nubby pencil stuck behind her left ear. The bright red hair had lost a bit of its luster. That may well be because of the receding light outside.

After the kids received their change and walked away, she saw Lucas and Darwin standing there, bandages and all. Despite being tired, she smiled from ear to ear.

"Welcome back," she said. She looked up at Darwin. A blot of blood had seeped through the piece of gauze. "How can I help you . . . guys?"

Lucas said, "We'd like to have dinner. Been a long day."

She cocked her head to the side. "Lunch and dinner with us? Not even our most dedicated customers eat here more than a couple times a week. We're honored. Here, let me get you two some dinner menus."

Darwin didn't have much experience with women, although he could tell when someone was flirting. He scratched his head. What was Lucas up to?

She led them to a booth over by the wall under a retro sign advertising delicious, fresh-brewed coffee anytime. Sounded good to Lucas.

They sat and Lucas scooted over on his bench to sit next to the wall. Darwin sat in the middle on his side, which he mostly filled.

"You know, earlier when you asked what time I was getting off tonight," the red-headed waitress said, "I thought you might come back."

Darwin could do nothing but stare at the two of them. Here they were with no car, nowhere to stay, it was getting late, and Lucas was wanting to play footsie with a waitress. Just as he started to get angry and speak his mind, Lucas said, "Hey Lynn. You get off here in a minute, right?"

"Yeah," she answered.

"Mind if we buy you dinner?"

Darwin wondered where the "we" part came from. He'd never seen this woman before.

She stared at Lucas for a long moment, glanced at Darwin, and let out a deep breath. "Sure. Why not? I have nothing else going on tonight." She stopped. Seemed to think of something else. "Look, you're not going to try to kidnap me or anything? You're not a couple of weirdos looking to get your rocks off on some diner waitress are you?"

Lucas held out a hand and laughed. "No, nothing like that at all. I assure you. I want to ask you a question."

"What's that?"

Lucas shook his head. "That'll take a little explaining. Nothing kinky. That's why we wanted to have dinner with you. So there'd be time to explain."

She wore a skeptical expression. "Okay. Give me a minute. What do you want to drink?"

Darwin ordered a Coke. Coffee for Lucas. He had the feeling it was going to be a long night.

***

She left to get their drinks. Darwin tried to keep his composure. He'd been double-crossed, lied to, and nearly killed, and now Lucas seemed to have his own agenda.

"What are we doing here, Lucas?" he asked between clenched teeth. "Come on. We need to get on the road or find a hotel or something, and here you are, trying to hook up with some waitress. What gives?"

"No, I'm not. Look, you say we need to get on the road. How are we going to do that? We have no car."

"We could rent one. Doesn't your insurance company provide a rental in case of a wreck?"

"They don't. That's what took so long on the phone. Besides, what if some idiot finds us and crashes it into a harbor again? We might need to put some serious miles on a car between now and when we're done. That gets expensive with a rental. Don't think the insurance company would pay for an extensive trip anyway."

"So what?" Darwin's volume started to rise. "You're going to try to woo this girl and borrow her car? What if we end up wrecking it? What then genius?"

"Do you know what type of car she drives?" Lucas asked, to which Darwin shook his head. "I saw her digging in it outside earlier. It's a white Toyota Corolla. The thing is maybe twenty-five years old. Looks like it's powered by hamsters. Can't be worth much."

"What are you saying? Try to talk her into taking us to—where was it—Edisto Island? And if something happens, you just buy her a new car?"

"Something like that."

Darwin glared at him in disbelief. "I can't believe you. If you have the cash to buy her a new car, why not just spring for the rental?"

"Because we're talking a difference of thousands of dollars." Lucas paused. "Also, consider this: how did Riddick's guys track me to that library at that time?"

"Well, he knew what library you were going to be at," Darwin answered. "Simple."

Lucas wagged a finger. "No. Not so simple. Have you paid attention to the types of cars on the road around here?" Darwin shook his head. "Right. A four-door Jeep looks like it's a popular ride on the island. How many black Jeeps such as mine do you imagine there are here in Hilton Head? Ten? Twenty?"

Darwin conceded the point. "Yeah, although they knew you were going to be there at some point today."

"They did. I agree. But what if there was another identical one here? How would they have known which was which? They arrived after I got there and were waiting on me."

"Dunno."

"Let me put this out there. You said on the way over here that Riddick told you he's a treasure hunter. Right?"

"Yeah."

"Okay. We also know he has a lot of money, right?"

"We do."

"Do you know anything about treasure hunters such as Riddick?"

"Can't say I do."

"Many are honest. But some, some are modern-day pirates. Ruthless. Will stop at nothing to find treasure, even resorting to violence and sabotage. Whatever."

"Riddick certainly looks the part of a pirate."

"Exactly. Remember, he's shown flashes of anger towards us in the past two days," Lucas said. "This lost treasure of Blackbeard has got to be his personal holy grail."

"I'll agree with that."

"He showed us back there at the harbor and yesterday out in Rose Bay that he'd resort to violence to get his way. Hell, Darwin, we could have been killed back there."

"He did. How does this tie back to those guys knowing your Jeep and you not wanting to get a rental?"

"What if Riddick has connections with the police and can track my license plate number? He could have gotten that at several points before we left Bath."

"Right, now that Jeep is sitting in a salvage yard somewhere," Darwin said. He saw Lucas flinch at the image. "I'm sorry. What I'm saying is that we no longer have a license plate number for him to track."

"We don't. We would if we rented a car."

"Huh. Good point," Darwin said and scratched the hair on his chin. "How would he know what we rented?"

"Well, if, if he has connections with the police department, who is to say he doesn't have similar ties in with credit monitoring services, or a network of shady informants within various government agencies? Those who sold information for the right price? What if he can track our transactions every time we swipe our credit or debit card? We sign our name to a rental, and then he could conceivably track that back to a license plate number and make and model of the car."

"Come on Lucas. That's stretching it."

Lucas shook his head. "Call me paranoid. Call me overly cautious. Whatever. At this point, with the stakes so high, we can't afford to have our names and whereabouts out there. You saw what happened back there. Darwin, we're in danger."

His big friend seemed to have simmered down. What was supposed to have been a fun excursion had turned into something much more serious. "Why not just quit?" he asked.

"And what? Go into hiding? Riddick knows we're on to something. Do you think he'd stop until he got the treasure?"

"No, I don't," Darwin admitted.

"Do you want the treasure to fall into his hands?"

"I don't. That would be a disservice to the world. If I found it, I'd make sure a museum somewhere would be able to preserve it and display it for many generations of people to enjoy."

"Do you believe Riddick would do that?"

"No. He'd keep it for himself locked away in a basement some-where."

"Awesome. We're on the same page here. Do you have any other ideas?"

After a minute, Darwin begrudgingly said, "I don't."

"Ok. Then let's try this," Lucas pointed in the direction Lynn had disappeared. "If she doesn't go for it, then I'll pull money out of savings and go the rental route as a last resort. Happy?"

"Not really, but what other choice do I have?"

"That's my Darwin."

"Wait. You asked her what time she was getting off tonight before all that happened at the marina. I thought you said you weren't here to pick her up."

Lucas smiled. "Hey, you've gotta admit she's cute."

Darwin shook his head, and then smiled. "You dog."

***

A million stars hung over Riddick's head as he pulled the speedboat into one of the many shipping centers owned by his company along the East Coast. The briny smell of the sea clung to him.

He needed to put on an Oscar-worthy performance for any employees who might be around the office. A shift-change had just occurred, and the night crew would be in. If they were doing as they were supposed to, they should be busy. He hoped his employees would move even faster upon seeing him.

Perhaps they'd be too busy to notice his foul mood. If this were the early 1700's, he'd select a random employee—a smaller one—take him into a backroom somewhere and beat him senseless. Blow off some steam. The real Blackbeard could have done that back in his day. Today, Riddick would have to worry about lawsuits and getting arrested.

He wanted to take out his frustration on something or someone. He was so close to attaining the treasure he'd been after for over thirty years. Then, those morons—his henchmen—may have ruined everything. He didn't know what he had wanted them to do when he had directed their attention back at the marina. But destroying both cars in an attempt, to what? Run them over?

Unless those idiots squealed, they couldn't be traced back to him. Both the speedboat and yacht were in his name. Unless someone at the marina had seen his men pilot the speedboat in, Riddick could claim that he'd never seen them before. A friend of a friend who wouldn't want the attention of the authorities owned the car. If that friend knew what was good for them.

Riddick still had a few things going for him. Not all hope was lost. While Darwin piloted the yacht along the Hilton Head coast, Riddick took a moment to riffle through the young man's backpack. In it, he'd found the printout of a treasure map. What was shown on the map appeared to fit the same description Darwin and Lucas had said they'd read in the diary of Mary Ormond. Lucas must have made that part up rather than revealing the existence of the map. Riddick couldn't believe his eyes. They'd kept it from him.

What it depicted didn't look like it was anything in the direct vicinity of Hilton Head. He'd folded it and placed it in his back pocket before zipping up the backpack.

If he could figure out the general area shown on the map, he would be able to find the X that marks the spot. Without being able to keep an eye on Darwin and Lucas, Riddick needed to ascertain their whereabouts from elsewhere.

As luck had it, he had a line on how to do that as well . . .

# CHAPTER THIRTY

L UCAS HAD TAKEN A shot in the dark propositioning Lynn to transport them to their next destination. He hadn't thought about what he and Darwin would do if they didn't find the treasure there. They couldn't have her chauffeur them back to North Carolina. Darwin and Lucas would cross that bridge when they came to it.

She drove them back to her apartment. It was across the street from an outlet mall just off the island. She went in, packed a few things for an overnight stay, and returned to her car. Lucas remembered that he and his partner had nothing but the clothes on their backs, so Lynn took Darwin and Lucas to a Target where they bought some inexpensive clothes, underwear, socks, toiletries, and a cell phone charger for Lucas. Darwin had the chargers for his devices in his backpack.

When Lucas laid out the scenario and the problem he and Darwin had, he expressed to Lynn a need to get on the road and head north as soon as they could. He wanted to be on Edisto Island at first light tomorrow. There was a small town named Walterboro just off I-95 where he could get everyone hotel rooms. It was the last stop before Edisto, an hour away from the interstate.

Lynn jumped at the opportunity to earn a quick five hundred dollars in cash. For once, she could have an adventure of her own. Rushing home and grabbing clothes and items from her bathroom and skipping town right away was no big deal to her. She was ready for something unexpected to happen in her life. Here was her chance to be in a story such as one out of her books.

As they were on their way from Hilton Head to the interstate, Lucas said, "Lynn, I never caught your last name."

"Oh, I'm sorry," she said while concentrating on the dark road ahead. "Russell. What are yours and Darwin's?"

"Mine is Caine. Darwin is a Trickett."

"Gotcha. Nice to meet you all."

"It's a pleasure to meet you too," Darwin called from the back seat.

Lucas felt sorry for the guy. Darwin rode in the backseat where there wasn't enough room to accommodate his bulky frame. Lucas, while not as big as Darwin, was still above average size. He still felt cramped in the front seat.

*Could have been worse*, he thought. *She could have driven one of those tiny Fiats.*

He purchased a charger at Target that plugged into a cigarette lighter or in a traditional power outlet. With his phone almost dead, he plugged it in and searched for a hotel in Walterboro. At least it wasn't a long drive to get there from Hilton Head. From there, it would leave them with about a sixty-minute trip in the morning to Edisto Beach.

Early in his relationship with his soon-to-be ex-wife, she had introduced him to Edisto Island. It seemed like most people in the Charlotte area went to Myrtle Beach when going on vacation. Lucas had been there several times, and always thought it was too busy. His brother and his wife went there all the time. They shopped, dined at a variety of restaurants, played putt-putt at amusement parks, or caught a show. The beach was an afterthought. Many people who went to Myrtle enjoyed the attractions over the surf and sand.

Lucas was different. When he went to the beach, he went to the *beach*. All he wanted to do was get his toes in the sand, sitting low in a beach chair, with a cool beverage in hand, watching the waves roll in.

That was paradise itself. He could block out everything else going on with his life and just zone out.

Kristen took him to Myrtle Beach and noticed he did not seem to care for the glitz, glamour, and horrendous traffic. She suggested a place her family went to when she was young that didn't have the same hustle and bustle. In fact, the place she proposed was unincorporated to guard against just that and had a laid-back way of life. The local islanders referred to the lifestyle as "Edis-slow."

There was a different vibe to Edisto Lucas enjoyed. It was un-incorporated, the only town on the East Coast that he knew of to hold that distinction. The island did not suffer from the inevitable creep of hotels, chain restaurants with neon lights, high-rise hotels, putt-putt courses and other trappings of normal tourist destinations. The grocery store and mini mart on the corner were allowed because of necessity. The island is off the beaten path. The closest stoplight is thirty minutes away. The closest McDonald's took an hour.

Lucas fell in love with the place the first time he went. Since then, he has been back a dozen times. Sometimes a couple times a year. He'd met interesting people there and made some contacts. One, he knew, might be able to help.

Lucas booked two rooms at a Microtel Inn in Walterboro. A room with two queen-sized beds for him and Darwin and a king size bed-room for Lynn. He was financing this venture and was glad to see the hotel offered a free continental breakfast.

They all got acclimated to each other on the trip up the interstate. Lynn told them about what brought her to Hilton Head—leaving out the being broke part and the thoughts of moving home to Mis-souri—while Darwin and Lucas filled her in on their backstory.

"Lucas, tell her about what happened with the Mahoney's," Darwin said, noting that Lucas had not mentioned that.

"Ah, it's nothing," Lucas said.

"Don't be so self-deprecating," Darwin said, and then to Lynn, "Lucas here came to work one morning and found his boss dead in the parking lot."

"What?" Lynn asked, eyes bulging.

"Yeah," Darwin continued, "a security fence surrounded the complex with just one way in or out. You had to have access codes to get in. Lucas was the last person to see him alive—other than the killer, of course. So, Lucas became the prime suspect."

"Wait," Lynn said, knitting her eyebrows. "Was this the thing that happened where the owner of that big Mahoney's restaurant chain was shot by his wife?"

"It was. Lucas solved it."

She took her eyes off the road for a second and glanced at Lucas. "That was you?"

He shrugged. "It was."

She didn't know what to say. She remembered that story. It was national news for about a week. She double take. *Oh my*, she thought, *this guy was a real-life storybook character*. Now she was very glad she came along.

***

The next morning, they all met in the dining room adjacent to the Microtel Inn lobby. Lynn was freshly showered. Her hair was still damp. Lucas thought she looked and smelled wonderful.

After checking in the night before, they adjourned to their separate rooms. Lucas made a call while Darwin cleaned up. After Lucas climbed out of the shower, they fell asleep almost at once. The events of the previous day took their toll on them. Lynn had stayed up well into the night, swept up in the frontier of the Canadian West while reading *When Breaks the Dawn* by Janette Oke. She imagined Lucas in the role of Wynn Delaney, the hunky hero of the tale.

While Lucas was in the shower, Darwin researched their destination. When he compared the area Lucas saw with the map Blackbeard had drawn three hundred years ago, he knew they were on the right track. With a few exceptions, which would be due to human error on Blackbeard's part, the two maps were almost an identical match. It would be difficult to get there by land. There were no roads to or from the area.

Darwin then shared several texts with Lisa back at the museum telling her what they discovered and thanked her for her help in them getting this far.

Lucas poured himself a cup of hot coffee from a carafe, grabbed a bland-looking muffin and a waxy apple before joining Lynn and Darwin at a small table in the corner of the dining room. A Belgian waffle, eggs, bacon, sausage patties and a healthy covering of thick syrup sat in a pile on Darwin's small Styrofoam plate. Lynn nursed a steaming cup of coffee in both hands as though trying to stay warm. The remains of a bowl of Fruit Loops sat in front of her. Several purple and green cereal fragments floated in the milk.

"Morning," Lucas said as he sat.

"Good morning," Lynn smiled.

Darwin couldn't speak. His mouth was full of food.

"Did you sleep well?" Lucas asked.

She nodded. "I did. You?"

"Like a log. Except for Darwin's snoring."

His big friend glanced up with a mouthful of food at the comment with a scowl on his face causing Lucas and Lynn to laugh.

"So what's up?" she asked. "What now?"

Lucas took a bite of his muffin, chewed, then said, "After we finish here, we'll check out and get on the road. I called a guy I know down there that has a fishing business on the island. He has a big shrimp boat called the *Sarah Jane*, and rents out other boats to tourists. He's going to hold us one until we get there."

"Great. What then?"

It was Lucas's turn to smile. "Go find treasure."

***

Before leaving the sleepy town of Walterboro, they stopped at a Wal-Mart that was open 24 hours and bought a couple of shovels, which they stowed in Lynn's trunk.

From Walterboro, they took mostly two-lane roads to Edisto Island. Thick, dark clouds kept the sun from appearing. The air was thick. They didn't smell the ocean yet, although Lucas knew they would before long.

The route took them through several small towns. Groups of houses tended to huddle near the many churches along the way. Like oases in the desert. The region wasn't well populated. At one point during the hour drive, Darwin asked Lucas if he was sure he knew where he was going.

He told Darwin to have a little faith in him. A few miles later, the car burst out from a line of thick trees and crossed over a long, arcing bridge spanning the Intracoastal Waterway. On the other side, a sandblasted wooden sign welcomed them to Edisto Island. After that, the route meandered over and around fields and swampland. The same pattern of churches and groups of houses continued.

Darwin figured that only about ten people attended a few of these churches. And some of them were enormous. Religion must be a large part of these people's lives.

They rounded a corner and saw another big, white church standing by itself to the left at the edge of one of the many lakes in the marshland. Darwin had his eyes on the church almost until they passed it.

As they passed by Botany Bay Road on the left, a dirt road leading past the church, Lucas pointed to their right.

Darwin's head jerked over just in time to see . . . well he wasn't sure what it was he saw.

About a hundred feet from the road, in the middle of the marsh, a dead tree stood. Hanging from its branches was a speed limit sign with a posted speed of "35 miles per hour," a pink toy Volkswagen Beetle sat on top of the sign. A fuchsia beach chair hung from one limb; orange and pink inner tubes, streamers and assorted floatation devices dangled from others. On top of everything, an American flag fluttered in the strong salty breeze.

"What in the world is that?"

"They call it The Mystery Tree," Lucas answered. "Someone has been decorating it for years. No one knows who does it. What is on it changes with the seasons and holidays. I bet if we come back here next month, you'll see vampires, ghouls, and ghosts for Halloween."

"And no one knows who does it?" Lynn asked.

"Nope. They must do it in the middle of the night. They've never seen anyone messing with it that I know of. It's dangerous too."

"Why's that?"

"There are alligators around here."

"Oh," Darwin said and then sunk deeper into his seat and into silence.

They passed a gas station with a gift shop and a Domino's Pizza all in the same building. Businesses and homes became more concentrated as they drove. Although Darwin thought, recognizable names were rare to see. He saw an Ace Hardware. That was about all he knew. Everything else seemed locally owned. He wondered if that was by design.

Then, all at once, they were there.

They passed by the Edisto Beach campground on their right and crossed a short bridge. Another sign that read "Welcome to Edisto Beach" waited for them on the other side.

# CHAPTER THIRTY-ONE

LUCAS HAD WANTED TO reach the island by first light. He wanted to have the entire day to devote to exploring the area on the map and if everything worked out, finding the treasure. As they put the bridge behind them and passed a grocery store, the sun broke through the clouds and its rays reached down to the ocean as though God was dipping his fingers in the water.

It promised to be a picturesque day. Perhaps they would make history as well, Lucas thought.

A quiet four-lane highway ran the length of the beach, behind a single row of ocean front houses. Only a few vehicles were out at this hour. Men going out to the beach to claim their spots for fishing. Employees of the island's large timeshare coming from off the island to work. Restaurant workers arriving to prep for the lunch rush.

The densely packed houses along the ocean to their left concealed most views of the ocean. From time to time, Darwin spied green waves over the sand dunes. He almost remembered seeing a few of these homes as he and Riddick cruised past this place the previous day. He was amazed to find that there weren't any large hotels along the water. He mentioned that to Lucas.

"Yeah, when tourists started coming to the island years ago," Lucas said, "the townsfolk kept it unincorporated. They allowed one grocery store and gas station. Everything else had to be small. No bright lights. They were isolated and wanted to keep the quaint, laid-back way of life they enjoyed unlike their neighbors to the north and south."

"Nice," Lynn and Darwin both said.

Lucas sat back in his seat. "That's why I like it here."

After about three miles, the road narrowed to two lanes and began to curve around the southern end of the island. They passed the different areas of the sleepy resort complex and a well-manicured golf course rising from the marsh as they came about to the sound side of the island. They saw mostly older people out for an early morning walk, jog, or bike ride.

As they approached a large sign for the resort on their right with an entrance road splitting two holes on the golf course, Lucas had Lynn pull into a parking lot on their left. To the right was a squared two-story building with gray siding. The sign above the door read "The Dockside Bar & Grill."

To the left of that was a small building with blue wood siding covering the top half of the structure. The area below the siding was made of cinder blocks painted white. Large murals of shrimp, a fishing boat, swordfish, and crawfish covered the front of the building. A covered entry way came out from above the door with "Fresh Edisto Seafood" painted in flowy letters across the façade. A wood sign hung down advertising "Fontaine Fishing Charters" in bold white letters.

The restaurant's parking lot was empty. The smaller building had two cars parked in front of it. "Pull up right there," Lucas instructed. "I've used these guys a bunch of times. Nicest folks you'll ever meet. They love to have a good time too."

Darwin practically jumped out of the car now that he had a chance to stretch out from its cramped confines.

Alone in the car with Lynn for the first time, Lucas said, "I can't thank you enough for all you've done for us."

Her smile made Lucas's heart skip a beat. "Sure thing," she said. "I needed a break from the monotony anyway. Glad I could help."

Lucas reached into his pocket and pulled out a wad of twenty-dollar bills. "Look, here's the five hundred I said I would give you for bringing us."

She took the money from his hands and held it carefully. She almost cried. This was a lifesaver for her. "Thank you," she said.

"No, thank you. We wouldn't be here if it weren't for you." He noted for the first time that her eyes weren't brown. Up close, they appeared hazel. "Look, you can go back to Hilton Head if you want. I know people around here and I think I can get us back to North Carolina."

She shook her head. "What would I go back to?" she said. "I already told my boss I wasn't coming to work today. I'm off tomorrow. All I would do is go sit in my apartment and watch sappy old romantic movies or read a book. If you don't mind, I wouldn't mind tagging along with you guys for a while longer."

What she said delighted him, but not without reservation. "I just want to warn you, if this Riddick guy comes around, it might get dangerous."

She gave him a self-assured smile and then said, "What good would an adventure be without a little danger?"

***

They followed Lucas inside. The strong smell of fish struck them as they entered. Built-in white shelving containing folded souvenir shirts and other trinkets ran along the left side of the small space. Before them was an empty glass case. Later in the day, after the *Sarah Jane* returned from the waters surrounding Edisto, the case would be full of crab legs, clams, and shrimp, and varieties of locally caught fish.

The backdoor behind the counter was open. A man of about average height wearing a beat up and sun-stained Fontaine Charters hat came through it when he heard the bells above the door chime as it closed behind Darwin.

He smiled and said, "Help you?" Then he recognized Lucas. "Hey man. Good to see you again."

"Good to see you too, Jeremy," Lucas said, shaking the man's hand. "Were you able to hold *The Marsh Hen* for me?"

"I was. Getting into the slow season. It's around back," he said, jerking a finger in the direction of the back door. "Got it ready for you."

"Thanks man. I appreciate it."

"Hey, I appreciate you. If you hadn't called me last night, she might have sat out there by herself all day today. Not good for business. How long do you suppose you'll need it?"

"Dunno. Couple of hours."

"No worries. You can keep it for longer if you need to. I'll just charge for the two-hour price."

"Great. Thanks. Every little bit helps. If someone calls wanting to reserve it, call me and I'll be back."

He turned his head to the side. "Nah. This morning I doubt it. It might rain and most of the tourists went home on Sunday. But I'll let you know."

"One more thing," Lucas said, "think you'll be able to do that favor for me I mentioned on the phone if it comes to it?"

"Absolutely, just let me know."

Lucas led Darwin and Lynn through the back door and onto a dock protruding from the back of the Edisto Seafood shack connecting to the Dockside next door. A 21-foot Mako offshore fishing boat floated beside the dock. It had a covered center console behind a clear acrylic windscreen, a swivel helm seat and two seats behind on the port and starboard sides.

"Much better than that jon boat we took out yesterday," Darwin observed.

"That it is," Lucas said and climbed aboard, stowing the two shovels in the floor of the boat. He extended a hand for Lynn to grab as she crossed over from the dock. He didn't extend the same courtesy to Darwin. He could handle himself. The boat dipped when he set both feet in the boat causing ripples to move across the still water.

The opposite bank was about fifty feet away from the dock. Sea grass swayed in the breeze along its length. Two older men floated past in a small fishing boat on their way out to the A.C.E. Basin to catch crabs. They smiled and waved. Lucas knew he and his friends would be close behind them. A group of kayakers glided by from left to right in the opposite direction in search of dolphins.

"This is nice," Lynn said as she sat down.

"I agree," Darwin said.

"Just a little slice of paradise," Lucas said.

"I see why you said you like coming here. A bit of a different pace than Hilton Head. Slower. At least this morning."

"Truthfully, it doesn't speed up much from here. Just the way I like it," Lucas said.

Darwin reached into his backpack and started digging. He became agitated after a minute, and said to himself, "Come on, where is it?"

"Where is what?" Lucas said.

"The map. It's not here."

Lucas cursed himself. "You don't think you left it back at the hotel, did you?"

"No. I couldn't have. I didn't even look at it last night."

"Have you seen it since you got to Hilton Head?"

Darwin gave him a vacant look. "No, I haven't."

"Damn. You don't suppose Riddick stole it did you?"

Darwin shrugged. "I guess he could have. He might've done it while I was steering the ship."

"Hmm. I wonder if that's why he had you do that," Lucas said. "To get you away from your backpack?"

"I don't know. He's manipulated us every step of the way until then."

"Sounds like he's a bad guy," Lynn said.

"You could say that," Lucas said. "He owns a shipping company and it turns out he's also a treasure hunter."

"There are still people like that still around?"

"Oh yeah. Some strike it rich big time. This treasure of Blackbeard's could be his ticket to that." Lucas paused to start the outboard motor. "See, treasure hunters can start as honorable men and women. Then the prospect of treasure and fortune can make them greedy. It can bring the worst out in people. It causes men to sever friendships and even marriages. When silver and gold mixes with human instinct, it creates a volatile recipe."

"Oh," Lynn said, thinking about the bad men in her books. Early people in the Canadian West faced similar circumstances during the gold rush. She understood the mentality.

"Trust me, you wouldn't want to meet him," Lucas said.

"I hope not."

"Yeah, I hope you don't get to either." He turned to Darwin. "Don't worry about the printout. Remember, I have a picture of it on my phone. I know where we're going anyway."

Lucas started the skiff and eased out into Big Bay Creek at idle speed. After they passed the Edisto Marina and the choppy waters of the A.C.E. Basin opened before them, he opened the throttle. They saw many varieties of birds flying across the marshes and wetlands.

The broad expanse of water came from the Ashepoo, Combahee, and Edisto Rivers combining to create the A.C.E. Basin. It is one of the largest estuaries along the Atlantic Coast. It combines with the larger St. Helena Sound to the south. A private-public partnership was formed in the 1980's after outside development pressures crept in. The residents of Edisto petitioned local, state, and federal authorities to help preserve the basin.

That partnership is one reason why Edisto hasn't become as gentrified as other beaches along the Atlantic Coast. Large development companies couldn't come in, cultivate the land, and build it up as they wanted to. They took their business elsewhere.

That lack of attention from outsiders may have also kept any would-be treasure hunters from coming around too, Lucas thought.

"Why does the water look like black tea?" Lynn asked, looking at the seawater passing by the hull of the boat.

"I believe that comes from the Edisto River," Lucas answered. "There's tannins in the water coming from the decomposing tree leaves of the surrounding hardwood forests causing that."

"Yuck. Is it safe?"

"I don't worry about it. No one else near here does. When you get in the water on this side of the island, you can see the small, black particles floating around. They're not harmful."

The shore of the approaching island lay before them, coming closer. They were soon able to make out details. The tide was low, exposing twenty feet of wet sand. Beyond the high tide barrier were clumps of sea grass, rocks, and other bushes. A dense line of palm trees concealed the view of the rest of the flat land. There were not any signs of civilization. It was a barren place.

Darwin pointed a meaty thumb at behind him and said, "If that's Edisto Island back there, what's this in front of us?"

"This is Pine Island. It is connected to Otter Island to our left and Fenwick Island to our right. There's a creek running down the center of the three that makes it look like a big kidney from the air."

Darwin looked up from his phone. "This is amazing. I'm looking at where we are on Google Earth right now. Lucas, this is the spot. It looks almost identical to what Blackbeard drew."

"Well, you have to imagine the sands shifted over the centuries, although I don't think Blackbeard was too bad of a cartographer. Seems to have hit it dead on."

"What about the sun?" Darwin asked.

"What about it?"

"There was a half sun drawn on the map to the left of this island. What do you think that means?"

Lucas thought about it for a moment. He turned and pointed to the opposite shore of Edisto. Darwin and Lynn turned and looked. "Do you see that resort complex over there? With the palm trees?"

"Yeah."

"They call that area Dolphin Lookout."

"Ooo, I love dolphins," Lynn said.

"Well, if you stand over there on that beach for any length of time, you'll usually see several. They come into these shallow waters to feed and give birth."

"Amazing."

"Wait, did you say dolphins?" Darwin asked.

"Yeah."

"Remember the notation Blackbeard made on the bottom of the map?"

Lucas's eyes went wide. "Ah, I'd forgotten about that. He said the treasure was 'where the dolphins gather.' That means this must be the place."

"I want to know," Lynn said. As she began to realize this may well be one of the biggest moments in all their lives, she became excited. "What did the notation say?"

Darwin enlarged the image on his phone so he could read it verbatim. He cleared his throat. "Blackbeard wrote, 'Treasure buried twenty-three paces in by the large oak under a falling sun near the cove where the dolphins gather.'"

"Huh," Lynn said.

Darwin started to tick off the points with his fingers. "One, this place looks like what Blackbeard drew. Two, it's close to where he may have gotten the treasure from the *Atocha*. Three, it's got dolphins. This is it. We're here."

"Wow," Lynn said.

"And if you're over there during the evening," Lucas said pointing to the beach by the Dolphin Lookout, "you often see a spectacular sunset over where we are now. I bet Blackbeard was here for one of those and drew that half sun to help remind him where to find the treasure."

"That seals it." Darwin looked from where they were and to the left and where the open waters of the Atlantic would be if a hump in Pine Island wasn't blocking their view. "You know, if I were running from the Spanish Navy with my holds full of their gold, this wouldn't be a bad place to hide a ship, tucked here into the crook of this island. Passing ships wouldn't be able to see them."

Lucas agreed. "And you can imagine that maybe Blackbeard might have been slightly afraid to see a much larger warship with many more guns approach. I bet he took off from the *Atocha* and high tailed it here, not knowing where "here" was. Could be one reason as to why there are no place names on the map. He knew the general area, so he drew that half sun to remind him this was a spot to catch a beautiful sunset."

"How about that?" Lynn said. "Maybe Blackbeard had a romantic side to him."

"You're probably right. He only had fourteen wives."

"Eww," Lynn said. "Maybe not."

Lucas scanned around and said, "Right now with it being low tide, we could cruise on over to Otter Island and find a ton of sand dollars."

"Sand dollars? Really?" Lynn asked.

"Yeah, there's a watersports place that runs tourists out here during low tides to do nothing but look for sand dollars and seashells. The water isn't deep around here. When the water recedes, it leaves long sand bars exposed. You walk out and you just find sand dollars everywhere sticking out of the sand."

"I love those things. I didn't know you could get them from water that way."

"It's crazy. People go back with buckets of them. You could make money from selling them if you wanted to."

"Remember, we're in a hurry," Darwin reminded them.

"Right."

Lucas had Darwin hand him his phone so he could see the image of the map. He checked his position and moved the craft along the shore to the right about twenty yards and into a concealed cove before grounding the boat into the sand. "This should be our starting point," Lucas said.

The sand along the shore came out about ten feet from where a line of seagrass ran. Behind that was a dense line of palm and oak trees interspersed with large sandstone rocks.

Lucas cut the engine and hopped out of the boat, grabbing both shovels. He helped Lynn climb over the side and onto the soft sand. Darwin followed.

"Okay," Darwin said, "no one really knows how tall Blackbeard was. I know he was described as well over six-feet tall."

"Right and the average height of people back then were several inches shorter than they are now," Lucas said. "Darwin, we're both over six feet. I'm six-three. What about you?"

The large man wiggled a hand. "Six-seven, six-eight. I'd say you're a little closer. Someone as tall as me they likely would have described as a giant."

Lynn stood in between both men, looking up at the conversation. "Hey! Maybe I would have been average size way back then."

Darwin gave her an awkward, condescending pat on the head. "There, there little lady. We all have dreams."

She gave him a playful punch in the stomach. Her hand disappeared. "Be good, mister."

"Alright, alright," Lucas said, this time it was his turn to get everyone refocused. "So, we agree that he was about my height?" They nodded. "Okay, he said twenty-three paces in. We don't know if that was during low or high tide, so I'm just going to start walking. Keep your eyes peeled for a larger than average oak tree."

"If it's still here," Darwin said.

"Let's hope it is."

Lucas turned and walked onto the beach and into the trees, counting his steps. Two, three, four, five. The maritime forest was thick, and he couldn't see in front of him past a couple feet. He wondered if there were more trees here now than there were then. Ten, eleven, twelve. They climbed over a fallen palm tree. The salt air became intermingled with the smell of eucalyptus. Twenty-one, twenty-two, twenty-three. Stop.

Lucas cast his eyes about, taking stock of their position. "Anyone see it?"

"No," Darwin answered.

"No," Lynn started to say, then, "Hold on. To the right." She pointed. "See that clearing?"

Her head was below the branches of the surrounding trees. Those same fronds obscured Darwin and Lucas's view. She had a different perspective. They ducked down to her level and peered to where she pointed.

They saw an area of sand perhaps ten feet in diameter surrounded by trees. In the middle of the clearing was a fallen tree, its trunk pointed away from them. Gossamers of Spanish moss hung from the long-exposed roots.

"That qualifies as a big oak," Darwin said.

"Yeah, but is it the right one?" Lynn asked.

A large, tan-colored stone sat near where the tree once stood upright. Lucas noticed something odd on the rock's surface. He walked over to it, crouched, and studied it. Lucas laughed.

"What's so funny?" Lynn asked.

He didn't answer her but directed a question to Darwin. "What was it Blackbeard said on the night before his death when he was asked where his treasure was?"

Darwin frowned. "You mean, "Only he and the devil know where the treasure is?""

Lucas stood aside and pointed at the face of the stone. "What do you think that is?"

Lynn and Darwin crowded in for a view of the spot where Lucas pointed.

The markings were faint. An image was carved on the side of the tan rock.

They saw a skeleton with horns, holding a goblet in its right hand and a spear in its left.

"What is it?" Lynn asked.

Darwin answered. "That, my friend, is the same image Blackbeard used on his flag. That is his depiction of the Devil."

The carving faced the fallen oak.

The proverbial X that marked the spot.

# CHAPTER THIRTY-TWO

THE THREE WHOOPED AND cheered when the realization hit that they had located where the treasure was buried. Now all that remained was to locate the exact spot and start digging.

"I hope all that cheering is to mark my entrance," a voice called through the palms.

Now on high alert, Darwin and Lucas had their eyes focused on the section of the trees where the voice came from. Lynn hid behind them. They saw a dark shape coming towards them. It pushed between two large palm fronds and there he was.

Riddick.

This time, however, he was dressed in his full pirate regalia. When Darwin and Lucas first met him, he was dressed in modern clothing. Today, he wore his entire Blackbeard costume: Tri-point hat, long brown frock coat, strands of the hair on his beard twisted together with red ribbons. Billowy, tan pantaloons were tucked into long, brown boots that came almost to his knees. A cutlass hung from his left hip, and he had four gun holsters wrapped around his torso. Two of which held guns.

The other two guns were in each hand and pointed at Darwin and Lucas.

He had a Devil's grin on his face. "Miss me?"

Lucas didn't answer his question. "How did you find us?"

The smile didn't leave Riddick's face. He gestured with one gun off to the side. "First, toss your shovels over there. It wouldn't do to have you guys wielding weapons." Darwin and Lucas complied, their shovels landing with a *thump* in the sand. Riddick turned and addressed Darwin. "Darwin, I'm afraid you've been betrayed."

"What do you mean?"

"Your friend at the museum, Lisa, gave you up."

Lucas sensed Darwin's anger rising. "How do you know her?" he asked.

Riddick smirked. "It's simple. For the past ten years, my company has been one of the largest contributors as far as donations to the museum you work at. So, you might say, I have connections and influence." He approached Darwin, and held one pistol to Darwin's chin, causing the thick skin to mold itself around the barrel. He aimed the other pistol at Lucas. "If it weren't for me and my generous donations, that fancy new wing of the museum, for which you were hired for, may never have been built. I wanted to fund most of it should something such as this happen. I needed them in my pocket."

He swiveled to Lucas. "You see, I know all about Travis Cole. I was the one who granted him permission to comb over Blackbeard's estate. My family owns that land. Let's just say he balked at our arrangement. He had found something in Bath, and he may have hidden it somewhere at the museum. I wanted to have influence in case whatever it was ever surfaced." He turned his gaze to Darwin. "Thank you for that, lad."

While the pirate explained how he arrived on Pine Island, Lucas reached back and rubbed Lynn's arm. She was shaking. He didn't want Riddick to get suspicious of his movements and took his hand off her skin, not before giving her an "OK" gesture with his fingers. At that, he felt her making furtive movements he hoped his and Riddick's bulk covered.

"I remembered you telling me you worked there," Riddick was saying. "I made some calls, applied some pressure, and threatened to pull my funding. They knew you had been in contact with this Lisa during the past two days by looking at the recent calls made to and from her phone on her desk."

Riddick adjusted his grip on the pistol causing the folds on Darwin's chin to shift. "You better not have harmed her," he said through clinched teeth.

"Oh, rest assured son, she's fine. I sent two, uh, employees out to her house before she woke up this morning to . . . ask questions."

Sweat began to drip from Darwin's face onto the cold metal barrel of the pistol. Lucas watched. He didn't dare make a move. Yet. He knew why pirates during that era fought more with knives and swords in close quarters than the more deadly flintlock pistols.

"Don't worry. We didn't have to rough her up too much. And she didn't say anything that led me here."

"What do you mean?" Darwin gritted out.

"She wouldn't talk, although her cell phone did. We looked at the text messages you two exchanged last night, pointing to Edisto Island."

Lucas felt as though he had been punched in the gut. He told Darwin to stay off the grid. This is what Lucas was afraid would happen. He couldn't fault his young friend. He had been excited, almost killed, and, for all his loneliness, had a girl talking to him. If it hadn't been for Lisa, they wouldn't be here now.

Unfortunately, being "here" at this moment meant having a weapon pointed at him. There could be an opportunity to make a move if the situation presented itself. Lucas felt horrible for getting Lynn into this situation. The five-hundred dollars he had given her for bringing them to Edisto wasn't going to be nowhere near enough.

"Once I knew the name of the location, all I had to do is compare it with the map I took out of Darwin's backpack—thank you for that."

"You're welcome," Darwin said, his tone dripping with icicles.

"When I learned you were headed here, it was as obvious to me as I'm sure was to you when I compared the maps. Then, it's just my luck that you were here ahead of me to get the work started."

Riddick removed the gun from Darwin's chin and stepped back, pistols leveled at the three of them. "Ah, I see you have a new friend here," he said. "Why don't you step out from behind these two lugs and introduce yourself."

Lucas felt her arm clinch him tighter. "It'll be okay," he whispered to her.

Lynn gulped and took a tentative step and moved out to where Riddick could see her. The evil smile on his face somehow morphed into a Casanova smile.

"Well, well, well. Aren't you a lovely little thing? How did you get mixed up in this?"

"I drove them here," she said.

"You drove them here? Where did you come from?"

"Hilton Head."

"Ah, of course" Riddick said as though everything now made perfect sense. He turned to Lucas. "I'll have to give you credit. You move fast, and you have good taste." He licked his lips, sending a wave of revulsion through Lynn. "Tell me gang, what were you cheering about before I stepped over? Oh, and thank you for doing that and allowing me zero in on your location."

In a millisecond, Lucas explored a dozen options on how to answer. He could come up with no believable reason to give, knowing that Riddick knew why they were on this small island.

"I offered you the opportunity of a lifetime," Riddick said to Darwin. "Regardless of what has happened that offer is still on the table."

"Shove it. I don't want your job you piece of filth."

Riddick took a cautious step back. He did not want to be within arm's reach of Darwin, gun or not. Another reason Riddick wanted Darwin in his fold was because of the potential added muscle he could bring if honed properly. "Be that as it may, I wish you'd reconsider. I feel that we would make a formidable team in the world of treasure hunting. Your research and my resources could make you rich."

"Yeah, but at what cost? Having to resort to violence, theft, and even murder to get there?"

Riddick shrugged. "Comes with the job."

Lucas noted that Riddick did not dispute the part about murder. He asked, "So what now? Are you going to kill us?"

"No. Not yet at least," Riddick said. "Now tell me, what were you three whooping about a moment ago?"

Taking the lead, Lucas answered, "We may have found it."

"Fantastic."

To show he was willing to cooperate, Lucas explained how they located the large fallen oak and the devil symbol scratched into the nearby rock.

"So, the devil did know where the treasure was after all?" Riddick said, then laughed, "Who would have known Blackbeard was being literal when he made that statement?" He paused for a moment. "Okay, start digging."

"That would be pointless," Darwin said.

"Why is that? You said this is where the treasure was?"

"Wouldn't it make more sense and save time if you let me get my metal detector out and scan the area? Narrow it down."

"Makes sense," Riddick submitted.

"Okay then," Darwin started to unsling the heavy backpack from his shoulder.

Riddick stepped forward shoving a gun in Darwin's ear and aiming the other weapon at Lynn. "Don't try anything funny or the girl dies first."

Darwin had to restrain himself from lunging at the pirate. "I won't. Just stand back and let me assemble this."

Riddick did as Darwin suggested, although he kept both weapons trained on his three captives. "Do what you need to."

Darwin dug in his pack and brought out a metal disc with a folded pole attached. The pole extended to make a long handle. Darwin pressed a button on the disc, and it beeped once. Lucas and Lynn watched as Darwin walked to the oak and started moving the metal detector back and forth over the sand. It beeped sporadically as he walked around the circumference of the fallen tree. He got to the trunk, climbed over, and resumed scanning on the other side. When he got to the area between the rock and the tree, the detector began beeping faster.

"We got a hit!" Riddick shouted.

"Maybe," Darwin said, looking at the LCD display on the handle. "Doesn't appear to be much. A foot or two below the surface."

Riddick studied where the metal detector pinged. "Well, what are you waiting for? Start digging."

He kept his guns trained on Darwin and Lucas as they retrieved the shovels they had thrown off to the side. He didn't have anything to fear from the small woman, although he kept her within his direct eyesight.

The two men started digging. In a short amount of time, they had a good-sized hole made in the sand. Lucas stuck his spade in the sand and pushed with his foot on the back edge to help thrust the triangular tip deeper.

*Chink!*

Everyone froze and stared in rapt attention at Lucas.

Lucas pulled the shovel from the sand and then dug a spot a few inches behind where they'd heard the sound. There was no metallic clink as before. He strained and pushed the shovel deeper before pulling down on the handle. That caused a shoebox size of sand to be lifted from the hole.

As the exposed sand fell away from either side of the shovel, a single gold coin tumbled out, rolled around in a tightening spiral twice before settling face up on flat ground.

# CHAPTER THIRTY-THREE

T HE FOUR OF THEM stared at the coin in disbelief for almost a minute before looking at each other with mouths wide open. In that moment, all the animosity and threats and gun pointing were forgotten. The enormity of what just happened was lost on none of them, even the newcomer Lynn.

The first piece of a treasure thought lost for over three-hundred years lay in the sand before them.

Riddick stashed the gun in his left hand into one of the holsters on his stomach, walked over, and picked up the coin. He held it between his thumb and forefinger and gazed closely at it. He used his thumb to clear away most of the sand on the coin's surface.

"Oh my," he said reverently.

"What is it?" Lucas asked, looking over the pirate's shoulder at the coin.

"To this day, coins from the Spanish Treasure Fleet of 1715 still wash up along parts of Florida they call the Treasure Coast. Boxes of treasure have been brought up from some of the wreckage. People sell them online," Riddick explained. "In almost all cases, those coins have eroded to a degree. The faces may have rubbed off, or the edges worn away."

He pulled the coin away from his face and held it up for everyone to see. He said, "As you can see, this coin looks as though it is in near mint condition. To me, it looks like a four-escudo Philip V. I believe these were minted in Mexico. I've seen ones in okay condition sell for five or six thousand dollars."

"Wow," the three captives said at the same time.

"This one?" Riddick said. "I'd say this one would easily snag ten thousand at auction."

"And there might be hundreds or thousands of these where this one came from," Darwin said. "Jewels too."

While the others thought about the amount of treasure beneath their feet, Lucas recognized that a bad situation for him and his two friends was about to get worse. Before that coin tumbled from the sand, he saw a scenario where Riddick just somehow abandoned them here and let them find their way back to civilization. They could have accused Riddick of Travis Cole's murder, although there wasn't any solid proof. If it came to it, Riddick may have gone to court had the Raleigh police decided to press charges. He would have hired a team of expensive defense attorneys and been acquitted.

When the coin tumbled into the sand, the bad situation got worse. Much worse.

For the first time, Lucas feared for his life. He, Darwin and Lynn were witnesses. They knew. After what happened leading up to this moment, Lucas didn't see Riddick wanting to split the treasure with any of them. They were expendable. That would dawn on Riddick soon.

"What now?" Lucas asked.

The wicked smile returned. "Keep digging."

He glanced at Darwin who was studying him and nodded. "You heard the man, Darwin. Let's get at it."

Riddick backed away to allow Darwin and Lucas to resume their work. Over the next ten minutes, the hole deepened, and they unearthed two more coins in excellent condition. Riddick pocketed them. They had yet to find the mother lode, so to speak.

The pirate was becoming fidgety. Lucas realized the weapons Riddick kept in his hands began to weigh heavy. They drooped now and then before coming back to level. Lucas saw that Darwin was getting fatigued. It was hot, damp, and sticky out here. They needed water. He was starting to feel it a little himself.

"Where is it?" Riddick demanded. "Where is the rest of the treasure?" He patted his pocket. "Surely this can't be all."

Lucas stopped digging and leaned against his shovel. "I have no idea. Would you let Darwin scan again with his detector?"

Riddick walked to Lucas and gestured with a gun at the hole they had dug. "Why? It already pinged. We know this is the spot."

"I have a feeling. Just let him."

Riddick removed his hat and swiped the back of his hand across his brow to remove the beads of sweat. He shook his head. "Alright, go-ahead lad."

Darwin dropped his shovel and retrieved the metal detector from beside Lynn. He went back to the dig area and resumed his scan. This time, however, the equipment failed to erupt in a chorus of loud beeps. He moved across the entire clearing. The detector discovered nothing further.

Seeing the lost look on Darwin's face when he fished his rounds of the clearing, Riddick said, "Well tell me, where is it?"

Darwin shook his head in exasperation while returning to the group. "I don't know. It's not here. The scanner's finding nothing."

Riddick's mouth opened and closed without speaking. His face turned red. He was at a loss for words. The guns dropped slightly. He was standing five feet from Darwin. Lucas stood about the same distance off Riddick's left side "So you're telling me these three coins are all that's left of it?"

Darwin shrugged his beefy shoulders. "That's what it looks like."

Riddick's mouth tightened beneath the thick black beard. An evil gleam came over his piercing blue eyes. With frustration etched on his face, he said, "Then all of you are worthless to me. As we pirates say, "Dead men tell no tales.""

It was now or never. Lucas saw Riddick start to raise both weapons above level to point at Darwin's chest.

Lucas grabbed the handle of his shovel and swung the sharp edge of the spade at Riddick's neck with all his might. Riddick saw the motion coming and dodged just enough for the blow to hit him in the shoulder. His hat flew off to the side. Lynn screamed.

The blade plunged into the pirate's shoulder several inches in an explosion of blood. He still managed to turn and aim both weapons at Lucas and pull the triggers.

The two flintlock pistols boomed. Sparks flew. Lucas felt a bolt of lightning strike him and went down.

# CHAPTER THIRTY-FOUR

For the first time in his life, Darwin faced death as Riddick brought the two guns to bear on his chest. He'd always thought the phrase "seeing your life pass before your eyes" was just something people said for effect. That it wasn't a true statement.

In that moment, as he saw the bitter disappointment on Riddick's face and the two guns begin to rise, Darwin reflected on his childhood. How he sometimes didn't know where the next meal would come from. The father he never really knew. The loneliness he felt in school as other kids shunned him because he was different.

The jubilation he felt when he got the job as a busboy at Mahoney's as soon as he was old enough to get a job. Of meeting Lucas and the conversations they had as Darwin neared graduation. How Lucas may not know it, but he was instrumental in encouraging Darwin to pursue his dreams of being an archaeologist.

He remembered that incredibly long ride on his moped as he traveled the back roads from Concord to the North Carolina State campus in Raleigh the summer after graduating from high school. How he never thought he'd get there. But he did. He got there. Went through four years of college and graduated. No friends or family came to the graduation ceremony, which saddened him. Still, he pushed on. He thought of the sense of accomplishment he had when the hiring director at the museum had called him and told him he got the job.

Flashes of the adventure he had been on over the past two and a half days went through his mind. Out of everything, these had been the best days of his life.

Now he was afraid it was all about to end. He had been around many unsavory characters in his life: drug dealers, pimps, thieves, and murderers. The man who stood before him was perhaps the vilest person he'd ever met.

Darwin watched the black circles at the end of the barrels rise and point at both of his eyes. He saw Riddick's fingers begin to tighten on the triggers. Then, out of the corner of his eye, off to the right, he saw Lucas swing his shovel and hit Riddick.

The black circles of the guns lurched, disappeared from his view, and swung at Lucas and fired. Orange embers and smoke filled the air as a deafening explosion erupted. One shot went wide over Lucas's head. The other hit his left shoulder, spinning him around and down into the sand.

Riddick tossed both weapons to the ground and started to reach for the other two weapons holstered on his torso. He was now turned side on to Darwin.

Darwin raised his big size sixteen Nike shoe and brought it down hard on Riddick's right knee. The bones and tendons in that knee stretched and broke with the impact. His leg bent at a sharp angle sideways, causing the femur to burst through the skin. He yelled out in pain as he started to go down, although not before Darwin landed a punch on the right side of Riddick's head with his big fist.

Riddick was unconscious before he hit the ground. It was the first punch Darwin had ever thrown.

The sheer rush of adrenaline and protective rage coursing in his veins made Darwin want to get down and break all the bones in Riddick's body. Somehow, he stopped himself.

Blood covered the sand near both Riddick and Lucas.

Seeing that the danger had passed, Lynn rushed over and tended to Lucas. Blood rushed between his fingers where he held his hand against his shoulder. He squeezed his eyes closed as he fought the pain.

Lynn had taken a semester of emergency medical training in college. She yelled for Darwin to take off his shirt and toss it to her. He complied and she ripped it into strips to help control the flow of blood and stabilize the wound. The gunshot wound didn't look too serious. Just a graze.

"Here let me," she said to Lucas and lifted his hand off the gash. She took one strip of fabric and wiped the seeping blood away. She used the others to create a makeshift bandage and sling. "There, that should hold until we can get you to a doctor."

"Thanks," he said between pursed lips. "I owe you one."

Before she could respond, they heard someone shout from the trees from the direction that they had entered the clearing, "Everybody freeze!"

Two men with shotguns drawn burst into the clearing. They wore dark blue buttoned-up shirts and matching slacks with matching baseball caps with the words "U.S. Coast Guard" embroidered in gold on the front.

Help was here. They were safe.

***

Two ambulances were waiting at the Edisto Marina when they arrived on the Coast Guard patrol boat half an hour later. One whisked the still unconscious Riddick to a hospital in Charleston. There were no such facilities on Edisto. A paramedic gave Lucas a shot of antibiotics, stitched his shoulder up, and put a thick bandage on the wound. The laceration wasn't severe enough to warrant a trip to the emergency room. The paramedic told him that if the pain got too bad, to head to a clinic where a doctor would prescribe medication for him.

Someone gave Darwin a t-shirt from the golf course across the street to wear after Lynn had used most of his old, tattered shirt to treat Lucas. He received a new t-shirt as well because of his other one being covered in blood and having a large hole blasted in the shoulder.

A TV news van from Charleston was already at the scene.

The police were also there to sort out the mess. They got the accounts of Darwin, Lynn, and Lucas and told them there may be further questioning in the near future before releasing them. Jeremy at Fontaine Charters was also questioned when Lucas informed them about how he had put the charter captain on alert that there may be trouble. When Lynn and Lucas were in her car before getting on the boat, he had instructed her to send a quick text to Jeremy in case of trouble. That was what she was doing behind Lucas and Darwin's backs when Riddick entered. The police spoke to the two Coast Guardsmen to coordinate how the case would be handled. The police investigators had to head north to Charleston and wait for Riddick to get out of surgery before they could speak with him.

Before leaving, one officer said to Lucas, "That was a gutsy thing you did back there. Not many would take that risk."

"I couldn't just let him shoot Darwin. I knew Riddick would get one shot with those flintlocks. They only fire one round before needing to be reloaded. That's why pirates strapped multiple pistols to them. Once expended, they weren't likely to get three minutes to load again in the middle of a battle."

"What if he would have gotten to the others in his belt?"

"Then we'd be dead," Lucas said. "As I said, it was a risk I had to make."

Darwin came over and hugged Lucas, careful not to further harm his shoulder. "Thank you for saving my life. I can never repay you enough."

Lucas stepped back and smiled. "Hey, I'd be dead too if it weren't for you putting that beat down on him."

Lynn came over and tried to put her short arms around both large men. "And I'd be dead if it weren't for you two."

"We wouldn't be here if it weren't for you," Lucas said. "Besides, I might've bled out had you not been a battlefield medic. I meant what I said back there. I owe you anything."

The Coast Guard patrol boat towed *The Marsh Hen* back to the dock behind Edisto Seafood. They had already left to retrieve Riddick's powerboat.

Lucas paid Jeremy for use of the boat and apologized for the trouble.

"Hey, don't worry about it," he said. "This'll be on at least the local news. Free advertising for me. Who knows? It could go national."

Lucas didn't like that thought. He didn't want the attention. Although it would be good for Darwin's career and Jeremy's business.

They walked out of the small storefront and climbed into Lynn's car. They all felt as though this had been the longest day of their lives, even though it wasn't even noon yet. They needed to go somewhere, fill their empty stomachs, and figure out if it were time to give up and head home.

Lucas knew just the place to do that.

***

The thick cloud layer that kept the sun hidden for the most part during the morning had moved out to sea, leaving behind a bright sun with scattered clouds.

Lucas took them to a place near the northern end of Edisto along Jungle Road that served incredible fish tacos named McConkey's Jungle Shack. The restaurant consisted of a pickup window on the street side where passersby could pick up a quick hot dog or ice cream cone. On the other side was a screened-in covered porch with four tables on a deck. You could smell the ocean and hear the waves from there.

After years of coming to Edisto, Lucas began to recognize the people who worked in the various small establishments on the island. He'd made friends with several people and looked them up when he was on the island.

Angie had been his server many times at McConkey's. She was not quite average height, but a little above average weight. She had pudgy cheeks that looked as though they'd been pinched way too much as a child. She had a long, blonde ponytail running most of the length down her back.

Lucas opened a screen door on one side of the dining area and poked his head in. Angie heard the small cat's bell jingle when the door opened and poked her head from the kitchen to see who her visitors were. Her smile faded and soon returned when she took note of their disheveled appearance. She served grizzled fishermen and contractors every day, so she was used to patrons showing up who looked worse for wear.

At present, Lucas imagined he, Darwin and Lynn gave any of those people a run for their money in the "you look ran over" department.

"Hey, I'll be right with you all. Just have a seat anywhere." Before ducking her head back into the kitchen, she blinked twice and stared hard at the two. His head swiveled from Lucas to Darwin down to Lynn and back. "Oh my God! Lucas? Is that you?"

Lucas was surprised she remembered his name. He remembered her telling him that her family had lived on Edisto for several generations. She took the dishtowel that had been on her shoulder and tossed it back through the doorway, presumably onto a countertop. She rushed out to greet them.

"What the hell happened to you?" she shouted, and then covered her mouth realizing there were other customers who could hear her. Then quieter, "I mean, you look horrible Lucas. What happened? Gosh, it's been too long since I've seen you on the island."

"Let me sit down first," Lucas said. "Been a long morning."

"Of course, of course," she said and pointed to an empty picnic table on the patio at the edge of the railing. "You all have a seat there. I'll go get you something to drink. What'll you have?"

Everyone asked for the Southern specialty of sweet teas, and she scurried off to the kitchen.

It hurt for Lucas to swing one leg over the bench seat of the picnic table. With his shoulder in a sling, Lynn helped him get situated before taking a seat beside him. He groaned with the effort as Darwin sat down on the opposite side. It felt great to sit, Lucas thought.

He had his back to the main road and had a view of a wide parking lot McConkey's shared with the island's only grocery store. Beyond that was a line of houses followed by Palmetto Boulevard running along the shore down the entire length of the island. On the far side of that, Lucas could just make out a narrow strip of blue that was the Atlantic Ocean.

A wood fence spanned the back of the parking lot. Tall palm trees dotted the perimeter of the asphalt. The palm fronds swayed in the gentle sea breeze. Families together on bicycles or rented golf carts leisurely made their way along Jungle Road. No one was in any hurry. Wherever their destinations may be, it would still be there when they arrived. Edis-slow indeed.

People come to Edisto to spend time with family and friends at the beach. The local eateries, such as McConkey's and The Seacow across the street were all great in their separate ways. The food was excellent and the restaurant decorations had a charm of their own. There were various gift shops and boutiques peppering the island. If you wanted a Wal-Mart, you had to drive an hour up Route 17 back to Walterboro to find one.

Edisto reminded Lucas of the small town he grew up in West Virginia named Summersville. Except you traded the lakes and mountains for the beaches and ocean here.

Angie returned, bearing three sweet iced teas in matching clear plastic cups with no lids. The thick humidity created beads of perspiration that had already enveloped the cups' surfaces. She set the teas between them on the wooden surface and laid down two straws in paper wrappers.

"Here ya go folks," she said, taking a pen from behind her ear and drawing a ticket pad from her apron. "Specials today are grilled Mahi sandwiches and she-crab soup."

None of the three, overcome with exhaustion, had thought to look at the menus yet. They were trying to get their bearings and compartmentalize the insane forty-eight-hour period they just survived.

"Get us three orders of the fish tacos," Lucas said. Darwin gave him a look. Lucas assured him, "Trust me."

"Okay guys and gal. I'll put this in and tell them to rush it. I can see you need it. Be right back."

"Thanks," the three sitting at the table said in unison.

Angie returned later after another server had appeared from the kitchen to service the four or five parties already seated. She squeezed in beside Darwin and said, "Told the boss lady I was taking a break." She extended a meaty hand to Darwin, who shook it. "Don't believe we've met. I'm Angie. Lived on this island all my life."

"Darwin," the big man returned, looking intimidated by the small woman sitting next to him. "Lived in North Carolina all my life. First time I've been to South Carolina."

"Really?" she asked, surprised. "You look what, twenty-three or twenty-four years old and have never been to South Carolina?"

"Correct. Never been out of that state until yesterday."

She looked at him as if he were an alien visiting Earth for the first time. "Well, welcome to Edisto. One day here, and you'll never forget it."

Darwin gave a painful smile. "Ain't that the truth?"

Lucas and Lynn couldn't help but laugh at that.

Angie turned to Lynn and gave her a skeptical look. "You're not the same woman he was here with last time."

Lucas nearly choked on his tea in mid-sip. "No. No, she's not," he said. "That person is, uh, out of the picture."

It was Lynn's turn to be confused. "What person?"

For an uncomfortable moment, Lucas didn't want to respond. He hadn't mentioned his soon-to-be ex-wife to Lynn yet. He felt as though he had a connection to her but did not know if this was the time to bring that up.

Darwin did it for him. "Oh, Lucas is married."

"That's interesting," Lynn said in a disappointed manner.

Lucas placed a hand on her wrist and cleared his throat. "What my friend meant to say is that I'm getting divorced."

She held the other hand up to her mouth. "Oh, I'm sorry to hear that."

"Not as sorry as I am for going through it," Lucas said dryly. When the subject of his impending divorce came up, people were curious as to why. It was not as if he had done anything wrong. "She cheated on me and walked away. Simple as that."

She rubbed his hand. "I'm sorry to hear that," she repeated and then added, "Her loss."

Sensing she had perhaps touched on a sore subject that may have nothing to do with why they were here, Angie changed the subject. "Tell me, what happened to you this morning?"

Lucas gave her the amended version of the events from the past couple of days, culminating with Riddick riding to Charleston in an ambulance.

Angie shook her head in disbelief during the telling. After Lucas finished, he took a long sip of his tea and said, "We all saw the cop cars and ambulance tear down Jungle Road earlier. Wondered what was going on. Whoever would've thought Blackbeard had set foot near Edisto Island?" Her eyes lit up as a thought struck her. "You know, it's not that crazy."

"What makes you say that?"

"Well, because pirates destroyed the Grimball plantation a long, long time ago."

The three adventurers' eyes went wide at the same time.

"When was this?" Darwin asked.

Her brow furrowed in concentration. "Dunno. Early 1700s I think."

The two men looked at each other and shared the same thought: Could it be?

She explained that Paul Grimball was the first person granted ownership of land on Edisto Island from the Lord's Proprietors. He settled on the opposite end of the island on the banks of the North Edisto River. His plantation thrived from the sale of indigo and Sea Island cotton.

The estate was situated in a strategic spot with easy access to the Atlantic Ocean and the Intracoastal Waterways to Charleston and Port Royal.

Sometime in 1717, unknown pirates thought to be Spanish sacked, pillaged, and burned the house to the ground. Only a twelve-foot-tall portion of one of tabby corner walls remained.

"What's a tabby wall?" Darwin asked.

"It's a form of concrete used back then made of water, sand, ash and oyster shells used by early settlers in this region."

"Oh, that's cool."

"Yeah, they had to use what was available to them back then."

"What happened to this Grimball guy? I assume he had family, too."

"I think he died, but his kids were able to escape," Angie said.

"How did they do that?"

She shrugged her shoulders. "I'm not sure."

Darwin, Lynn, and Lucas shared a look, as though trying to read each other's thoughts.

"This is the end of the line," Lucas said to them. "We traced the map and found its location. The treasure wasn't there. I don't know about you, but I'm not ready to go home yet. This may be our last chance."

"I don't see where else we would go with this," Darwin said. Lynn agreed.

Lucas nodded. "Okay then. I say we follow this lead." Lucas turned to Angie. "You wouldn't know how we can get out there, family, would you?"

She smiled conspiratorially. "As a matter of fact, I know the person who owns the estate now."

***

They savored their fish tacos, paid their bill, thanked Angie for her help, and then set off for Point of Pines Road at the northern end of Edisto Island, back along the same two-lane road they traveled on earlier.

It was this or nothing.

# CHAPTER THIRTY-FIVE

AFTER CALLING AND SPEAKING to the owner of the Grimball Estate, the man agreed to meet them at the entrance to the Point of Pines Plantation at the end of that road. They traveled up Route 174 and almost passed the road. The access to it was just past a restaurant named The Old Post Office on the other side of a small bridge that spanned two islands in the marsh.

Point of Pines Road meandered over three miles of flat country with alternating fields of cotton plants and sunflowers at the foot of an ancient oak forest. The limbs of the trees had wisps of Spanish moss hanging from them, fluttering in the soft ocean breeze. The paved road ended and continued as hard-packed sand mixed with gravel. The small Toyota skidded and swerved on the looser parts of the sandy road. With sadness, Lucas thought his Jeep would have fared much better, but that wasn't going to happen.

Near the end of the road, they left the dense woods and came to a clearing covered with sea grass interspersed with oaks. A silver gate spanned the road adorned with various strongly worded "No Trespassing" signs. The message was clear: enter at your own risk.

An older man with a long-sleeved Guy Harvey fishing shirt, cargo shorts, sunglasses, and flip-flops leaned against the bed of a new Chevy pickup beneath the gate, blocking entry. His name was Earl Grimball. The seventh great-grandson of Paul Grimball.

Lynn pulled to a stop behind the truck. They got out of the car and walked up to the man.

Lucas shook Grimball's offered hand and introduced Lynn and Darwin.

"Nice to meet you all." Grimball regarded the three of them and said to Lucas, "I assume it was you I spoke to on the phone?"

"It was."

"So, you believe there's treasure on my grandpop's farm?" Earl Grimball said in a thick Southern drawl.

Lucas looked at Darwin and Lynn before answering. "We do. We have reason to believe that it may have been Blackbeard himself who destroyed this place."

Grimball placed a hand over his mouth and ran it down his chin. "That'd be something. We were always under the impression the culprits were Spanish pirates from the south of here. The old man traded goods with them from time to time. We thought it was maybe done in revenge for a deal gone sour."

"Angie told us your ancestor died during the attack." Darwin said.

Grimball's features saddened. "He did. Just three of his kids survived. One son and two daughters."

"How did they escape?"

"They found some place to hide," Grimball said. "Where that was, they never revealed. The pirates were here for three days and killed Paul and his wife and their servants as well as over three thousand heads of livestock. They razed cotton fields and destroyed the house with cannons from their ship."

"We're that close to the river here?" Lucas asked.

Grimball jerked a thumb in a general direction over his shoulder past the gate. "Yeah, the North Edisto winds past here just beyond those trees. The house was set right on the riverbank."

An idea began to form in Lucas's mind. He asked, "Were there any Indians around here when he settled?"

"There were. Of course, we had the Edistow tribe here on the island. Then there were the Toogoodoo's on the other side of the Intracoastal Waterway."

"What type of Indians were they?"

"What do you mean?"

"Well, were they peaceful or warlike?"

Grimball scratched his chin. "The Edistow's were mostly peaceful, I believe, but they would fight about protecting what was theirs if it came to it. The Toogoodoo's, now they were aggressive. They didn't like or trust anyone or trade with anybody and crossing them often led to violent results. Why do you ask?"

"Just trying to get the lay of the land. Get a picture of what your ancestors were dealing with when they settled here," Lucas said. "So, you'll allow us to take a look at where the plantation house used to be?"

"I will, although if you find any treasure, remember who owns this land. I'll be the one to decide what gets done with it."

The night before, Lucas researched the laws and regulations of South Carolina concerning the finding of treasure, artifacts, and antiquities. If a person finds something on state owned land, they must seek the proper permits before digging. On the other hand, any treasure discovered on privately owned land—such as the Grimball Estate—was finders' keepers. If you found something and weren't the rightful owner of the land, you had to take it up with the person who held the deed.

If they located Blackbeard's treasure somewhere on this estate, then it was up to Earl Grimball to decide its fate. If he wanted to keep it for himself, then that was his prerogative. If he desired to split or donate it, it was his right. Lucas wanted to stay on good terms with Grimball after Angie warned them that he could be ornery.

Darwin knew this as well. He said, "Absolutely. If nothing else, I just hope you'll allow us to catalogue and report what we find. If we find anything, that is."

The older man studied the three for a moment. "Okay then. Just so we have a basic understanding. Follow me."

He climbed in his truck and Darwin, Lynn, and Lucas got back into her car. They followed him through the gate down the sandy road by a narrow field with short grass. Lucas imagined a herd of cows grazing here three hundred years ago. At the end of the grassy expanse, the road turned sharply to the right into a thick canopy of oaks.

A moment later, they emerged into a clearing overlooking the North Edisto River. The water sparkled in the sunlight. The site rested on a small peninsula jutting out into the water offering grand, sweeping views of the salt marshes on the opposite side. The open range of land was roughly a hundred yards long and fifty feet back from the riverbank. The ground was flat. Near them, to their left stood the remaining wall: a whitish corner formed with cement made of oyster shell. The tabby wall. Other than that, the area was barren besides a few spots dotted with grass and bushes. The sour smell of the river floated on the breeze.

They climbed from their vehicles, and Grimball led them to the edge of the ruins.

"This is it," he said. "All that remains."

"Wow," Lynn said. As was her nature, she had been quiet throughout much of the day. Never in a million years would she have figured she would be on a treasure hunt. She didn't truly believe what Lucas and Darwin were telling her until she saw the devil image scraped into that rock on Pine Island.

"How much have you all been out here?" Lucas asked Grimball.

"Not very often to tell the truth," he said. "Not much here as you can see."

"Anyone ever come and research this place, you know, from a historical standpoint?"

"Well, to tell you the truth, not this spot." He pointed over their heads where the road emptied out into the ruins. "There used to be several slave cabins over there that people from the Smithsonian and people in Columbia took a big interest in. They even tore one down piece by piece and reconstructed it in D.C. at the Smithsonian. Although no one ever asked about this piece of land right here," he said, pointing at their feet.

"That's interesting. I would've thought they'd want to check out a place destroyed by pirates," Lucas said. Now that he saw the house's setting, the premise Lucas imagined for the way the Grimball children hid and escaped the pirate attack seemed a real possibility.

"Well, they never did," Earl Grimball said.

Darwin set about getting his metal detector going. Lynn went and sat in the shade under an oak to watch. Lucas and Earl stood together as he pointed out various locations where he believed different structures used to stand, such as an outhouse, a barn, servant's quarters, a bathhouse, and a dock and boathouse. The dock was on the side of the peninsula facing out to sea. They couldn't see the Atlantic from here, although Grimball assured them it wasn't far. The location of this strengthened the theory Lucas had in his mind as he gazed across at the opposite bank of the finger of land.

After the metal detector started chirping in a staccato rhythm, Darwin began to scan around the home's foundation and barn. They figured those areas would be the most probable locations to hide treasure. He crisscrossed those regions and came up empty.

He started to expand his search when Lucas asked, "You know Darwin, I never did ask. How deep can your detector find metals?"

Darwin stopped. "Depends on a couple things. The type of metal, soil and how much there is. This thing can find a coin a foot or two deep."

"Okay. What if there were a large concentration of gold and silver?"

Darwin contemplated for a moment. "Dunno. Down several feet. The bigger the amount the better your odds of finding it if it's deeper."

"What if it's below rock?"

"Below rock? Like bedrock? No, you would need ground-penetrating sonar for that. Why?"

Earl and Darwin looked at Lucas expectantly. Lynn got up and walked over from the tree to hear Lucas's answer.

"If this was Blackbeard's doing, he would have torn up everything trying to find his treasure." He said to Earl. "Your ancestor somehow found where Blackbeard buried his treasure on Pine Island, dug it up and brought it back here and hid it. They were the only family here in Edisto, and you say he traded with pirates. Blackbeard may have known who Paul Grimball was. Before Grimball figured out what to do with treasure, the pirates killed him. Everyone here who knew about it died with him."

"What about his kids?" Earl asked. "They made it out somehow."

"That is why I asked you about the natives in the area earlier. If there were any aggressive ones nearby."

"Okay. What of it?"

"Bear with me here," Lucas answered. "During the early days of colonization, when settlers built homes, sometimes they had to prepare to escape or hide should they get attacked by Indians. If they lived on a river such as this place, then they would build an escape tunnel that let out into the river."

"Wait," Darwin said. "You mean like Governor Eden had in Bath? Where Blackbeard allegedly smuggled goods into his home?"

"Exactly," Lucas said with a point of his finger. "Earl, I bet when Paul Grimball had this house designed, he had tunnels added to protect him and his family." He let that settle in. "When Blackbeard arrived here, Paul knew he was in trouble and had his kids escape into the tunnels. He and his wife didn't make it."

"Then wouldn't the kids have known about the treasure?"

"How old were they?"

"Young," Earl answered. "The oldest boy was ten at the time."

"Just old enough to know how to get a raft on the river and get him and his siblings to safety. Maybe not old enough to know what the treasure was. Or perhaps they never saw it. Possibly it was hidden in a closed off spur of the tunnel."

"Then how come Blackbeard didn't find the tunnel if it's here?"

"Well, one, we don't know he didn't. He might have and the treasure may well be somewhere else entirely." Earl got a disappointed look on his face. Lucas went on, "Listen, this is it for us. We have no real proof that there is anything here. Just circumstantial evidence. What we do know is that after Blackbeard attacked a treasure ship returning home to Spain and then stashed the treasure somewhere, unknown pirates destroyed this place. Those pirates may remain nameless because the children who escaped may not have known who they were.

"To answer your question," Lucas continued, "the entrance and exit to the tunnel may have just been very well hidden."

Earl cocked his head to the side. "You know, you might be on to something there."

"So, do you want me to keep scanning?" Darwin asked.

"Yeah, you can. You never know. If it's here, then it could be near the surface."

"Okay," Darwin said and set off to scan in a different zone.

"How can we find out if there are tunnels underneath us?" Lynn asked.

Lucas looked out over the full river and turned to Earl. "Do you know when low tide is supposed to be today?"

"Ah, about five, six o'clock I believe."

"You wouldn't happen to have a boat I could borrow for about an hour around then do you?"

He smiled. "If it leads to treasure, I absolutely do."

# CHAPTER THIRTY-SIX

L ATER, AFTER THEY HELPED Earl get his boat in the water at Steamboat Landing close by, they motored back down the North Edisto River towards the Atlantic to the Grimball Estate ruins. The four of them crowded into Earl Grimball's old fishing boat. The tide was on its way out, exposing the riverbanks around the peninsula. Tall, puffy clouds rolled in from inland as the heat of the afternoon energized the atmosphere. Lucas wished those clouds wouldn't develop into thunderstorms while they were out here.

Lucas hoped his theory proved true with the tunnels. If not, it would be time to go home and get back to life. He had divorce proceedings to deal with soon as well as figuring out what would happen with the insurance company and his Jeep. What happened with Riddick could keep him bogged down with a police investigation and court proceedings for the foreseeable future. He had wanted to open a second bookstore, although with all that was going to happen, he might have to push that plan aside for now. There was also the bullet wound on his shoulder to worry about. He had taken some Aleve he had picked up from the grocery store just before Earl arrived with his boat. That medication felt like it was beginning to wear off, leaving a dull ache in his shoulder.

This journey had managed to distract him from the horrible sequence of events with Kristen leading up to the night Darwin had called. Even if they didn't find treasure, he was happy to see Darwin and spend time with him. The young man had never had much to look forward to or had the means to pursue his dreams. He hoped this adventure would give Darwin the confidence he needed to get a new outlook on life.

And Lynn, well he didn't know much about her. Yet. He'd have to wait and see what happened there.

Lucas directed Earl to guide the boat along the bank where the part of the peninsula facing away from the ocean was. The ruins of the tabby wall materialized from the ground. Near there was a part of the bank that curved in a U near where the peninsula returned to the riverbank headed upstream. Tall sea grass grew up from the riverbed, concealing most of the wall made of rocks and sand.

Using Google Earth earlier, Lucas saw this island from above where he imagined a tunnel entrance. The shape of this small crease in the riverbank would be concealed from anyone floating by on the river. Barely noticeable, although just big enough in which to launch an escape craft.

The tide was now at its lowest point. They could see the riverbed beneath the green water. Lucas directed Earl to pull the boat up close to the depression in the bank. There was just enough water to keep the boat from running aground. Shallow water lay in front of the riverbank.

"Darwin," Lucas said, raised his injured arm in the sling and pointed to the section of the bank obscured by sea grass. "Can you hop out and check out that place right there, could you?"

Darwin barely contained his excitement. "Sure thing, cripple," he joked and climbed out over the side.

Darwin landed in the water with a splash.

"Be careful," Lynn said.

Darwin felt his heart pumping. The sense of discovery he felt at first discovering the map back at the museum and finding those coins on Pine Island paled in comparison to what he was feeling now. This was it. The absolute end of the journey.

He didn't want to go back to Raleigh yet, although he would have no recourse if they came up empty here. Back to his dull job. Back to his boring life. He didn't want that. Since setting out on this trip, he imagined what would happen if he found this treasure. Riddick was right; Darwin would become famous overnight. He hoped he'd be able to do whatever he wanted to in the field of marine archaeology. This could open doors previously unknown to him. He wanted to do his part to help the world understand some elements of the past. That was his goal when choosing a college major.

"Look over there on the wall on the side of the curve nearest the home," Lucas called to Darwin from the boat.

Darwin waded into the depression. Small crabs darted away and into the water. He pushed into the seagrass and started moving his hands over the surface of the bank. He moved to his right, going deeper in. His hand hit something. He stumbled. Lynn made a noise while Earl and Lucas looked on. Darwin regained his balance and investigated where he had stopped. They saw his hands moving around the sea grass, lost from their view.

With his eyes focused on the bank before him, he shouted, "Guys, I have something here!"

"What is it?" Lucas asked, the pitch of his voice rising with every syllable pronounced.

Earl eased the boat to the right to give them a better view of what Darwin was seeing.

With his hands still buried in the grass, Darwin looked back at them and gave the biggest smile of his life.

With both hands, he parted the grass revealing a large, dark opening.

***

Earl dropped an anchor to keep the boat from floating away. Darwin helped everyone climb over the side of the ship and into the shallow water, taking special care with Lucas and his shoulder. Darwin pulled two flashlights from his backpack and handed one to Lynn. Lucas needed his right arm free to help him keep his balance. Lynn would help guide Lucas. She handed Darwin a shovel. Earl Grimball had a lantern for camping he had brought from home when he went to get his boat earlier.

Darwin parted the grass on one side while Earl grabbed it from the other, allowing Lucas and Lynn to enter the tunnel. She shined her beam around a grotto not much bigger than a bedroom. Water covered the floor. The walls were made of dark bricks. The sounds of moving water echoed in the space. Darwin and Earl followed close behind. The combination of his lantern and Darwin's flashlight greatly increased the level of light in the cave. Along the left side of the grotto was a raised platform.

"I wonder if that's where they kept their raft," Lucas said. "If it were made of wood, keeping it elevated would have prevented it from rotting."

"Could be," Darwin agreed.

Along the wall behind the raised area, toward the rear, was another opening.

Lynn stood on Lucas's left side—his injured side—and kept an arm around his waist to help keep him steady. She held the flashlight in her left hand. She helped him step up onto the platform and down the length of the wall.

They stopped at the opening at the back of the cave. She raised her flashlight and shined the beam down the tunnel. The glow illuminated the general direction of the where the house would be up above.

"Go on," Lucas urged. Her arm tightened around his hips. She trembled. "There's nothing to be afraid of," he whispered into her ear. "We've got you."

Relieved and determined, she pressed forward.

"This is remarkable," Earl said from behind them. "No one was aware of this tunnel for three hundred years."

"There are probably old tunnels such as this all over this side of the United States," Lucas said.

"They've just been lost in time. Like this one," Grimball said.

They had traveled down perhaps twenty feet of the tunnel when the floor began to angle upward. The walls of the tunnel here were made of faded red bricks. The passageway terminated at a rotten, door made of wood faded with age. Its doorknob had long since rusted in the damp, salty environment and disappeared.

"Is the treasure behind there?" Earl asked.

Without answering, Lucas reached forward with his good arm and put his hand in the opening left in the door by the missing doorknob. He pulled. The door creaked on ancient hinges as it swung open. Behind it was a solid wall of brown dirt.

Dead end.

Lucas punched the wall in frustration. Everyone else echoed his sentiment in their own way.

"Earl, do you know where we might be in relation to the old house?"

The older man tried to get his bearings. He examined the shaft ahead and back in the direction from which they came. "I would say if the home didn't have a basement, then this would have been behind the kitchen probably. In the butlers' pantry. That would have been a fine spot to hide the entrance to this tunnel, I reckon."

Lucas didn't know why, but he had expected a warren of tunnels running in many directions. Like one of those ant farms he played with as a kid. Instead, the tunnel was just a single long room leading to a small cave. That appeared to be it.

Darwin seemed to share the same thought. "This can't be it can it?"

Lucas shook his head. "I hope not."

"What if there is more to it?" Lynn asked. They regarded her, waiting to hear an explanation. "I mean, what if other parts of the tunnel are hidden."

"Like, did Paul Grimball put the treasure in another part of the tunnel and then seal it shut?" Lucas said. "I had that thought too. That could be why his kids didn't know about it."

"I'm thinking the same thing," Darwin said.

"Yeah, me too little lady," Earl—who had the most to gain from finding the treasure here—said. "How do you all think we can find any additional spurs to this tunnel?"

Lucas gazed back behind Earl and Lucas along the long walls leading back to the entrance by the river. He looked to the wall beside him and *thwacked* it with the meat of his fist, making a solid *thump*. "We go back and pound on the walls all the way down, listening for anything that sounds hollow or any section where the bricks look to be a slightly different color or don't quite fit in properly."

They nodded and started hitting the wall with the meaty side of their fists, where the action wouldn't hurt so much. As they moved back towards the entrance of the cave, the sounds of fists hitting walls resonated in their ears.

*Thump.*

*Thump.*

*Thump.*

*Thump.*

*Thwunk!*

Earl, Lucas, and Darwin stopped what they were doing and looked over at where Lynn stood staring at the section of the wall where her small fist made the muffled sound. Darwin stepped over and hit the wall three more times to make sure it hadn't been a mistake.

*Thwunk!*

*Thwunk!*

*Thwunk!*

"Guys," he said he said to Earl and Lucas. "You might want to come over here."

They all gathered around the big man. The bricks on the section of the wall where the noise came from didn't fit together perfectly. They were the same color as the rest of the bricks, likely from the same batch. However, in this spot, the mortar in between the bricks was noticeably darker. The area went from floor to ceiling and was about three feet wide.

"This part was bricked in at a different time," Earl said. Everyone agreed.

"Step back," Darwin said, hefting the shovel.

The three moved aside, giving Darwin room to work. He handed his flashlight to Lucas and then turned the shovel to where he was gripping the wood near the spade end. He reared back as much as the width of the tunnel allowed and plunged the wooden end of the shovel into the wall. The tip of the handle made contact on a junction of mortar between four bricks, causing a loud noise. The wood of the handle splintered from the force used by Darwin.

Where the shovel handle hit the wall, the bricks caved inwards at an angle, exposing a thin crack of open air on the other side.

A strong, musty scent bled through the opening causing the four of them to move back involuntarily. Earl held the lantern in front of the opening, giving them better light.

Darwin threw the broken shovel aside. It clattered down the tunnel. He lifted his big foot and stomped at the exposed area causing four of the bricks to crumble under his strength. The space of the opening was now about the size of a baseball.

Lucas dropped down to his knees and shined the beam in the opening. The small size of the opening and the power of the flashlight limited his vision. He had the sense that the room behind the bricks was large. Larger than the grotto at the cave entrance.

"What do you see? What do you see?" an excited Darwin asked. "Is it in there?"

Lucas stood, dusted off his knees, and handed the flashlight to Darwin. "You tell me big guy."

Darwin's hand was shaking as he accepted the handle of the flashlight from Lucas. He kneeled, wiped dust off the edges of the hole, and pointed the flashlight through the opening.

Inside the hole, light reflected off objects of many varying shapes and sizes. Straight edges, rounded curves and more. Much more.

Gold. Gold was everywhere! Gold bars. Gold coins. Gold ingots. Gold jewelry. He saw the dull gleam of silver and copper in places as well as the sparkle of different colors of jewels. Underneath it all was dozens of wooden crates about the size of shoeboxes.

Overcome with joy, tears flooded his eyes. He began sobbing, lowered the flashlight in one hand, and covered his face with the other.

Lynn and Lucas got down beside him and wrapped him in an embrace. Lucas said to him, "There, there big fella. You did it. You discovered Blackbeard's treasure."

Darwin ran the back of his arm across his nose. "No Lucas. We discovered Blackbeard's treasure. I couldn't have done this without you, or Lynn, or Mr. Grimball."

Getting antsy, Grimball pushed forward, moving them away from the hole. "Gimme one of those flashlights," he said. Lynn handed him hers. He turned with it and peered into the hole. He gulped. "Holy hell. I'm rich!"

He handed the flashlight back to Lynn and did a jig, singing, "I'm rich, I'm rich, I'm rich."

Darwin, Lucas, and Lynn shared a smile and watched the man dance.

***

Earl left them there. He owned a construction company and said that he thought he had a sledgehammer in the back of his truck. He would go retrieve it and come back.

Lucas and Darwin sat side-by-side on the floor of the tunnel facing the new hole in the wall while they waited. Lynn sat close to Lucas.

Their conversation had little to do with the treasure on the opposite side of the wall or the events leading them to this point. At some point, Lynn's hand crept over, and she intertwined her fingers with Lucas's. They laughed. They joked. They were happy. They were relieved it was over.

After a few minutes, Darwin turned serious. "So, what do you suppose he's going to do with the treasure?" he said of Earl. "Think he'll donate it? Give us some, or keep it for himself?"

"Darwin, I don't know what to tell you," Lucas shrugged. "It's out of our hands now. I hope he does the right thing, although in this situation, there is no clear-cut answer to that. It's on his land. By what the South Carolina state law says, he is the rightful owner. Maybe he has a philanthropic side and donates it to a museum. Who knows? He could give us all equal shares. I don't know anything about this man other than what we've seen today and what Angie told us back at McConkey's. That he can be cantankerous.

"Whatever he does, Darwin," Lucas continued, "know this: we helped shine a light on a lost chapter in history today. All of us."

Darwin leaned his head back against the wall and thought, *that's all I wanted.*

***

Earl Grimball returned a bit later, hefting the sledgehammer when he appeared in the tunnel as though it was the Super Bowl Trophy. He came in and handed it to Darwin who set to work on demolishing that part of the wall. Quickly, he created a space large enough for all of them to step through.

As was his right, Earl went in first. The treasure almost filled the back half of the cave. Lucas estimated the space was about four-hundred square feet. Tons of gold and silver coins, statues, jewelry, and trinkets made up the treasure.

***

Later, they celebrated with Earl's wife at the restaurant above the marina. They watched a dramatic sunset go down over the A.C.E. River Basin behind the windows of the eatery. A group of dolphins played in the waters beside the docks of the marina while a dozen seagulls floated by overhead. Families going out for an evening cruise in the waters of Edisto floated by.

Lucas sipped a beer with his arm around Lynn gazing at the grand vista. His shoulder was already feeling better. He had discarded the shoulder sling in Lynn's car on the way here. He remembered the half sun Blackbeard had drawn on his map indicating a sunset and laughed.

"What is it?" Lynn asked.

Lucas tilted the bottle at the sunset. "That," he said. "Just consider about all the tales of Blackbeard and how he was supposed to be this big, bad pirate who brought terror to the New World during his time."

"What about it?" Darwin asked.

"I was just thinking," Lucas said, "that it's humanizing to believe that a salty, vicious and violent pirate who became famous for his fearsome persona could still take the time to appreciate something as beautiful as that sunset."

Everyone agreed.

They celebrated well into the night.

# EPILOGUE

R IDDICK WOULD NEVER WALK without a cane again. The kick from Darwin saw to that. Riddick may never see the outside of a jail again either.

Because he fired his guns, the police charged him with attempted murder. After speaking with Darwin, Lucas and some of the other townspeople of Bath, they discovered his many transgressions. The entire town lived in fear of him. No more. The police investigators attained a warrant from a local judge and searched his home. In it, they discovered evidence tying Riddick to several missing persons cases, including correspondence and valuables previously belonging to those who had disappeared. He would be tried in those cases and for the murder of Travis Cole.

When they went back and seized Riddick's yacht at the Harbour Town Marina, they discovered that he stole it a year earlier from an elderly couple in Key West.

Blackbeard the pirate created a persona to make people believe he was something more than he truly was. Riddick impersonated the pirate in more ways than one. Riddick apparently didn't have as much money as he let on. The board of directors of the shipping company figured out long ago that he spent money with reckless abandon and placed a limit on how much he could spend. He resorted to theft and piracy to get the rest of what he wanted.

That greed was now going to send him to prison for the rest of his life.

The day after they located Blackbeard's treasure, Darwin and Earl Grimball negotiated how to deal with it. They called an appraiser to come down from Charleston to estimate the value of the treasure. The man was astonished at what they had unearthed. After looking through several of the shoebox-sized chests and studying their contents, he placed a conservative estimate of one hundred million dollars on the treasure's value. Possibly much more depending on what they found as they sorted the chests.

Grimball wanted to keep most of it for himself. He wanted to retire and set up his family to lead comfortable lives for generations to come. He donated a portion to the South Carolina Maritime Museum in Georgetown near Charleston with the provision that Darwin lead the research.

As for the three who led him to the find, Earl Grimball let them choose one sealed treasure chest apiece. They couldn't look at the contents beforehand. He told them to imagine they were opening a box of Cracker Jacks. They didn't know what surprises might be in store. They figured each chest was worth at least a million.

They each selected a box for themselves, gave him a hug and promised to stay in touch. They departed Edisto in Lynn's Corolla and returned to her apartment on Hilton Head.

Darwin and Lucas appeared on the Charleston news for the second time in three days. By morning, their story had gone national. Media and museums all over the southeast were calling for interviews. It wasn't Lucas's style to seek attention or have it on him. Thankfully, Darwin elected to speak for the group. Lucas agreed to do one interview with a local station in West Virginia near where he grew up. Darwin already agreed to be on NBC's Today Show followed by an appearance the same day on the Tonight Show with Jimmy Fallon to discuss their quest.

They crashed at Lynn's place the following night. The next morning, they took Darwin to a barber to get a fresh cut and shave. They then took him to two of the upscale big and tall clothing shops on the island to pick out new outfits. He wanted to look his best going forward. No more ratty clothes and unkempt appearance.

They celebrated again by going to an expensive restaurant on the island for lunch. Lynn took them to a rental car business at the airport where Lucas rented a sedan to take him and Darwin home. Cost wasn't much of an issue now.

Darwin thanked her for everything but recognized that she and Lucas wanted a moment alone. The big guy folded himself into the subcompact rental car and shut the door.

Lynn's red hair shifted back and forth across her face as she looked up at Lucas. He reached out his hand and tucked an errant strand behind her ear. She closed her eyes and breathed the cologne on his wrist as he did so.

"I want to thank you for everything you did for us," Lucas said reaching out and grabbing her small hand.

She squeezed his in return, knowing that he was a hero who had stepped out of one of her books. "You're welcome. I wouldn't have missed it for the world. It was amazing."

They shared a long embrace, followed by a quick kiss. They promised to see each other again. Soon.

***

Four nights later, finally back home, sitting in his office in Concord, Lucas heaved a sigh of relief. The past several days had been some of the most difficult of his life. He had gone on an adventure of the sort that few people ever would and lived to tell about it. The bullet wound on his shoulder still hurt, although he had his full range of motion back.

It would leave behind an interesting scar to talk about.

He came home to find a Notice of Hearing from Kristen with a date set for the next week to have their divorce finalized. He took the thick envelope to the post office, had the divorce decree notarized and dropped it in the mail.

That would spell the end of his relationship with Kristen. He would wish her well and hope to not see her for a long, long time. The insurance company offered him full value on his Jeep. Despite having almost unlimited funds, he decided he was going to buy a Jeep like the one he had before, just brand new.

He didn't know what he would do with the rest of his newfound wealth. He hadn't had time to consider it. Owning a bookstore no longer excited him. The thrill and sense of adventure he received from all of this was something he felt he wanted to do again in the future. Perhaps he and Darwin would find a similar mystery from the past to solve.

He didn't know what tomorrow would bring. He thought back to his drive along the North Carolina coast on the way down to Hilton Head. He had imagined floating on a raft with a beverage in his hands, riding on the calm waters of some tropical locale, letting the soft breeze propel him across the crystal-clear water.

Perhaps he'd look into flights south for the day after the final divorce hearing. Perhaps he would see if Lynn wanted to come along. The thought brought him peace and happiness.

He logged off his computer, stood up, went to the corner of his office, and tugged the cord to shut off the antique wooden lamp, casting his office into darkness. Lucas smiled and closed the door behind him as he exited the room. He would sleep well tonight.

The now empty office was quiet and dark. A faint beam of light punctured the darkness of the room. It came through the blinds from a streetlamp on the opposite side of the neighborhood street. The light fell on the middle of the three full bookshelves against the wall opposite the desk.

The ray of light spotlighted the display of state quarters left for Lucas by his grandfather. Now, all the display's slots were full. The South Carolina slot now had an occupant. However, it wasn't the quarter meant to fill it.

You see, Riddick didn't make it to the hospital with the three gold coins in his pocket they uncovered on Pine Island. Darwin had one. Lynn possessed another.

The third gold doubloon fittingly occupied the once blank slot on the display set aside for South Carolina—where the coin had rested for three-hundred years—now gleaming eternally in the streetlight.

# ABOUT THE AUTHOR

Caleb is the author of the award-winning and critically acclaimed *Death on the Boardwalk*: Book 1 of the Myrtle Beach Mystery Series. He is a member of the Mystery Writers of America, the International Thriller Writers, and Southeastern Writers Association, the author of six novels, including the breakout hit, *Death on the Boardwalk*: Book 1 of the Myrtle Beach Mysteries. He is also an occasional woodworker, occasional golfer, reacher of things on tall shelves, beach walker, shark tooth finder, coffee snob, and munchkin wrangler.

His two Lucas Caine Adventure novels, *Blackbeard's Lost Treasure* and *The Search for the Fountain of Youth*, were both Semi-Finalists for the Clive Cussler Adventure Awards Competition.

He is currently at work on the next book in the Myrtle Beach Mystery Series.

He lives in Myrtle Beach with his wife and son (the munchkin).

**Visit Caleb online at** www.CalebWygal.com.